Catching Echoes

CATCHING ECHOES (RECONSTRUCTIONIST 1)
Copyright © 2016 Meghan Ciana Doidge
Published by Old Man in the CrossWalk Productions 2016
Salt Spring Island, BC, Canada
www.oldmaninthecrosswalk.com

Library and Archives Canada
Doidge, Meghan Ciana, 1973—
Catching Echoes/Meghan Ciana Doidge—PAPERBACK EDITION

Cover design by Damonza
Bracelet (pictured on front cover) designed by Jill K Davis Jewelry

ISBN 978-1-927850-53-4

MEGHAN CIANA DOIDGE

Published by Old Man in the CrossWalk Productions
Salt Spring Island, BC, Canada

Author's Note

Catching Echoes is the first book in the Reconstructionist series, which is set in the same universe as the Dowser and Oracle series.

While it is not necessary to read all three series, *in order to avoid spoilers* the ideal reading order is as follows:

Cupcakes, Trinkets, and Other Deadly Magic (Dowser 1)
Trinkets, Treasures, and Other Bloody Magic (Dowser 2)
Treasures, Demons, and Other Black Magic (Dowser 3)
I See Me (Oracle 1)
Shadows, Maps, and Other Ancient Magic (Dowser 4)
Maps, Artifacts, and Other Arcane Magic (Dowser 5)
I See You (Oracle 2)
Artifacts, Dragons, and Other Lethal Magic (Dowser 6)
I See Us (Oracle 3)
The Graveyard Kiss (Reconstructionist 0.5)
Catching Echoes (Reconstructionist 1)

Other books in both the Reconstructionist and Dowser series to follow.

Though the Oracle and Reconstructionist series can each be enjoyed on their own without having read the Dowser series, readers are warned that the Oracle and Reconstructionist books feature characters from and discuss certain events within the Dowser series—and thus might contain spoilers for the Dowser books that appear before them in the preferred reading order.

More information can be found at:
www.madebymeghan.ca/novels

For Michael
My white picket fence personified.

I preferred it when life came in tidy packages. When it didn't—when something went awry—I was exceedingly skilled at packaging it back up. It was my job to do so, after all.

I was a reconstructionist.

I collected the puzzle pieces, then I gave those pieces to an investigative team to sort out. I didn't ask questions. I didn't offer answers. I saw, I recorded, and I moved on.

I didn't dwell or obsess. I didn't hunt down suspects. I didn't follow clues to find a killer. And I certainly didn't work side by side with anyone—least of all a vampire who I strongly suspected might turn out to be the major missing component when the case was complete.

Then I saw something I couldn't forget. It wasn't the bloodiest thing I'd ever seen—it wasn't even close—but it haunted me. I didn't like being haunted.

But I couldn't figure out how to get it out of my head.

Someone was killing teenaged boys in the Pacific Northwest. Despite my misgivings, if I could help catch a killer, I had to at least try.

Chapter One

"Who found the grave?" I asked, sidestepping around the site. I was wearing the Oxfords I put on when working so my heels wouldn't sink into the well-trimmed, damp grass, which was the greenest I'd ever seen. The Vancouver rain obviously promoted striking greenery even in early October, but I was glad it was currently only misting.

"Caretaker," Dalton said. "Phoned it in as vandalism to the West Van police yesterday. It filtered down from there. Any disturbed gravesite draws attention, of course. They sent out a necromancer first, then us when she didn't pick up anything unusual."

Dalton was an unusual witch name, so I assumed it was his last, not his first. Though I didn't recognize it as a founder surname either. He was the secondary investigator, probably more skilled technically than magically. His main duties included collecting evidence and securing the location while the lead investigator interpreted the facts and clues, then decided when a case needed the attention of a specialist.

A specialist like me.

I'd arrived in Vancouver at half past four in the afternoon, secured a rental car at the airport, and immediately followed my GPS halfway up the mountain on which the suburb of West Vancouver was situated. I'd parked by the administration building rather than blocking the single paved lane that wove through the cemetery. The CAUTION—BEAR IN AREA! sign at the entrance had left me momentarily disconcerted, but thankfully I was able to easily spot Dalton among the rows and rows of flush-mounted headstones.

I'd arrived just before five thirty. The sun would be setting around six forty, so I needed to be efficient with my collection. But I was always efficient. So as long as the team hadn't bungled anything before my arrival, I had no expectation of any problems with making my 7:00 P.M. dinner reservation.

This was my second time in Vancouver, and I wasn't going to pass up the opportunity to indulge in some great food. Even a reconstructionist had to have priorities.

"The site was scorched like this when you arrived?" I eyed the irregularly contoured burn that had seared the edges of the fresh turf running along each side of the gravesite. The burn appeared to be of mundane origin, but I wouldn't know for certain until I activated my circle. The necromancer who'd accessed the grave earlier wouldn't be an issue, because death magic was completely different from my own. But anything else would be important to know about ahead of time.

Dalton was still hovering over my shoulder, as if he thought I'd never set foot around a crime scene before.

"Yes," he said, but the sandy-haired investigator sounded unsure.

"If this was done by your team afterward, I need to know," I said, circling the burned patch. The interment was so fresh that the cemetery maintenance crew hadn't sodded over the burial site yet. So new that there wasn't even a headstone. The scorch marks were contained to a single grave. The remainder of the cemetery was pristine—untouched by vandals or time or magic. "Any spell might interact or introduce—"

"Is there a problem, reconstructionist?" a snippy woman's voice called out from behind me.

I turned.

Carolina Medici, the stout, forty-five-year-old lead investigator, strode across the blanket of grass between the gravesite and the path that led to the northern section of the cemetery. The late afternoon might have been cloudy, but the superior curl of the uppity, salt-and-pepper-haired witch's lip was plainly visible.

"I was determining that, investigator." I kept my tone even and crisp, professional though not particularly friendly. As was my preference when interacting with anyone of the magical persuasion. It was an investigator's job to rattle cages until clues fell out, but I didn't have to let the senior witch ruffle me.

"We aren't interested in your observations or concerns, Wisteria Fairchild." Carolina stepped close enough that I could see she had a smudge of chocolate on her upper lip. "Just do your reconstruction as requested."

I smiled at Carolina's sneering use of my family name. The forced expression was tight on my face. Though the Medici coven held a seat on the Convocation—the international governing body of the witches—they were not among the founding three families of Fairchild, Godfrey, and Cameron.

I was absolutely certain that the chocolate smear on Carolina's lip came from icing. Cupcake icing, specifically. No witch came to Vancouver without visiting Jade Godfrey's bakery, Cake in a Cup. Actually, I doubted whether any member of the magical community of Adepts would pass through without stopping in to pay respects to Jade's grandmother, Pearl, and to get a treat. The fact that Jade was a dowser and an alchemist—at least to those in the know—probably did wonders for business.

A Medici witch wouldn't be on the list of those 'in the know.' Hence, the posturing that was currently hindering my ability to do my job.

"Step back, Carolina," I said. My informal use of her first name was as overly familiar as her use of mine had been.

"What?" she sputtered.

"You're standing exactly where I need to construct my circle, investigator. So please, step back so I can get you your reconstruction."

I paused, plastering a pleasant smile on my face while I waited patiently for her to remove herself from my personal space.

Carolina twisted her lips. "Some respect would be expected."

"Yes, it would. Especially since I understand your usual reconstructionist already failed to collect at this site. The chair of the Convocation specifically requested that I drop everything and attend to your problem."

Carolina narrowed her eyes at me, refusing to be easily put in her place. "One might wonder how you came to be on Pearl Godfrey's speed dial in the first place."

"One might wonder, or one could do one's job, effectively and efficiently. Then perhaps one wouldn't need to be bailed out."

Carolina snapped her mouth shut, tamping down whatever nastiness desperately wanted to spew loose. She took two deliberate steps away, moving closer to the path.

I thought about forcing her farther back, then let the posturing game drop. I wasn't a Fairchild witch defending her coven reputation. I was a reconstructionist with a job to do.

And I actually wasn't affiliated with the Fairchild coven at all—by choice—though my Aunt Rose sat on the witches Convocation. But my estrangement from my family, and therefore one of the main reasons I was on Pearl Godfrey's go-to contact list, wasn't common knowledge.

My family's reputation and standing within the Adept community was both a hindrance and an unwanted, unwarranted boon. That a professionally higher-ranked Medici witch would instantly loathe me was a given. Even without proof or knowledge of a specific incident, I was certain some Fairchild had greatly wronged one of Carolina's ancestors. It practically went without saying.

I turned back to the gravesite. Underneath the scorched earth, the compacted, trampled dirt was freshly dug. Whatever had happened must have occurred in the last couple of days, because even in the absence of sod, the dirt and the black ash worked into it hadn't been washed away by Vancouver's infamous fall rain—rain that was well known for extending year round. Not that I was complaining about the weather. When I lived anywhere in particular, I lived in Seattle. Plus, I wasn't a fan of how shorts looked on me.

I wasn't picking up any elements that made this appear to be a difficult site to reconstruct. So the fact that Clay Dunkirk had fainted earlier today while attempting to do so was perplexing. Clay was a first-rate reconstructionist. This was his crew. They all had, at minimum, ten years experience on me, and I wasn't some novice.

But Clay did have a habit of letting his magic run wild. His sloppy-though-efficient technique had gotten him in trouble during a couple of Convocation tribunals. It left an opening for the defense to try to dispute the veracity of the reconstructions he produced. A suggestion that elements might have entered the reconstructions to muddy the process of collection. Which was ridiculous, really. Because even if an Adept skilled in illusion was on site at the exact moment of the collection, the magic would have a different tenor or lack depth. Unconnected magical events that occurred in the same area but at isolated times could and would intermingle in unfocused reconstructions in the same way, but they were always easy enough to spot and edit out.

I reached into the massive Christian Dior vintage briefcase that I wore perpetually slung over my right shoulder, then pulled out the first of four pillar candles. Green for earth. The black bag came from the 2010 spring collection and was made from crocodile skin. I'd removed the silver chain and decorative emblem. I wasn't a fan of labels. I just needed a bag that would stand up to constant use and could hold everything I needed to carry with me at all times.

I set the green candle at the north side of the witches' circle I'd been pacing out around the site. Then, keeping the area between as contained as possible—so that it just encompassed the scorched dirt and grass—I placed my blue pillar at the western edge. Blue for water.

No advocate or magistrate poked holes in my reconstructions. I was exceptionally precise.

The sky darkened further and the wind picked up. The weather report I'd checked to learn the exact time of sunset had indicated that it was going to rain in earnest tonight. I hoped I would be done with my collection before that and well into my first course at Bishop's Restaurant. I'd made the reservation online during the flight up from Seattle.

I would pay my respects to the Godfreys tomorrow when the bakery was open. If I was really fortunate, Jade would be out of town or busy. I was oddly uncomfortable around the dowser. Her magic was intense, and she'd featured in too many of my reconstructions in the past three years, often in terrible pain and seemingly close to dying. That reconstructed Jade was impossible to reconcile with the pretty pertness that seemed to be Jade in everyday life.

However, I knew my duty—as a reconstructionist and a witch—and visiting the bakery was not a social call I could avoid or delay.

Carolina was an annoyingly proficient and thorough investigator. I knew this because I kept brushing up against her persuasion spell—she'd placed it too close to the gravesite for my comfort—and it kept messing with my head. Investigators used certain spells to stop those lacking magic from wandering into an area that was under investigation. It shouldn't have bothered me so much, but Carolina was irritatingly skilled.

After the third time I found myself suddenly needing to rush home to check that I hadn't left the stove on, I was ready to start complaining. Except that complaining would call attention to the fact that it was bothering me in the first place. As a witch, I should have had no trouble blocking it out, except I had to lower my personal shielding in order to call forth and wield my reconstruction spell. I also didn't carry any personal charms or artifacts that would deflect the magic. Such items didn't last long around me. I eventually eroded everything I touched—magical or technological. Interacting with electronics was a challenge for a good portion of the Adept population, but the specific way I held and wielded my magic also ate away at magical items and spells.

After placing a red pillar candle at the southern point—red for fire—I leaned over to light the fourth and final candle at the eastern edge of my circle. White for air. I managed to avoid brushing against the persuasion spell, then returned to stand between the south and west candles.

I could feel Carolina eyeing me and my use of a mundane lighter. She'd probably write it off as an odd ritualistic propensity. But I was actually incapable of simply snapping my fingers to create a modest flame, though that was considered a basic witch spell.

My magic was more honed and specific than that. Well, it was now. I did one thing and I did it exceptionally well.

I'd paced a circle about three feet on either side of the scorched grave. I didn't salt or draw my circles as some witches did, but this wasn't a traditional witches' circle. My reconstruction circles were flexible, mobile, though that wasn't a common skill. And the few reconstructionists who could work their magic so flexibly weren't known for the accuracy of their collections.

I'd seen Clay Dunkirk work once. He had stood at the apex of the scene and cast in all directions. It was powerful and flexible, but sloppy. His technique allowed him to be extremely mobile, but was also prone to picking up contrary or overlapping residual events.

My reconstructions were acutely precise. My technique was an adaption of a spell passed down through generations of Fairchild reconstructionists. It was the only thing I'd taken with me when I walked away from the Fairchild coven at sixteen. The only ancestral tie that I accepted and exploited. It had been twelve years this autumn equinox since I'd been to Connecticut. Twelve years since I'd practiced any magic other than reconstruction.

Without this magic, I would have been destitute and at the mercy of my family.

With this magic, I'd been top of my class at the Academy, challenging the exam after a year rather than taking the typical four years to complete the training. I'd then quickly accumulated a first-class reputation among the Adept, despite being the youngest reconstructionist at the time. It helped that I was known to be open to freelancing, rather than being attached to a specific team or territory.

I carefully removed a platinum charm bracelet from my right wrist and tucked it in the pocket of my dark-navy, midlength Burberry trench coat. The bracelet wasn't magical, but it held two tiny reconstructions that I would have been dreadfully upset to lose by accidentally exposing them to corrupting magic. The tiny cubes were of my own creation and completely compatible with any reconstruction I might cast, but I always preferred to be prepared for whatever might be lurking behind even the most mundane of situations.

I spread my hands to the sides, fingers outstretched, as if cupping the edges of the invisible circle I had just paced out. If I looked for it, I might have been able to spot the crushed grass where I'd walked, but I didn't need to see in order to feel the magic I had laid in my wake.

I inhaled as I gathered the circle closed. Magic spread from my fingers, through the candles and circling back to me.

Carolina stifled an impressed gasp.

I ignored her, reaching for the residual magic now wholly contained within the circle. I beckoned the glimmer of energy to me. It flitted closer willingly, but it was weak, insubstantial.

"There is not a lot of magic here," I murmured.

"The ash read positive," Dalton said. He pitched his voice low, not knowing if I was talking to myself or initiating a conversation. Chatting wasn't generally conducive to casting.

I nodded, still focused on the fine threads of magic I could feel floating before me.

"Show me," I coaxed. "Show me where you began."
Normally I didn't have to speak to direct my reconstructions,

but this magic was immature, for lack of a better way to classify it.

The residual capered across and hovered over the grave. Then it drifted down into the scorched earth and grass.

For a breath, nothing more happened.

Then the dirt burst aflame before liquefying into a sickening pile of blood and pus. That pile rose up, reforming into a dark-haired young man of seventeen or eighteen, dressed in a funeral suit. He had a pink sparkly pencil jutting out of his chest in the area of his heart. The pencil sported a fluffy pink ball in place of an eraser. The teen's eyes whirled with red blood.

"Vampire," I said. "Perhaps seventeen before he was turned, newly risen. But..."

"Yes?" Carolina prompted. The investigator couldn't see the reconstruction as it played out in reverse before me. Not unless I invited her in, which I rarely did. I did my job, so she could wait to do hers.

"It looks as though he was killed with a pink pencil."

"A pencil?" Dalton echoed. "Someone killed a vampire with a pencil?"

"Obviously not," Carolina snapped.

Within the circle that surrounded the gravesite, the reconstruction continued to unfold from back to front. A chef's knife flew into the teenager's hand—as if he'd flung it away—then he reacted to being stabbed in the chest with it.

"He's talking to someone," I said. "But they...they don't exist."

That didn't make any sense. I should have been able to see any Adept standing within the circle. Not even someone exceedingly skilled at cloaking themselves could completely hide from me, and such magic would still register within a reconstruction.

Unless the person the vampire was conversing with was nonmagical? But I immediately rejected that thought. Though I wasn't well versed in vampire lore, I was fairly certain that even a fledgling would have ripped the throat out of any mundane they encountered on the eve of their rising. And actually, even the magically inclined would be at risk.

I watched the fledgling vampire read from a rolled-up note, then tuck that note back into his inner suit pocket. Then two pieces of a headstone flew into his hands and miraculously mended themselves. He must have torn the stone from the ground and smashed it. I'd seen no evidence of a broken headstone at or near the gravesite before I cast the reconstruction. The caretaker must have removed it for repair or replacement. Perhaps the reconstruction would make more sense when I watched the events again in the proper order.

The boy's dark hair fell across his high, pale forehead as he bent forward, replacing a broken corner of the now-flush-mounted headstone, then twisted back in a flip. He crouched at the base of his grave, again conversing with someone I couldn't see. Then I watched him—still running in reverse—dig his way out of his grave. Or, as rendered in the reconstruction, into his grave. The ground within the center of the circle smoothed, then was still.

The magic dissipated.

I stumbled forward in response to the sudden void of energy. Residual magic customarily ebbed and flowed, but minimal though it was, all the power fueling the reconstruction had simply disappeared.

"One minute he's a vampire, and then he's...not," I said.

"That's usually the case with a first rising," Carolina said snootily. As if she'd ever seen a vampire rise.

"You misunderstand, investigator," I said. "He wasn't magic, and then he was. He was human. A dead human, then a slaughtered vampire whose remains were purified by fire." I gestured to the scorched earth at my feet.

Carolina and Dalton glanced at each other skeptically.

"Vampires rarely pick humans to be their…children," Dalton said. "Or anyone so young, even Adepts."

I shrugged. None of the Adept knew vampires or their motivations particularly well…except for their need to drink blood to survive. And even those lacking in magic knew that rule, at least in their fantasy fiction and horror films.

"The boy was human," I said again. I rarely commented on my reconstructions, but this one was highly unusual. "I can't figure out why else the magic would be so immature."

"It's not your job to figure things out, reconstructionist," Carolina said. "Get your collection and we'll interpret it, as always."

I didn't bother arguing. Carolina was correct. I had a job to do and nothing more.

I pulled one of my handcrafted oyster-shell cubes out of my bag. Then I stepped through the dormant circle to set it in the center of the scene, placing the translucent three-inch-square box directly over the section of the grave where the fledgling vampire had risen.

The cubes I crafted were a further extrapolation of my reconstruction magic and unique to me. They were a product of a spell learned as a child from my uncle, then refined over years and years of tutelage. I coaxed the cubes out of finely crushed oyster shell, layering magically polished layer upon layer to create each vessel. As far as I knew, no other witch wielded her magic this way. It was the one and only thing I could create. Everything else I touched gradually eroded into nothing.

Stepping back out of the circle, I called the residual magic I'd previously accessed into the cube. The reconstruction played out again, but this time from beginning to end in real time. A brief moment from the teen's rising to his final death.

Again, I couldn't determine who the fledgling vampire was speaking to, though it was obvious he knew the person well enough that they could get close enough to kill him with a chef's knife and a pencil. A feat I would have thought impossible.

The replay paused oddly after the fledgling vampire dissolved into an oozing pile of blood and guts, almost as if a chunk of time had been removed. Which—again—didn't make any sense to me. Then his remains were set on fire by unseen means and turned into ash.

I'd never heard of a vampire turning to gooey mush when killed. But then, I had only textbooks, historic reconstructions, and one incident I'd personally reconstructed in London as references. Like most of the Adept, I had never been face-to-face with an actual vampire. Not only were they a rare subspecies of magic user, they were also traditionally xenophobic.

I kept the remainder of my observations to myself as I channeled the reconstruction into the oyster-shell vessel. Jade Godfrey had once referred to these handmade boxes as 'YouTube cubes,' and she wasn't far off. When Pearl's number had appeared on my phone, I'd felt momentarily ill, concerned that she was about to ask me to reconstruct another scene from her granddaughter's ever-turbulent life.

Thankfully, there were no demons or blood-crazed sisters to be reconstructed in the Capilano View Cemetery in West Vancouver. Simply a human teenager turned vampire, then turned to a pile of goo and set on fire. His murderer—or savior, depending on perspective—was obviously a human female. Obviously human because she carried no magic to imprint the reconstruction. Obviously female, and specifically a sister or girlfriend, by the note in his pocket and the pink pencil. Though even as I thought it, I realized that assumption could be construed as gender profiling, and therefore wasn't particularly professional of me.

But I surmised girlfriend, keeping the opinion to myself as I closed the circle and crouched down by the collection cube. The seemingly delicate oyster-shell box was practically unbreakable with the addition of the collected magic.

How a human had killed a vampire was intriguingly on the edge of impossible. How a teenaged boy had been turned into a vampire, then had apparently been abandoned by his maker to rise in a human cemetery, was disturbing and haunting. And not at all my business.

I placed a second oyster-shell cube beside the first.

"What are you doing?" Carolina snapped.

"You'd like a copy of the reconstruction, wouldn't you?"

The investigator frowned.

Ancestral history with the Fairchild coven or otherwise, I didn't know what was going on with the witch. Apparently, I couldn't avoid rubbing her the wrong way.

"The Convocation requested the original?" Carolina might be pissy and bossy, but she was also quick. Though good investigators were usually as intelligent as they were magically skilled.

I nodded.

Carolina pursed her lips, but she made no further protest.

I placed the fingers of my right hand on top of the cube swirling with the magic of the collection, and the fingers of my left hand on the duller empty cube. Then I touched my thumbs together, allowing the magic to flow through one hand, into the other, and down into the empty cube.

The scene I'd reconstructed from the residual magic at the grave replayed through my mind as it was copied. Yes, I also functioned as a magical video recorder. It was only really strange if I thought about it too much. I'd been collecting reconstructions for so long that the spell work was practically instinctual, so thankfully there was no need to really think about it at all.

I never kept a copy of my professional reconstructions. When residual magic was collected in the course of an investigation, doing so was against Convocation policy. But also, reconstructionists could become addicted to their collections, similar to how someone might be haunted by a memory—except that magic was involved. And magic made everything more potent, especially addictions.

Sienna, Jade's sister, was dead because she'd become addicted to blood magic and had gone on a killing spree to fuel the dark rituals she'd used to harvest the power of other Adepts. I had collected many of the reconstructions surrounding the deaths of her victims, but I was fortunate that I hadn't been commissioned to collect the scene of her own death. Thankfully, I really didn't know much about the particulars. Because even though three years had passed, the scenes of Sienna's life—the ones fueled by her addiction—still stalked my nightmares, awake and asleep.

While it was true that the members of the Fairchild coven weren't exactly poster children for the good side of the scale of good versus evil, I'd never been forced to reconstruct any of their magical incidents. They kept their darkness buried deep within. And, if it ever came to it, I could cite a conflict of interest. But I absolutely refused to let my family haunt me, not for one minute more than they'd already damaged my heart and soul.

It wasn't unusual for the Convocation to request an original reconstruction for incidents such as this, though I was fairly certain that Carolina didn't like having her investigations so closely observed. It was more difficult to sweep in and announce that she'd miraculously solved a crime when everyone else had access to the puzzle pieces.

That this was the scene of a crime was obvious, though which crime would be investigated and what charges might be leveled, I didn't know.

A teenager had apparently been killed and turned into a vampire. That could be a crime, if he'd been unwilling.

A teenager had been turned into a vampire in Pearl Godfrey's territory. That was definitely frowned upon, if not actually illegal according to Adept law. No vampire of power resided in Vancouver, which was and always had been witch territory.

A vampire had been seen in Vancouver in the company of Jade Godfrey, though. But again, only those in the know—or who had reconstructed the crimes of the black witch Sienna—knew that. However, that vampire had been destroyed by Sienna's hand in London almost three years before.

So Kettil, the one-time executioner of the Conclave—the collective that governed the vampires—couldn't have been the one turning human teenagers into fledgling vampires in Vancouver, British Columbia, Canada.

But I knew only what I'd seen within the magic I'd collected. I didn't ask questions about things that didn't concern me or my ability to do my job. Life among powerful Adepts was much safer under those circumstances.

"I walked the cemetery on my way in," I said, pushing away thoughts of dead teenagers and vampires while handing the duplicate cube to Carolina. "There are no other residual spots."

The lead investigator took the oyster-shell container, holding it gingerly by the edges. "I'm aware of that fact," she said.

"It won't break," I said, referencing the cube. "Not with normal handling."

"I'm accustomed to glass," she said stiffly, twisting away and passing the cube to Dalton.

He awkwardly placed the reconstruction in a six-inch thick, foam-lined metal carrying case. The cube didn't fit into the circle that had been cut out of the foam.

"We are accustomed to crystal," Carolina said, repeating herself unnecessarily.

I smiled politely. Most reconstructionists stored their collections in crystal balls. Some witches also used crystal to amplify seek or seeing spells, but crystal was heavy, unreliable, and expensive.

"The cube is responsive to my magic," I said. "I make them by hand."

"Yes," Carolina said. "I've seen them at trial. Most effective."

I tried to accept the praise—begrudgingly given or not—with a more genuine smile. It was difficult working with a new team member. I wasn't overly pleased to be filling in for Clay Dunkirk either. Though now that I'd felt the insubstantial magic and the way it had dispersed when the fledgling vampire returned to his grave, I wasn't surprised that Clay had fainted. If he contained his collection sites as I did, he wouldn't have had a problem when the magic just dropped away.

I glanced down at the cube I still held. It was oddly dim for something filled with magic. Red-tinted gray energy sluggishly swirled within it. Perhaps there just hadn't been enough magic for Clay to collect. Perhaps I was just that much more powerful. The notion quashed the smile I was attempting to maintain. My mother would be pleased that I was upholding the Fairchild reputation, but I wasn't a fan of how such power was wielded by the Fairchilds in general.

"I hope Clay recovers quickly," I said, shaking off the thought and tucking the dim cube into my bag.

The rain had intensified and evening had fallen while I'd been occupied with the collection. Drizzle was steadily wetting my cheeks. Dalton was currently placing tiny pinpoints of light around the gravesite to combat the darkness. I wondered if he was using a spell or premade charms.

"Clay is already on his way home," Carolina said, pulling my attention back to our stilted conversation. "On a well-deserved short vacation."

"Of course. Shall I stay in town?"

"No need." Carolina gave a dismissive wave toward the administration building where we'd parked. "I doubt we've happened upon a rash of risings. A vampire powerful enough to turn more than one fledgling wouldn't leave his child unattended."

"Then I'm pleased to have met you both."

"And you, Wisteria." Carolina smiled tightly. "I'll include it more formally in my report, of course, but please thank Pearl Godfrey for me. You were very…efficient."

Dalton stepped closer, grinning as he reached to shake my hand.

I hesitated at the friendly gesture, then grasped his hand firmly. Adepts weren't big on touching. You could never be certain what a magic user of unknown power could do to you through even the most minor contact. But an upstanding member of a Convocation investigative team wasn't likely to be going around collecting magic for nefarious purposes.

"Good night," Dalton said pleasantly.

I nodded, releasing his hand as swiftly as I could, and undoubtedly coming off as reserved and snobbish in the process. But I couldn't help it.

"I wish you well with the investigation," I murmured. Then I all but fled across the wet grass to my rental car.

Thankfully, I could use the rain as an excuse for my swift pace.

The rain began to hammer down in earnest as I pulled out of the cemetery and headed down the mountain and back into the city proper. The houses—mansions, really—were all well protected by tall cedar and fir trees from the probing of my twin headlights as my GPS guided me through a shortcut out of the affluent British Properties residential area.

The sporadically spaced streetlights did little to illuminate the winding, narrow road until I hit Taylor Way. Once on that main road, I slipped down the steep hillside, traversed the Lions Gate Bridge, and was cutting through Stanley Park on my way into the city within fifteen minutes. I'd missed rush hour, but would still have to forgo changing at the hotel so I wasn't late for dinner.

A text message on my cellphone lit up the car interior. I'd placed it within easy reach on the passenger seat. At a red light at Denman Street, I leaned over to see a text from Jasmine.

>*Looking forward to mac and cheese. Oh! And some of those frozen cheesecake balls.*

I laughed, pulling through the drenched intersection as the light turned green. Jasmine, my lifelong best friend and cousin on my mother's side, was flying into Seattle on Friday for a girls' weekend. It was also her twenty-eighth birthday. She was almost exactly one month younger than me. We'd been inseparable since birth and had apprenticed together at the tender age of nine.

When we were apart, I missed her in a way that made me lonely for all the things I'd never actually had…like a family that loved me more than power, money, and prestige within the Adept community.

Unfortunately, neither Jasmine nor I had that family, but we had each other. She made up for a lot of the rough times. She'd been there for me, as I had for her. And though I hadn't spoken to him for over twelve years, both of us also had Jasmine's half-brother, Declan, for better or worse, for good and evil, forever and after.

Traffic crawled in front of me along Georgia Street. Every light pouring out of the city—from storefronts, restaurants, and traffic signals—was reflected in a blurred rainbow of golds and greens and reds on the wet asphalt. My windshield wipers appeared to be having trouble keeping up with the deluge as my thoughts drifted to Declan...as my thoughts always drifted to him. I probably could have turned right at Denman, but I didn't know the city terribly well.

The next time I stopped for a red light, I texted Jasmine back.

Beecher's Cheese and the Confectionary, yes!! My treat. Miss you.

>*I miss you but I'm leveling up. Enforcer, baby.*

I snorted. Jasmine was a witch with an affinity for technology. In fact, the only reason I could even text with her was due to the protection spells she regularly placed on my phone. Otherwise, I would shut down the cellular—or any other technology—with a single touch. Jasmine's affinity for technology also translated into an obsession for gaming and social networks. If it was online, my cousin would play it—and then usually reject it as trite and dreadfully programmed within twenty-four hours.

I had no idea what she meant by 'leveling up' and 'enforcer,' but apparently, she had a new online role-playing game to obsess over.

I texted back.

Good luck with it.

>Luck? Who needs luck when you have magic in your fingers?

I laughed. Who could argue with that? Not me.

After I made my way over the Burrard Street Bridge and found parking just off West Fourth Avenue, I tucked my phone back into my bag and pulled my platinum charm bracelet out of my trench coat pocket. I allowed my fingers to linger on the two tiny oyster-shell cubes hidden among the bracelet's miniature houses, trees, and picket fences.

I carried those reconstructions with me everywhere since having had the bracelet made six years before. It was an acknowledgement that I would never have a life that contained a loving family, a dutiful husband, and two-point-five perfect children. Instead, I wore my white picket fence on my right wrist…in celebration and in defiance.

The oyster-shell cubes contained scenes from my past. Pieces of my heart, really. Large pieces. Reconstructions I'd replayed so many times that I had no idea anymore what parts were pure memory and what parts were actual events.

Declan. And Jasmine.

I clipped the bracelet onto my wrist. Then reaching into the back seat for my bag, I focused on swapping out my practical flats for heels and putting on a touch of makeup. I might be dining solo, but this level of fine dining called for an effort. In lieu of a hotel stopover, a teal pashmina stole, a strand of pearls, and a darker maroon lipstick paired with my practical-but-classic, dark-navy flutter-sleeve sheath dress would have to do.

Chapter Two

Bishop's Restaurant was located in the neighborhood of Kitsilano, ironically only a block and a half east of Jade Godfrey's bakery. Thankfully, Cake in a Cup was closed for the evening, so I could skip the societal niceties and wait until morning to drop the reconstruction off to Pearl.

I had a room booked at the Pan Pacific Hotel, which was situated over the Burrard Street Bridge and back through the downtown core. The hotel contained a fantastic four-diamond restaurant, the Five Sails. I'd eaten there on my first visit to Vancouver three years earlier, when I presented my reconstructions before the tribunal assembled to pass judgement on the murders committed by Jade's foster sister, Sienna. At the time, everyone had assumed Sienna was dead. She wasn't. And more reconstructions had followed in the wake of her bloody killing spree across Britain.

But I wasn't interested in dwelling on blood-frenzied black witches. I was seeking fantastic West Coast fine dining. And I was going to find that, and surround myself with regular humans, at Bishop's.

The restaurant was small and tastefully decorated. First Nations art—prints, carvings, and masks—dominated the white-painted walls. The tables were swathed in white linen, with a fresh posy and a glassed votive candle at the center of each.

"Ms. Fairchild?" The hostess, who I thought might also be the manager, greeted me in the tiny glassed entrance-way. Apparently, she knew exactly who each and every one of her reservations were as they walked in the door, which was utterly charming and boded well for the level of service over the rest of the evening. "May I take your wrap?"

"No. Thank you." I'd left my trench coat in the rental car, throwing the pashmina stole over my head and shoulders for the quick dash from the sidewalk into the restaurant. The evening held a slight chill, and I wanted the option of wearing the stole indoors as well.

"This way, please."

The tables at the front of the restaurant near the windows were all occupied by well-dressed patrons. The manager led me past the bar and up a short set of stairs to a second floor. Only a single table for two was empty, tucked into the corner of the waist-high wall overlooking the diners on the first level. Surprised that the restaurant was so full on a Monday evening, I was glad I'd made a reservation. I took the seat in the corner so I'd have a view of the room.

A hushed, happy murmur of conversation washed over me, unobtrusive and welcoming. I instantly relaxed.

The manager placed a two-page menu before me, along with a more extensive leather-bound wine list.

"Thank you," I murmured.

She smiled, then slipped away, weaving back through the close-set tables. I had a feeling the wait staff would be at my side the second before I knew I needed anything, but that they wouldn't chat my ear off in the process of serving me. I adored that style of service.

I glanced over at the nearby tables. Though the room was small, it didn't feel crammed. Perhaps it was the mixture of table sizes and shapes that created the sense of space. Or perhaps it was because all the decor was white, excepting the silverware and the artwork.

I carefully perused the menu, though I already knew I was going to opt for a seafood dish. As I'd noted from the website, and now the menu, the executive chef favored local ingredients and light sauces. I was already in heaven, and I hadn't tasted a single dish yet.

I settled on the dungeness crab risotto to start, and had just reached for the wine list to find a Pinot Noir to pair it with, when I realized that someone was sitting across from me.

Not just a someone. A vampire.

A white-blond, blue-eyed, exceedingly pale, tremendously powerful vampire who I'd thought was dead. Well, more dead. I had reconstructed the moment of his destruction myself. In London, three years before, I'd seen him stabbed through the heart with a magical blade. I'd seen him fall.

Kettil, the executioner of the Conclave, was swathed in expensive green cashmere so dark it was practically black, sporting what appeared to be a solid gold Apple Watch and lounging back in the seat across from me as if he'd been sitting there the entire time. His eyes were so light blue, they could practically have been called silver. He quirked his lips in a shallow, pleased smile.

I hadn't seen him sit down. I hadn't even seen him cross the room.

My server, who'd been approaching the table from the back kitchen area, flinched. Her human reactions were even more delayed than mine. Startled, she exhaled, pressing her hand to her chest.

"Wisteria Fairchild," the vampire said. His exceedingly straight teeth were even paler than his face. I couldn't see any hint of his fangs.

"Yes."

"Kettil." He reached across the table.

I lifted my own hand from the linen tablecloth. Pleased that it wasn't shaking, I grasped his outstretched hand as his gaze fell to my charm bracelet. He wasn't as cold as I thought he'd be, but perhaps I was still chilled myself. His fingers closed completely over mine, firm but not crushing. Still, I could feel the terrible strength that lay just underneath his hold.

He could tear me limb from limb, slaughter every human in the restaurant, bathe in our blood, and I wouldn't have been able to do a single thing about it.

I was panicking.

I never panicked.

But I could feel the adrenaline rushing through me as the vampire held my hand.

He lifted his gaze to mine, widening his grin. And without so much as a blink or a breath, he ensnared me. Idiotically, I'd been staring directly into his eyes.

He held his other hand up toward the server. She froze.

His presence flooded my mind in a warm, calming, and almost euphoric pulse.

"Steady," he murmured.

My heart rate settled. I felt as though my arm was suspended, stretched across the table, lightly cradled in his hand...cushioned by the awesome presence of his mind.

I could have stayed there forever. At peace...protected...cherished...

I could have been his forever.

No Fairchild is weak enough to be ensnared by a vampire.

I wasn't totally sure whether that was an original thought or a remembered edict of my mother's, but it was enough to wake me up to the situation.

I gathered my mental shields, imagining a barrier of magic between the vampire and myself. Evoking layers upon layers of magic, similar to the sides of my oyster-shell cubes. I blinked my eyes, then shook my head slightly.

I lifted my hand away from Kettil's.

He let me go.

I carefully placed my reclaimed limb on the table beside my place setting.

"May I get you a menu?" the server asked, as if she hadn't been standing motionless beside the table for over a minute.

"The wine list," Kettil said, though he didn't take his gaze from mine.

She laughed, thrilled by his request for some unknown reason. She picked up and handed him the list.

"You were thinking of a Pinot Noir?" His tone was intimate, as if we'd been discussing this selection and he hadn't simply plucked the thought out of my head.

I lifted my chin, affixing my gaze to his left cheekbone, then nodded as if I was in perfect control of the situation.

The vampire's lips curled into a smirk. He was dreadfully handsome, but in a way that might turn fierce and ugly with a single thought, a simple action. He pushed back the sleeves of his cashmere sweater, and I was surprised that the delicate yarn wasn't crushed by the casual gesture. His face, and what I could see of his wrists and forearms, was chiseled—honed from marble and centuries of dreadful deeds. Yet by candlelight, he looked exceedingly human. Though his spine was perhaps too stiff, and he held the menu a touch too formally.

"A bottle of the Blue Mountain," he said to the server. Though perhaps she was actually the sommelier.

"An excellent choice, sir," she said. "We only managed to get our hands on a single case this season. I don't recommend decanting it."

"Of course not," Kettil said.

The sommelier pivoted, crossing to descend the short staircase to the bar just off the entrance to the restaurant.

"Pinot Noir should never be allowed to breathe," Kettil said, maintaining his intimate tone. "In fact, it is best to cork it between pours. Yes?"

"Do not attempt to ensnare me again," I said, forcing myself to be pleasant while demanding his acquiescence.

"You were going to panic. There was no need to panic."

"The fact that you ensnared me shows that there was a reason to panic."

"You broke my gaze easily." Kettil settled back, one hand set casually on the table and the other on the arm of his chair. The pose was meant to appear casual, but it carried a sense of having been well practiced.

The vampire was being careful, considerate. That, more than anything else, should have been a massive warning sign. But it was my certainty that he had let go of his hold on me that chilled me even more. I had no idea whether I could have broken his control any other way.

Being powerless and feeling out of control were tenuous states for me. I avoided such situations, as if doing so was my religion and I was a zealous practitioner.

The sommelier returned with the bottle of wine—a deep, clear red from Summerland, BC, with subtle red berry and vanilla notes—and two globe wineglasses.

Kettil accepted the taster she poured, lifting it to his nose to assess the bouquet, then sipping as if he did such things every day. As if he was practicing being human in the twenty-first century.

Why would a vampire do such a thing? Why would he need to pass for human when the humans themselves had no idea what he was? And where was that wine going when he sipped it? Did vampires have working digestive systems? I had always assumed they just directly absorbed the blood they drank to survive.

Kettil nodded, approving the bottle.

The sommelier poured us two glasses.

My server, an older dark-haired man of fifty or so, stepped up to the table. He smiled at the sommelier as she slipped away. "In addition to our menu, tonight we are offering—"

Kettil cut him off midsentence. "The lady will begin with the dungeness crab risotto, followed by the Arctic char."

The server looked slightly startled, but he recovered smoothly. "And for you, sir?"

"I'm pleased with the wine and need no other sustenance tonight."

The server nodded, then hightailed it back to the kitchen. Humans might not have been able to understand they were conversing with a vampire, but unless ensnared, they instinctively preferred to avoid large predators. As did I.

My instincts screamed for me to run or fight, though I was fairly certain that I would die upon initiating either action. My upbringing compelled me to sip the wine and nod my approval of Kettil's choice. Then I stopped myself. I would be polite, but I wasn't going to allow anyone to rule me, from near or afar.

"Listening to the specials is part of the ritual," I said, as quiet and nonconfrontational as I could be.

"You already knew what you wanted."

I lifted my gaze to meet his almost-silvered eyes. "I might have changed my mind."

He nodded thoughtfully. "It has been many years since I've frequented a dining establishment. Even then, I wasn't there for the fish."

If it wasn't for the implied threat, that was most likely as close to an apology as the executioner of the Conclave got.

"I would like to view the reconstruction you collected at the cemetery this evening."

The hackles stood up on the back of my neck. A vampire wanted to see a reconstruction of a fledgling vampire's rising and subsequent destruction.

That wasn't suspicious at all.

Kettil raised a pale blond eyebrow at my silence.

"Pearl Godfrey requested my presence," I finally said, relieved to have the opportunity to foist the vampire off on the elder witch. "It is proper—"

"Fine." Kettil waved his hand dismissively, the motion creating a disconcerting blur. He was moving too quickly. "We will speak to the witches tomorrow if you insist on proceeding through proper channels."

I glanced down at my wine. Though I didn't want to appear submissive, I also didn't want to be caught staring at him strangely.

"But the Convocation will step aside," Kettil continued. "This is not a matter for witches."

"This is witch territory," I said, not knowing why I was bothering to argue. It really had nothing to do with me. I'd done my job.

Kettil laughed dismissively. "This is Godfrey territory."

I wasn't sure how his assertion was different from what I'd said—except maybe he was referring to Jade more than Pearl. Vancouver was changing, becoming more of a draw for Adepts in general. But Pearl Godfrey was still the force to be reckoned with in this area. Jade was too young, too inexperienced to hold territory.

Too dangerous.

And with too many dangerous friends, including the one sitting across from me.

I lifted my gaze to Kettil, watching his fingers curl around the stem of his wineglass as he lifted it, sipping and savoring the dark-red nectar.

The vampire was completely different in person than he'd appeared in the reconstructions I had collected of him. I wondered—for the second time—if that was somehow due to his connection to Jade. I'd posited that same thought in London when I'd watched him step between Jade and her sister to take a killing blow meant for the dowser. I'd watched him fall. I'd watched the magic in his veins appear to turn to ash underneath his translucent skin.

I had seen him die. I'd seen Jade's utter despair over losing him.

Yet he was sitting before me, seemingly unchanged but completely different.

"Pearl Godfrey will be appeased when we inform her that you will be helping with this investigation. You may report back to her."

"What…pardon me?" I'd obviously lost the thread of the conversation. "My work here is done."

"It is not."

The server returned, placing an amuse bouche before me—a delightful bite of tuna tartare with spring onion to whet my palate.

"There have been more risings?" I asked, pitching my question low so as to not pique the interest of nearby diners.

"One more. That I know of."

"But the investigative team—"

"Is no longer required."

I stared at him. More risings implied that a powerful vampire was involved, or multiple vampires. But I was a reconstructionist, not a vampire slayer. "I'm not a certified investigator. I don't put the puzzle pieces together. I only collect them."

"Perfect," Kettil said. "I just need the pieces I can't see. Then I'll do the rest."

I paused, choosing my next words carefully, even while knowing I should keep my mouth shut. For some reason, possibly because they were highly qualified, I felt compelled to defend the investigative teams and the unique skill sets of their members. "You are an...investigator for the Conclave, then?" I subbed 'investigator' for 'executioner'—Kettil's actual title—at the last second, not wanting to seem too pointed. I still wasn't sure how openly I could communicate with the vampire. Without getting my throat ripped out for my insolence, at any rate.

Kettil inclined his head.

"I had heard they refer to you by another title."

Kettil raised his eyebrow. Again. "Elder?"

My heart skipped a beat. I knew exceedingly little about the Conclave, but what I did know seemed to indicate that elders were...ancient. And that perhaps only a half-dozen existed.

"Breathe," Kettil whispered.

I exhaled, keeping my gaze firmly affixed to his left cheekbone and maintaining a polite engagement, but not staring directly at him, eye to eye. "I was referring to your other title. Executioner."

Kettil stilled.

Which was disconcerting, because despite him playing at being human, I would have described him as being perfectly still just a moment before.

I waited, aware of my heart beating slightly quicker than normal in my chest. The moment stretched between us, painfully stifled. I became uncomfortably aware that we were surrounded by activity and chatter, even as we sat awkwardly staring at each other.

"I was unaware you were versed in Conclave business," Kettil finally said.

"I'm not. Is anyone who isn't a vampire?"

"Yet you claim to know me."

"From the reconstructions, in the bakery basement and in London."

A slow, deliberate smile spread across Kettil's face. The expression transformed him into so-nearly-human that I momentarily forgot who and what he was. He was suddenly languid…approachable. Sexy.

The lower edge of my ribcage hit the table. I was listing toward him, infinitely eager for his next word, his next—

"Jade," he murmured. It pleased him to utter the dowser's name. As if he owned her somehow, claiming her just by naming her.

The weird connection between us snapped. I dropped my gaze to my wineglass. I'd been rotating it on the table in my right hand. I stopped. Though I knew that no matter how I tried to hide it, the vampire would know he unnerved me.

"Did she weep for me?" he asked. "As she was telling you all my secrets in London? Did the alchemist shed tears and tales?" His cool tone had warmed, become honeyed.

I wasn't sure how to answer. I wasn't sure what he wanted to hear. I had no idea how to maintain a professional demeanor around the vampire. "I don't believe Jade intended to share any secrets, as you call them."

Kettil shifted back in his seat and picked up his glass of wine, reverting back to playing human. He'd been leaning intimately forward as well. We'd been matching each other's body language.

I was certain that was a bad sign.

For me, at least.

"If Pearl Godfrey wishes it, I would be delighted to assist the Conclave in this matter," I said, erecting an impassible wall of professionalism between us.

Though I rarely needed to do so in the course of my job, I was more than capable of dealing with Adepts of power.

Kettil took a sip of his wine, then nodded. He slowly turned his silver-blue gaze on the rest of the room and all the humans in it. He held his glass in his palm, like other people held their brandy to warm it.

The server traversed the room, setting my dungeness crab risotto appetizer in front of me. I immediately retrieved my fork and took a bite, aware that the vampire was watching me. The dish was spotted with peas, three poached quail eggs, and served in a crab bisque. I'd been worried about the fennel I'd noted on the menu's description of the dish, but no one taste stood out above any other. It was creamy and delicious. The serving size was petite, perhaps six or seven spoonfuls. I applied myself to relishing each one. Once sliced, the quail's eggs revealed a perfect hint of soft yolk. I made an effort to get a tiny taste of every component in each bite.

I kept my focus on the food, and not on wondering what the vampire was thinking as he watched me eat.

"Whether or not we are to work together, I would recommend you allow the investigative team to continue," I said, since it was obvious Kettil wasn't done with the conversation. He was still sitting across from me, after all. And I wasn't completely sure he was actually drinking the wine, so I doubted that was what was keeping him.

"You didn't appear to be overly fond of Carolina and Dalton," he said, mockingly amused.

I whipped my head up so quickly that I awkwardly cricked my neck. He'd been at the cemetery, close enough to pick up my attitude toward the team, yet I hadn't noticed him when I'd been looking for residual spots of magic.

That was unnerving.

"It would seem prudent to have someone with you," I said. "Someone skilled in nonmagical investigation, computers and such. Unfortunately, my magic is a hindrance with technology."

Kettil flicked his gaze to my hands.

I resisted the urge to hide them in my lap, taking the final bite of my delectable risotto instead.

The vampire nodded thoughtfully, lifting his gaze to my face. Though he somehow looked past me, through me.

I stiffened my spine. If I was actually going to have to work with him, I couldn't be constantly cowering and casting my gaze to the side. "It's only logical with the victim being human, and his attacker obviously also—"

"I already agree, reconstructionist," Kettil said. "You have no need to press your point. I assume, if we are to work together, as you say, that you have a recommendation?"

"Jasmine Fairchild."

A slow smile spread across the vampire's face, but I had no idea what was so amusing about our conversation. There was something underlying all this that I was obviously missing.

"Your cousin, I believe," he said.

I set my fork down across my plate, then lightly pressed my linen napkin to my lips. Jasmine was well known, and not many witches worked with technology as well as she did. Pearl Godfrey commissioned work from her regularly. But it bothered me that the vampire had chosen to refer to our familial connection, instead of Jasmine's magical abilities.

The server slipped by our table, glancing at our full wineglasses, then bussing my empty plate without a word.

"Is Jasmine Fairchild as skilled at keeping secrets as she is at uncovering them?"

"She's been keeping mine for over a quarter of a century," I said flippantly, tiring of whatever game was being played even before I'd fully figured out the parameters or rules.

Kettil smirked, sipping his wine without looking away from me.

The thought of what he might rather be sipping drifted through my mind.

The vampire's smile widened, revealing the tips of his perfect teeth, as if he might be picking up on my thoughts. Though I felt none of the magical control he'd exerted on me earlier.

"Good," he said.

I racked my mind for a moment, trying to recall where the conversation had stopped. If this was his typical pace when exchanging information, spending too much time with Kettil would be exhausting.

"When and where would she need to meet us? Assuming our participation in the investigation is sanctioned by the Convocation."

"We'll be in Vancouver for another day at least."

"She was to meet me in Seattle this weekend. I maintain an apartment there."

"I know."

I ignored the vampire's statement. He obviously enjoyed intimidating me, but I wasn't willing to cede control of the situation any longer. "At some point, vampire," I said archly, "I will move beyond being frightened of you and simply walk away. I don't pay much heed to bullies."

"Good, Wisteria Fairchild. Otherwise, you will bore me utterly. I loathe being bored."

Jade Godfrey had thought that Kettil died in London. She'd mourned him deeply, bitterly. Yet he was in Vancouver, sipping wine, and seemingly challenging the Convocation's jurisdiction.

I despaired of ever witnessing what being bored might entail for him.

"Pearl Godfrey is expecting us at 10:30 A.M. tomorrow," he said.

So my participation was a forgone conclusion, was it? Though, honestly, that went without saying when it came to the Godfreys and the Convocation. I wouldn't have been able to legally separate myself from my family at sixteen or maintain a livelihood without either of them, even with my Aunt Rose maintaining one of the Convocation's thirteen seats. My debt was deep and undeniable.

Kettil glanced toward the kitchen a moment before the server stepped through the doors, then crossed into the dining room carrying my Arctic char. "I will leave you to your dinner."

"Goodnight, Kettil."

"Kett," he said, reaching across the table and touching the palm of my left hand before I'd had any chance to see him move. "It suits this century better."

He ran his fingers along mine, so lightly that I could barely feel his touch. Cool shivers ran across my wrist and up my arm.

Then the vampire was gone.

The server placed my main course before me. "Yukon Arctic char," he said. "With celery, swiss chard, gnocchi parisienne, and lemon caper vinaigrette."

"It looks delicious. Thank you."

He straightened Kett's chair, glancing toward where I assumed the bathrooms were. "Do you need anything else?"

"No, thank you."

The server nodded and retreated toward the kitchen, slowly checking on his tables as he walked away.

Kett had tucked a hundred-dollar bill underneath his still full wineglass. Canadian currency. He'd also just touched my hand as if it were...precious. I glanced down at my palm, but I could see nothing there that might have inspired an ancient vampire.

That he was ancient, I had no doubt. I knew little of substance about vampires, but I was fairly certain that a young vampire would never have recovered from the wound Kett sustained in London. And that a middle-aged vampire would have no need to adopt a nickname for a new century. Granted, I hadn't met a vampire of any age before. But I was willing to wager that an ancient vampire played at being human in order to not be bored by his unending existence.

I shuddered at the thought of such immortality. Then I applied my attention and my fork to the piece of art masquerading as food on my plate.

The delicately pink fish flaked underneath the lightest of touches. I swirled a bite in the vinaigrette, managing to capture a caper before placing it in my mouth.

Savoring the subtle, fresh flavors, I vowed to not worry for one extra moment about what I'd just seemingly agreed to. Pearl Godfrey would have the final say tomorrow. It would be silly of me to fret and ruin my dinner tonight.

I took a picture of my main course when I thought no one was looking, then texted it to Jasmine, who was the only other person I knew who reveled in food as much as I did.

Of course, Jasmine could cook.

I couldn't even boil water. Literally. I had to leave the kitchen after I set the kettle on the stove, then cross to the other side of the apartment just to make tea.

I was a skilled reconstructionist. But I eroded everything else I touched. Again, literally.

I housed my cellphone in a metal case coated in one of Jasmine's expensive spells—the workings of which I didn't even remotely understand—to protect it from my magic, and I still had to replace it every three months or so. I was exceedingly thankful that 'the cloud' was a thing these days.

Texting in a restaurant as lovely as Bishop's was unseemly, so I quickly tucked the phone away and applied myself to my food.

I always ate alone.

I lived alone.

Even my work was mostly a solo endeavor.

By choice. By preference.

Yet with Kett's departure, I felt uncharacteristically lonely.

After ordering the cheese plate for dessert, I contemplated wandering up the block and knocking on Jade's apartment door. Would the dowser invite me in and offer me cupcakes?

Except a witch like me—with a powerful but specific skill set—didn't become friends with someone like Jade. Being around people of her power level made me antsy to unleash my own magic.

And I didn't unleash.

I couldn't.

The cheese plate came with fruit. I paired a slice of camembert with a sliver of pear and tried to settle back into the comforting surroundings and chatter.

No. Powerful people—including Kett and Jade—got witches like me hurt or killed. Even worse, not all wounds were skin deep. Some dented the soul.

And my soul had been damaged enough for a lifetime. It had been that way since before I was sixteen, and was proving to be exceedingly slow at healing.

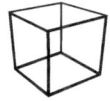

Built out of white steel and blue glass, the Pan Pacific Hotel sat on the edge of Vancouver's inner harbor, boasting one-hundred-and-eighty-degree views of the North Shore Mountains and the city skyline. The convention center and cruise ship terminal attached to the four-star hotel stretched across the foreshore, perched over the water on piles drilled deep into the ocean floor.

I left my rental car to the valet and gave my bag to the porter, strolling through the automatic glassed front doors into the grand entrance, then up the escalator to check in at the front desk. The hotel's contemporary decor was lush but not gaudy. Golden-lit cream pillars, sweeping staircases, sepia tiled floors, and light wood accents dominated throughout. A display of fresh-cut flowers easily four feet tall and two-and-a-half feet wide was perched on a large round table in the center of the atrium lobby. Glassed railings on every floor offered an inner view of the first five storeys of the building.

This trip was my second stay at the Pan Pacific. During my first visit, the service had been polite and professional, plus the view was spectacular. So I'd seen no reason to try another hotel.

I checked in without any fuss, finding my luggage tucked just inside the door of my room by the time I rode the elevator up to the twelfth floor.

I didn't bother turning on any interior lights. Immediately crossing to the windows, which practically ran from floor to ceiling, I gazed out at the night-shrouded harbor and the soaring mountains to my right. The lights of the city spread for miles on my left. A neon-lit filling station for boats floated between the hotel and the dark swath of trees that was Stanley Park. Beginning at the edge of the park, countless lights decorated the steel cables of the Lions Gate Bridge, creating the effect of a massive, single-stranded pearl necklace suspended over the inlet that separated the city from the North Shore. From my vantage point, I could trace the exact route I'd driven to and from the cemetery that afternoon.

I tugged off my heels, then curled up on the firm but comfortable high-backed armchair and ottoman combo that sat in the corner of the room. Still gazing out at the view, I retrieved my cellphone from my bag and dialed Jasmine.

Raindrops sprinkled across the window, blurring the downtown lights. But there was nothing forlorn about sitting alone in the darkness perched above the city and the ocean. It was comforting, inviting.

"Hello, cousin," Jasmine said, answering my call after a single ring. Her greeting was cheerful but slightly distracted, as always.

I tucked the phone between the side wing of the chair and my ear, holding it close and risking eroding the spells that protected it from my magic just for a moment. "So I just had dinner with a vampire."

"What?!"

Jasmine's shriek forced me to drop the phone into my lap out of deference for my eardrum. Laughing, I retrieved it, resting it on the arm of the chair, then tapping the speaker icon while my cousin continued to natter excitedly at the other end. So much for capping my evening with intimate, calm conversation.

"Tell me everything." Her demand reverberated through the phone's speaker. "I'm pausing my game. Start from the beginning."

"Pausing your game? That is serious."

"A vampire? A vampire! Was he seriously creepy and fangy? Or was he a she? Who set up the meeting? Pearl? Why a restaurant? That seems like an odd choice of location. Wouldn't it give the vampire ideas about what he or she should be eating? Have you ever met one before?"

Jasmine paused, inhaling as if to line up her next set of questions.

I took the opportunity to answer the final question of her first round. "You know I haven't."

"Please. With the secrets you keep? I can never know for sure."

The smile slipped from my face as my chest tightened at the implication beneath her words. I toyed with my bracelet, looking out the window again. From the lower vantage point of the chair, I could see the far third of a vibrant blue outdoor pool and its red-tiled sundeck situated below on the eighth level.

"I'm sorry," Jasmine said. "I know you don't keep secrets. Not really. I shouldn't have said it that way."

"It's okay."

We sat in silence together for another minute or so, then Jasmine tried to pick up the thread of the conversation.

"So was the meeting work related?"

"He wants me to work on a case with him, connected to the case I reconstructed today."

"For the Godfreys? With a Convocation-certified reconstructionist? That's not really a vampire thing, is it? Cooperation?"

"I'm not sure." I suddenly felt tired. The reconstruction in the cemetery hadn't been taxing, but all I could think about was how I wouldn't mind burrowing underneath the thick white duvet that topped the bed, then closing my eyes on a long day. "I think this vampire might be a bit different than we've been taught."

"What little we've been taught."

"Exactly."

"Wisteria." Jasmine paused again. "I'm sorry."

She hated it when I went quiet, but sometimes I just didn't have anything to say. Sometimes I didn't want to justify my past behavior or my current choices. My secrets, according to Jasmine. "I'm just tired."

"If you need me, I'm there."

"I already mentioned the possibility of you working with us to Kett," I said. "Assuming I accept."

"Kett? Is that his name? Brilliant. And, hell yeah, you're taking the job. Why wouldn't you?"

"I don't normally take contracts outside the jurisdiction of the Convocation."

"Which is exactly why you'll be saying yes," Jasmine said smugly. "Just tell me where to be and I'll be there. With bells on. Unless vampires don't like bells."

"I think that's bears."

When Jasmine laughed, the sound warmed my heart, and the tight spot in my chest eased.

"I expect you to describe every inch of this Kett, magically or otherwise. A vampire! I'm completely prepared to instantly like him."

I laughed. "He's not exactly likable. More along the lines of intimidatingly powerful."

"Even better. Why should we be like every other witch out there?"

"Some boundaries are in place for our own protection."

Jasmine laughed again, but snarkily this time, and we dropped the topic. No matter how much we cared for each other, our outlooks on life—and personal safety—were very different.

I could hear her fingers on her computer keyboard through my phone's speaker. She'd started playing her game again. Or she was researching vampires. Or perhaps both at the same time.

"Have you gotten an answer from the Academy yet?" I asked, prolonging the conversation even though I was weary. "About digitizing their records? Right now would be a really good time to have access to everything they have on vampires, instead of just trying to recall lessons I took years ago."

"Not yet," she said. "They've stalled me, saying I need a unanimous vote from the Convocation."

"So you have to table a motion?"

"Yeah. I'm working on it with Rose."

Rose, our aunt, held the Fairchild seat on the witches Convocation. Other than Jasmine, she was the only Fairchild I had any contact with, and even then, I tried to keep it to less than once a year and on business-only terms.

"Still," Jasmine said, "I doubt you'd uncover much more in their archives than you already know."

"But you might."

"You know it doesn't work like that. The information actually has to be available, no matter how deeply buried."

Besides being able to spell and work with electronics, Jasmine's magic brought the mundane definition of what a 'hacker' was to an entirely new level.

I yawned. "So the new game is fun?"

"Engrossing."

"Aren't they all?"

"Nope. And I can hear you yawning. Go to bed. I expect a full report in the morning."

"Morning?"

"Okay. Afternoon."

I laughed. "Fine. I'll email you some information in the morning and you can look at it whenever. Try to get some sleep."

"You too."

I ended the call. But then instead of heading directly to bed, I lapsed back into gazing out at the gorgeous city and toying with my bracelet again. I brushed my fingers over one of the two tiny reconstructions hidden among the platinum house and tree charms.

Effortlessly, I pulled a glimpse of a darkly tanned boy with golden-hazel eyes out from within it.

A sudden gust of wind hammered rain against the lower pane of the window, drawing my attention. And for a moment, through the blurred wash on the glass, I thought I saw a blond, pale figure standing in the rain at the edge of the outdoor pool, four floors down.

A figure that I would have sworn in that instant was Kett, gazing up at my hotel room.

Heart thumping, I threw myself out of my chair, pressing my hands against the rain-spattered window and scanning the wide, adobe-tiled patio below.

The image I'd pulled from the reconstruction winked out.

The area around the well-lit pool and hot tub was empty. The lounge chairs were all folded and tucked away along the edges of the sundeck. A slight haze of steam rolled off the tranquil light-blue water of the pool, and what little I could see of inside the hotel from this angle was devoid of people.

I had just imagined it.

Kett.

I was allowing the tension of the day to make me feel vulnerable, even hunted. And that was a state I knew too much about already. I didn't need to be randomly manifesting monsters stalking me in the dark.

Stepping to my right, then my left, I grabbed the edges of the curtains and swiftly tugged them closed, blocking out my view of the pool and of the city and the mountains beyond.

I was overtired to the point of wallowing in emotions I had no interest in revisiting. Enough was enough.

Chapter Three

Though it wasn't yet 10:00 A.M. on a Tuesday in October, there was already a line of five people outside Cake in a Cup. I'd scrambled to change after a private Pilates session at the Movement Studio just down the street, swapping out my workout tights and tank top for my second go-to work outfit—a navy-blue herringbone fitted sheath dress. It was minimal, modern, and deceptively dressy with a slight sheen, but the fabric was stretchy enough to move in. I paired the dress with side-zip knee boots in navy-blue suede, foregoing nylons and hoping the sun would eventually win out over the clouds that had been lingering all morning. The boots' two-inch stacked heels, squared almond toes, and rubber soles kept me in the functionally stylish arena.

I'd thrown my classic navy-blue Burberry Chelsea trench coat on over this ensemble—an investment piece that I wore pretty much year round—then hefted my massive bag over my shoulder and high-tailed it up the block. I wanted to arrive before Kett, and in general, I was a fan of being early for appointments.

Though the exterior of the building looked exactly the same with its white French-paned front windows and door, the magical shielding on the bakery had taken on a different, more intense tenor since I'd last been in Vancouver. The wards that coated the storefront—and, as far as I was able to tell, the apartments above—hummed with magic, prickling against my skin from over half a block away. And when Jade's assistant baker, a part-First Nations woman whose pink name tag declared her to be 'Bryn,' unlocked the front doors to open the bakery, I found that I couldn't pass through the entrance without an invitation.

I lingered outside on the sidewalk while the other nonmagical customers shuffled inside, already laden with brown paper grocery bags and Starbucks coffee cups. Through the windows, I could see the massive glass dome of the bakery case that occupied the center of the storefront, as well as the handful of round bistro tables and stools in the seating area. A number of trinkets—as Jade called them—hung in the windows and above the door.

These were comprised of pretty, cobbled-together items—coins, figurines, sea glass, and more—attached to silver chains. Each item carried a tiny hint of magic, so infinitesimal that only the dowser was capable of feeling it. Or, more specifically in Jade's case, of tasting it. But once twined together by Jade's alchemist powers, the trinkets became much more than the sum of their parts. Not simply the found-art wind chimes they appeared to be.

It seemed a safe guess that many Adepts came to the bakery with the hope of leaving with one of these trinkets, now that Jade's alchemist abilities were better known. But I understood that the dowser never sold any. I wasn't surprised. Jade's sister, Sienna, the black witch, had used these pretty trinkets to siphon the magic from the Adepts she'd murdered.

A tall, voluptuous blond stepped through the swing doors that led to the kitchen at the back of the bakery. Her ever-present smile widened as she caught sight of me loitering on the sidewalk through the open front door. She was wearing a light blue short-sleeved cotton T-shirt emblazoned with a pink Cake in a Cup logo, and a frilly pink apron over her jeans and dark-blue sneakers. Her curly hair was swept back and clipped up.

Jade Godfrey. The dowser herself.

Though I'd been anxious about the idea of seeing the alchemist again, an involuntary smile spread across my face. Even with the magic of the wards between us, it was impossible to not smile when the dowser smiled at you. Well, as long as Adepts weren't being murdered or I hadn't been tasked with trying to pull magic from a dead dragon's skin.

Jade wiped her hands on her apron, then beckoned me toward her. The magic of the wards shifted, allowing me entry. But instead of dissipating or opening as some magical barriers did, the energy slipped around me, coating my skin as I stepped onto the white-painted wooden slat floor of the bakery. I had a moment to wonder if the wards had somehow taken an imprint of my magic, and how that would have even been possible. Then Jade was before me, offering her hand.

"Wisteria," she cried, pleased to see me despite the fact that our last meeting had been strained, to say the least. Over two years had passed since then, though, and the bakery didn't exactly appear to be teeming with imminent danger.

"Jade," I said, more subdued but smiling nonetheless. It was impossible to not absorb some of Jade's enthusiastic energy when I was around her. "I'm meeting Pearl."

"Oh? I didn't know."

"Not until ten thirty, though."

"Ah, sit and have a coffee and a cupcake, then."

"That's what I was hoping to do."

Jade gestured, directing me toward a table beside the middle window. "I'd sit with you, but I'm not quite done baking."

I tore my gaze away from the thick wedding-ring-charm necklace twined around her neck. I'd seen the magical artifact a few times, but there was something mesmerizingly different about it this morning. However, staring at another Adept's magic—or even asking them about it—was considered exceedingly rude.

"Thank you." I set my bag on the floor beside the window, slipping off my trench coat before I perched on the high stool.

"What can I bring you?"

"I can wait in line like everyone—"

Jade stalled me with a raised hand. "How about baker's choice?"

"That would be lovely." No one in their right mind would turn down a cupcake that had not only been baked by the dowser, but also specifically selected by her.

"And a...mocha?"

"Triple shot?"

Jade threw her head back and laughed as if she found my coffee predilections delightful. "Of course."

As Jade slipped away, I folded my coat and laid it across my lap, tamping down on the impulse to touch the pretty trinket hanging by my shoulder. It was constructed of green and blue sea glass, a chunk of Wedgwood china with its sharp edges smoothly sanded, and a set of silver coins. I didn't like getting distracted by magic, and usually my personal shields filtered almost everything out. But Jade was particularly powerful, and intriguing. I knew if I looked at her without any shields, I'd see her blue-gold magic dancing all around her like an aura. But I never looked at anyone or anything unshielded, not without carefully constructing a circle to contain the magic first. Never.

Jade appeared beside my table, moving too quickly for a human. I managed to not flinch, and wondered if she knew she was doing it. I worried about her disconcerting her human customers, but it really wasn't my place to mention the gaffe.

"*Clarity in a Cup*. Apple spice cake with honey buttercream." Jade placed a cupcake before me, perfectly positioned in the center of a white, scalloped-edged side plate. "I'm developing some apple recipes for Rochelle. This one has nutmeg in it, so it's also perfect for you."

I didn't know who Rochelle was and wasn't exactly sure why the cupcake having nutmeg made it perfect for me, but I'd learned a long time ago that it was best not to question powerful people. Not even when they were technically younger than you.

"Thank you," I said. "It smells heavenly."

Jade smirked, then set a large pink ceramic mug down on a napkin, both of them emblazoned with the bakery logo. Happily, the mug was filled to the brim with a deliciously scented mocha. It was also sprinkled with nutmeg.

"Why nutmeg?" The question was out of my mouth before I could stop myself from asking.

"Your magic," Jade said, casting her voice low. "It tastes like fresh-ground nutmeg. I thought I'd mentioned it before?"

I contemplated the cupcake, suddenly not sure how I felt about eating something that tasted like my own magic tasted to the dowser. "Do all…my types…"—I carefully avoided using the word 'witch' in mixed company—"…taste of nutmeg?"

Jade laughed quietly. "No. You all share a grassy base. But the nutmeg is something unique to you, or perhaps your family."

I nodded, taking a tiny sip of the hot mocha. Rich, smooth chocolate and slightly burnt coffee slipped across my tongue and warmed my throat. I was fairly certain Jade hadn't met Jasmine yet, and no other Fairchild witch would enter Godfrey territory willingly. Except for Rose, but even then, I assumed my aunt would only come to the Pacific Northwest or Vancouver on Convocation business.

Jade Godfrey had another reputation developing among the Adept—one that Pearl had already enforced during her tenure as the chair of the witches Convocation. Anyone with any sort of darkness in their practice of magic would avoid Vancouver and the Godfreys like a plague of light and moral supremacy.

Though, apparently and interestingly, that didn't include Kettil, the executioner of the Conclave. Even with what little I knew of him, the title alone made it a safe guess that few Adepts came darker than Kett.

"Delicious," I murmured, reaching for the cupcake.

Jade's gaze fell to my hands, following my movement as I nibbled on the delectable cake and icing. She reached out and brushed her fingers against my left palm, similar to the way Kett had touched me the previous night. "You hold your magic so intriguingly," she murmured, as if she was suddenly mesmerized. "Also, your nails completely rock."

I glanced down at my hand. I'd opted for a sparkly topcoat over my white-tipped, pale-pink French manicure earlier in the week, but I had no idea what the dowser meant about my magic.

Before I could set down the cupcake and ask her to clarify her statement, she tilted her head as if listening to something. "Gran's here."

Moving slower this time, she wandered off through the seating area and into the kitchen without another word.

I was completely content to remain sitting at the window of the bakery, consuming buttery, moist apple-infused cake for the rest of my days. But as I ate, I wondered if Jade added more than just spices when she baked. She called this cupcake *Clarity in a Cup*. Was this feeling of contentment my version of clarity? Also, was Jade feeding magic to non-magicals? That was a major indiscretion among the magical community, but maybe the Adept were the only ones influenced by her bakery creations. Or had she just seeded the idea, so that now I was overthinking it?

Either way, I wasn't in any rush to move on with a day that seemed sure to be filled with tension and confrontation. The Adept never played well with each other, and any communication involving elders of the Conclave and the Convocation was sure to be volatile.

I managed to eat about three-quarters of the cupcake—and was already starting to eye the chocolate creations in the display case in contemplation of a second treat—when Pearl Godfrey strode into the bakery from the kitchen.

Her silver hair was braided and coiled into a perfect bun at the back of her head. It was only a few shades lighter than the gray of her cable-knit sweater, which somehow looked sleek and modern paired with charcoal wool crepe pants. But it was her deep-blue eyes, simmering with power, that truly defined the chair of the witches Convocation. Once Pearl met my gaze across the seating area, I actually had to force myself to not bow formally to her.

She closed the space between us with three quick strides, holding out her hand to shake mine firmly. "Wisteria."

"Pearl."

"Unfortunately, I only have a moment." The elder witch twisted her lips distastefully. "I've another meeting."

"With Kettil," I said, not bothering to offer up the vampire's titles in a room full of nonmagicals.

Pearl raised her eyebrow at me. "He's spoken to you? About the reconstruction?"

I nodded. "Last night."

Pearl sighed. "Then it was as expected? I suppose only so many events can occur in a graveyard. Come to the back."

She turned, walking off in silence. Adepts weren't big on finishing conversations all in one go. Most, if not all, of their interactions were about setting up possible power plays. But since I was a well-paid pawn in the system, I couldn't exactly complain.

I glanced down at my partially eaten cupcake mournfully. Then, hefting my bag over my shoulder, I decided to bring it and my mocha with me. Anything else would be disrespectful to the chef.

I wandered back to the swing doors that led into the kitchen, expecting Bryn, who was smiling and bustling around behind the counter serving customers, to question me. But she didn't even glance over as I followed Pearl through the doors.

Jade was baking. I wasn't sure what I'd expected, since the dowser had already indicated that she had things to finish. But it certainly wasn't the sweet magic that cut through my personal shields so easily that I could practically taste it floating through the air.

I gasped, drawing Pearl's attention. The elder witch smiled, then returned her attention to Jade.

The dowser was piping thick chocolate icing onto some sort of chocolate cupcake. Her movements were minimal and precise, yet I could feel the magic dancing around her without even opening my witch senses to it. Normally, feeling magic unintentionally sent me into a tailspin and heading toward the nearest exit. Adepts who boiled with so much power that I couldn't shield myself from them were dangerous.

But the magic Jade commanded while baking was uplifting and comforting.

"Here?" I asked Pearl, pulling my attention away from Jade and tugging the reconstruction out of my bag.

"Jade?" Pearl asked.

"Done," the dowser proclaimed with an easy smile. Then she licked a dollop of icing from her latex-swathed finger. I'd been so enraptured by the magic that I hadn't noticed she was now wearing gloves.

Jade followed my gaze, tugging off her gloves to reveal deep-garnet nails. "I just got a pretty manicure too. *We the Female*. I wish I could grow mine long enough to justify the expense of a French manicure, though. I always love yours. Gel?"

I nodded as I placed the oyster-shell cube holding the reconstruction from the cemetery down on the stainless steel workstation between us. "The color lasts about two weeks," I said. "But I do nothing with my hands."

Pearl leaned over the cube, frowning slightly.

Jade smirked, nodding toward the reconstruction. "I'd say that was something."

I smiled. Being proud of myself went against my upbringing, but I could be pleased with my efforts at least.

"Not much magic," Pearl murmured.

"Hardly any at all," I said, focusing on business instead of the friendly banter that Jade was so fond of. "The gravesite was scorched—"

Pearl flinched, then grimaced.

I followed her gaze. Kett was standing beside Jade on the other side of the workstation.

The dowser had already thrown her arm over his shoulders in greeting. Her laughter practically set off sparks in the magic that she'd been generating while baking. The vampire had appeared out of thin air, as if by teleportation. But I was sure I would have felt any spell that powerful. And I was also fairly certain that teleportation wasn't an ability vampires inherently possessed. At least I hoped they didn't.

The fact that he was mobile during the day reinforced my impression that he was ancient. According to the minimal amount of lore that the rest of the Adept world had access to, younger vampires were actually dead through the daylight hours.

Though Kett didn't return her embrace, he was smiling at Jade. Really smiling, not smirking or sneering. They were so obviously friends. Though I'd known this, or at least had thought it to be the case, seeing it in front of me was surreal. My admittedly patchy understanding of vampires made the idea of them forming friendships seem highly unlikely. Magical or not, we lesser Adepts were simply inferior. Weaker and mortal. Sustenance. Prey that might be otherwise useful for a short period of time.

Magic sparked off the right side of my face, neck, and shoulder. I took an involuntary step away from Pearl, glancing her way as I did to see that her eyes were glowing electric blue.

She was angry. Possibly in reaction to how Kett had snuck up on her.

"Pearl," Kett said, nodding toward the perturbed witch. His smile had vanished.

Jade huffed out a sigh, picking up the tray of frosted cupcakes. "Don't go without saying hi to Kandy."

Kett nodded, but he didn't turn his silver-blue gaze from Pearl as Jade swept out of the kitchen.

"Reconstructionist," Pearl said, not even bothering to greet the vampire as she gestured me toward the oyster-shell cube.

I nodded. Visualizing my personal shielding as a dense, protective layer between the witch, the vampire, and me, I stepped forward to place my fingers on one edge of the cube.

"I assume you've seen it, then?" Pearl directed the question to Kett without actually looking at him.

"Not yet," he said, distantly polite. "The reconstructionist was adamant about the chain of custody."

Pearl drew herself up to her full height, lifting her chin regally. "Wisteria is a fine witch."

"Indeed. Shall we proceed?"

Pearl placed her fingers on the edge of the cube perpendicular to mine. The vampire did the same across from her. I triggered the magic within the cube, calling it forward to play out the scene I'd collected in the cemetery. I could have chosen to project and play those events directly above the cube as well. However, with Pearl and Kett touching the cube, they would see the reconstruction unfold in their minds exactly as I'd seen it.

While I controlled the playback that way, I could also manipulate the image, zooming in on details or viewing the entire scene from a different perspective. Though only as I had witnessed it while collecting the magic. I couldn't highlight any details after the magic had been contained in my cube. Which was fine because I was thorough, keeping my reconstructions tightly confined in the first place.

After the scene had played through once, Pearl disengaged from the cube. "And the person wielding the knife and the pencil?" she asked. "Human?"

I hesitated. Technically, it wasn't my place to comment on collections. "I'm not sure Carolina has come to that—"

Pearl waved her hand impatiently, making her magic brush against me uncomfortably. I forced myself to stand against it. I was fairly certain the elder witch didn't know she was wielding her power so loosely. But the presence of a vampire in the bakery and a murdered fledgling vampire in a West Vancouver cemetery clearly disturbed her.

"I'd like to see it again," Kett said.

Pearl finally turned her attention to him. "This is Godfrey territory."

"This is Conclave business." The vampire's tone was as dispassionate as ever.

"There is no Conclave here," Pearl said. Her own voice became clipped, edged with anger. "Have you done this?" She gestured toward the reconstruction cube.

Her magic buffeted me again. I took a step away, drawing Kett's gaze.

"A child of mine would not be so easily slain," he said. "Nor would he turn into some sort of gelatinous mess."

"Have. You. Done. This?" Pearl wasn't yelling, but she was close to it.

Kett eyed her coolly. "I have not. But I will take care of it. With Wisteria's help, so as to—"

"What?" Pearl snapped, rounding on me.

I took another step back.

Jade appeared between the swing doors, hissing, "What the hell, Gran?"

Pearl turned her fierce scowl on Kett. "This one has sullied our territory." As she raised a hand toward him, some sort of electrical magic danced between her fingers.

" 'This one'?" Jade repeated. "That seems a little—"

"And now he is demanding the cooperation of a witch under the protection of the Convocation." Pearl was building up to a full-fledged rant, ignoring Jade's attempt to defuse the situation.

Then suddenly, there was too much magic in the kitchen.

The air became clogged with it. Energy from three powerful beings pressed against me, driving me sideways yet again.

Kett and Pearl were locked in some sort of staring contest. And Jade had stepped up between them, possibly to mitigate the situation. But for me, her involvement only increased the strain on my personal shielding. I was struggling to maintain the detachment I constantly strove for.

I tried to calm myself. None of the magic swirling around the kitchen was directed toward me. None of it was of malicious intent. Powerful people simply expressed themselves with—

Bright spots appeared before my eyes. I felt myself becoming lightheaded. I'd stopped breathing. I was being ridiculous. Cowering like some fledgling witch.

I took a deep breath, gathering my shields. Then I visualized those shields pushing the suffocating magic away.

Nearest to me, Pearl swayed under my unintentional assault.

Jade slipped a hand underneath her grandmother's elbow. Then all eyes turned toward me.

I smoothed my hands down my dress, lifting my chin against their shocked expressions. "Pearl, Kettil informed me that there has been another incident that he wishes me to look at, with your permission. And, of course, any way I can be of assistance to the Convocation and the Godfreys…" I allowed my words to trail off, hoping I had eased the situation enough without having to blather on about loyalty and friendship.

Pearl pursed her lips. "I see."

"I had no intention of superseding the Convocation entirely," Kett said. "I understood that you assigned the reconstructionist to this case specifically. That you trusted her to represent—"

"Of course." Pearl returned her gaze to the cube thoughtfully.

"Is this something I need to be involved in?" Jade hadn't taken her gaze from me. But I couldn't quite tell what she was thinking, which was odd, because the dowser was normally anything but oblique.

"If you wish," Kett said.

Jade snorted. "So, no."

He laughed quietly. "No. I imagine you are busy with wedding plans."

Jade grimaced, then smiled when Pearl glanced her way. "Yay! Wedding plans!" she said, far too brightly.

"Please, Jade," Pearl said. "I've already relented."

"Relented!?"

Kett stifled a smile. I didn't know Jade very well, and I knew the vampire even less. Which made it even harder to figure out what they could possibly have had in common. Perhaps simply shared experiences?

"I didn't know you were getting married," I said, politely inserting myself back into the conversation. "Congratulations. Have you set the date?"

"Yes," Pearl said.

"No," Jade said.

Pearl eyed her granddaughter, who smiled at her sunnily.

"There will be an engagement party," Pearl said. "I'll send you a save the date."

"Warner's schedule is difficult to nail down," Jade said, completely amused by Pearl's obvious frustration. "You know dragons. He'd get married tomorrow, or ten years from now. Time is relative."

I didn't really know any dragons, and I certainly didn't know that Jade was engaged to one. Though I had met Jade's fiance, Warner, in Seattle, I was pretty sure we hadn't said more than two words to each other at the time. And I was happy keeping it that way. Dragons and guardians were beings that featured heavily in Adept bedtime stories and morality tales. The fact that a few of them actually walked the earth was more nightmare inducing than comforting. Maybe that was an ill-informed opinion, but I assumed demigods had to be unpredictable. The fact that

Jade's father was one was a tidbit of information to be stored away and never discussed.

I smiled as if an engagement party filled with uncountable powerful Adepts didn't sound completely terrifying.

Pearl let out a deep breath, completely exasperated.

Jade patted her grandmother's shoulder. "I'm sure he'll come to the party. Just as long as there aren't any demon invasions that day."

"Keep me informed," Pearl said, changing the subject and turning her intensely blue gaze on me. "Hourly texts, and a phone call every twelve hours."

"Of course," Kett said, speaking for me.

Pearl ignored him. "Be careful, Wisteria."

I nodded.

The elder witch exited the kitchen.

Jade leaned back, resting her hip against the stainless steel workstation and crossing her arms as she regarded Kett, then me in turn. "Working together, eh?"

"So it appears," Kett said, reaching for the cube. "I'd like to view the reconstruction again."

"Old business or new?" she asked probingly.

The vampire ignored her, looking expectantly at me instead.

Not completely following their exchange, but also completely content to not get involved in anything Jade considered 'old business,' I obligingly stepped forward. Placing my hands on the edge of the cube opposite to Kett's, I triggered the scene from the cemetery.

Jade was eyeing the vampire thoughtfully, then her gaze fell to my right wrist. "I like your bracelet," she murmured.

Concentrating on the magic underneath my fingers, I smiled politely but didn't answer. The reconstruction finished playing out in silence.

"Again," Kett said.

But Jade spoke before I could comply. "Just a second." She curled her fingers around Kett's wrist, then wrapped her other hand over my bracelet. "Wisteria seemed a bit nervous earlier."

Kett raised an eyebrow in Jade's direction.

I opened my mouth to protest.

"I mean, who wouldn't be when faced with you?" she added, smirking.

"You," Kett said.

"Oh, I was scared. But Wisteria isn't foolhardy. And I owe her a gift."

"Do you?" Kett asked coolly.

"I believe I do."

I snapped my mouth shut. There was something going on between the two of them that I couldn't figure out. Some concern that Jade was trying to be flippant about.

"I have no intention of harming the reconstruction-ist," Kett said.

"Of course not. But you don't mind if I give her a little peace of mind, do you?" Jade dropped her voice to a whis-per. "When was the last time you walked the earth beside someone who considered you prey?"

A shiver ran up my spine. I clenched my fingers into a fist, but didn't attempt to free myself from Jade's grasp. Though she held me lightly, I knew there was no way I could have broken her hold.

"I have never walked shoulder to shoulder with any-one who..." Kett trailed off. Then he nodded.

Jade's hand on my wrist warmed. I forced myself to relax my arm. Then I realized she was doing something to my bracelet.

"Wait!" I cried, suddenly fearful for the two recon-structions hidden among the platinum charms.

"It's okay," Jade said. "I can taste the magic already held within."

She released my arm and Kett's wrist. "There. All good. Armed for vampire."

I glanced down. The bracelet didn't look any different.

Kett chuckled.

Jade smirked at him. "Test it, then."

He shook his head almost imperceptibly. "Your concern is noted."

"Well, that's good," Jade said. "I wasn't aware I was being subtle about it." She touched one of the tiny house charms on my wrist. "Is this supposed to be…what is this supposed to be?"

"A white picket fence," I said stiffly. "That I carry with me wherever I go."

Jade eyed me for a moment, then nodded. "You should be able to use it like a shield now."

"Against vampires," Kett said wryly.

"Thank you," I said politely, though I still wasn't following what was going on between the dowser and the executioner.

"My pleasure." Jade offered Kett a smile that was both challenging and playful. "See you later, alligator."

"I shall pay my respects before I leave," Kett said.

Jade turned away.

"Wait," I called out, suddenly remembering the magic that had surrounded Jade earlier. "Do you mind…I'd like to collect…before, when you were baking…" I stumbled around asking permission awkwardly.

Jade smiled at me, as open and friendly as she apparently always was.

"I create miniature reconstructions for my cousin Jasmine," I said. "For her birthday. I don't have one yet, for this year. But I collect moments, magical moments. Pretty or inspiring things. Just seconds. A glimpse. Not a scene, you understand. Not usually. I wouldn't be stealing anything or using your magic..."

"Wisteria." Jade interrupted me gently. "I'm overjoyed that you think a glimpse of me baking is a worthy moment to give to Jasmine for her birthday."

I nodded, feeling childish about my clumsy request. "Thank you."

Jade exited through the swing doors into the bakery.

I turned back to find Kett watching me, as if I'd done something terribly interesting. Or perhaps completely baffling. He was nearly impossible to read.

"Again," he said, indicating the cube.

I reached forward obligingly.

He hovered his fingers over my bracelet instead of touching the cube.

I froze with my hand extended, suddenly very aware that the long table between us was nothing to him. He wouldn't even need to bother tossing it aside if he came for me.

He pressed his fingers to the edge of the cube, lifting his icy gaze to meet mine.

I could feel the weight of the charm bracelet on my wrist. Normally, I never noticed it at all. Kett hadn't actually touched it. I wondered if he could feel or sense its magic.

I swallowed my trepidation, then lowered my hand and triggered the reconstruction for him once more. This time, I focused on the young teen rising from his grave. This time, I reminded myself why I was there, and why I'd be moving forward with this investigation.

Someone had murdered a human teenager.

Twice, by my reckoning.

Normally it wasn't my job to call for justice or to exact it, but that waste of life had to be answered for. Nothing was more precious, and nothing was more worth fighting for.

I knew.

Kett wandered off into the bakery storefront while I laid out my candles and quickly captured a brief moment of the magic that dwelled in the bakery kitchen. I channeled the dancing, almost capricious energy within a tiny oyster-shell cube. When I constructed cubes that small, I added a platinum locking eyelet to them so they could be clipped onto a chain. I commissioned the eyelets from a silversmith, so they were pricy but unbreakable.

I made only two of these special reconstructions a year, one for Jasmine and one for Declan. Jasmine collected her reconstructions on a necklace. I had no idea what her half-brother did with his. Perhaps he threw them away unwatched. But I sent him one each year in August for his birthday, usually after requesting his current mailing address from Jasmine.

Other than confirming his address once a year, I never asked after Declan. And I definitely never asked after my parents or any of the other relatives who Jasmine kept in contact with for some insane reason.

And I never would utter my uncle's name ever again. It had been twelve years this fall. Twelve years since I'd laid eyes on any of them, on Declan.

Yes, I accepted the little bits of information Jasmine dropped about her brother in casual conversation, hoarding those morsels, then running them over and over in my mind for months afterward.

But as far as I knew, he had never asked after me either.

When I closed my reconstruction circle, the magic that coated every surface of the bakery glistened in various shades of blue and gold. I didn't even need to coax forth a scene. The magic that played out around me was like joy and peace personified. Just watching it would bring a smile to Jasmine's face. And that was the point of my birthday gift reconstructions.

I collected the magic, clipping the glimmering cube onto the zipper tag of the inside pocket of my bag so it wouldn't get lost. Then I snuffed out the candles.

Kett was watching me from just inside the kitchen's swing doors. I hadn't felt him appear behind me. And I couldn't read his expression.

I involuntarily touched the now-fortified charm bracelet on my right wrist. The vampire's gaze dropped to the trinket. Then he smiled, amused and completely unfazed.

"You will stay out of my head," I blurted.

"I will."

"I won't let you bite me."

Kett raised his silver-blue eyes to meet my gaze. His smirk widened into a grin, revealing his impossibly white, impossibly straight teeth.

"You will," he said. "When the time comes, you will lift your hair from your neck of your own free will, of your own desire. You will align yourself with me, Wisteria Fairchild. I am your doom and your salvation."

I stared at him, angered and flustered by his words. By his utter arrogance. But I had no words of my own with which to refute his preposterous claims. I clenched my fists at my sides, opening my mouth as if to force myself to speak.

Kett raised one eyebrow.

I shut my mouth, turning my back on him. I collected my candles and slung my bag over my shoulder.

The vampire had moved to the large steel door at the back of the kitchen. "Shall we proceed with your actual job? I have a site for you to look at."

I lifted my chin, walking toward him and out the door when he opened it.

He wanted to play games, did he? He'd find that difficult with me.

I took no chances.

I made no bets.

I'd been foolish and weak once, and I'd paid for my folly. I had lost everyone I thought I loved, and one of the two people in this world who actually loved me back.

I would do my job. But I wouldn't gamble with what I'd salvaged.

Chapter Four

The sun was still attempting to break through the clouds overhead as Kett and I left the bakery and walked toward a white BMW SUV parked a block away on a side street. The vehicle was new and had a current parking permit in the front window, which seemed oddly permanent. Was the executioner of the Conclave living in Vancouver? If so, where? With Jade and her fiancé?

The SUV would have been flashy anywhere else, but in Kitsilano, it was almost nondescript. So what was a vampire in designer dark-wash jeans, a steel-blue V-neck cashmere sweater, and brushed suede oxfords doing driving an SUV and sipping Pinot Noir with me the night before?

My cellphone pinged.

I flinched, startled from puzzling out Kett. What he was doing in Vancouver really wasn't any of my business, but apparently, his suggestion that I was going to beg him to bite me in the near future had me on edge.

I retrieved my phone from my bag, glancing at the text message. It was from Jasmine.

>*Gravesite belongs to Colby Hansen. Attended Sentinel Secondary School. Boyfriend of Luci Jennings. Straight As. Big on moody poetry and gaming, on and offline.*

Kett opened the passenger door of the SUV for me, then stepped around to the driver's side.

"It's from Jasmine. She's tracked down some info about the teenager. I contacted her last night about the case and followed up with the few details I knew by email this morning."

"I saw," Kett said dismissively.

Not quite certain what he was talking about—other than intimidatingly suggesting he'd read my text message on the sly—I climbed into the SUV, tucked my bag behind my feet, and adjusted the shoulder strap of my seat belt to the recommended setting for my height. The vehicle still had that new car smell, and didn't contain a single personal item I could see.

My phone pinged with another text.

"Facebook page," I said, clicking the link that had appeared.

Kett started the engine, pulling out to circle the block, then turning left onto West Fourth Avenue, heading east.

I scrolled through Colby Hansen's Facebook profile. "Not used much by him. Serving as a memorial now. Sad. They think it was a suicide."

"As they should," Kett said.

"Drained of blood?" I said snottily. Apparently, maintaining professional detachment around a vampire was going to be a struggle. "That's how it works, isn't it? So where did his blood go?"

He didn't answer.

My phone pinged a third time. I tore my gaze away from Kett's chiseled profile, already admonishing myself for staring at him at all.

Jasmine had texted a second Facebook link. I clicked on it. "Luci Jennings."

Colby's girlfriend's page didn't have much on it that was public, but her cover photo was of a handwritten note on a thick piece of letterpress stationary embossed with pink flowers. The pink-inked note read: *Thank you for your condolences.*

"The pink pencil," I murmured.

Kett was looking at me, rather than the road. I glanced nervously ahead through the windshield. We were sitting at a red light. I hadn't noticed that we'd stopped.

"Yes?" he prompted.

"I think we should talk to the girlfriend."

"A human," he said derisively.

The light turned green.

"As far as we know. But perhaps a human who knew about Colby's suicide not being a true suicide—"

"Death is death."

I paused, assessing this statement. I wasn't sure what he meant or how it was relevant.

"Because of the pink pencil," he said.

"What? Yes. In the reconstruction the teen is…staked by a pink pencil."

"Pencils do not kill vampires. Pink or otherwise."

I smirked, then quickly smoothed my expression. "Perhaps it was a magical pencil."

"Perhaps the teenager wasn't a vampire."

That gave me pause. "What else could he have been?"

Kett didn't answer.

My phone pinged a fourth time.

>*Vancouver* 7:20 P.M.

"Jasmine's flight gets in this evening," I said, texting back a thumbs up and a quick 'Thank you' for the information.

"There are no direct flights from Connecticut?"

"She was in San Francisco, winding up a case."

Silence stretched between us. I placed my phone on the shelf above the glove box. Rain sprinkled across the windshield as the city around us flattened, and the real estate lining the wide boulevard became less polished and more serviceable.

Kett flicked on the wipers.

"So the other site?" I asked. "Another incident?"

"You will see."

I didn't attempt any further chitchat. I preferred to walk into scenes without preconceived ideas anyway. And silence was the best way to reinforce my unwillingness to participate in whatever game the vampire had going on.

I fingered the tiny oyster-shell cubes attached to my charm bracelet, hoping that whatever Jade had done to the bracelet hadn't somehow erased the reconstructions I kept housed on it. I could have viewed them just to make sure, but even though the vampire wouldn't be able to see the magic as it replayed, I didn't want to do anything so personal in his presence. I had a feeling that everything and anything I did around him would be used as leverage against me at an unnamed but looming date.

"Don't worry," Kett said. "The alchemist is exceedingly skilled."

"It's an extraordinary gift," I said, dropping my hand and turning to watch shops, restaurants, and pedestrians slip by outside my window.

"Jade Godfrey is a powerful ally."

"Not everyone sees the world as being so black and white," I said, bothered by the suggestion that I would view Jade's offered friendship as a means to an alliance. Mostly because that was exactly how my family viewed any and all relationships.

"True," he said. "But you and I do."

I kept my mouth shut, though it was a near thing. Not all Fairchilds were powermongers, but what did I care if the vampire thought my last name defined who I was? If he even knew my family, for that matter. Though his previous mention of Connecticut implied as much.

"Where are we heading?" I asked.

"Surrey."

Excellent. That was an urban sprawl east of Vancouver, and at least a forty-five minute drive trapped in a steel box with a vampire.

"Do you have any questions about the reconstruction?" I asked, trying to keep myself focused on my job and not my potentially claustrophobic surroundings and possibly homicidal companion.

"Do you have any answers?"

"Actually, I don't. Because, as I've stated previously, I don't look for answers. I leave that to other people."

"You were exceedingly clear."

I was tempted to let the discussion languish, reverting to the silence that was always my best weapon against power plays. But this was a job, and I was, at a minimum, attempting to be professional. "I still think we should talk to the girlfriend, Luci."

Kett nodded. "Afterward. If you don't turn up anything more substantial than the grieving recollections of a teenaged human female."

And with that declaration, we spent the rest of the ride in silence.

The rain grew heavier as we merged onto the freeway and drove into the city of Surrey. After trading one thrumming vein of traffic for another, then cutting directly through endless neighborhoods filled with large, cookie-cutter homes that occupied almost every square foot of their properties, Kett parked at the curb in front of a nondescript but massive apartment complex.

Without a map to lead me back to Vancouver, I'd have been completely lost in the surrounding urban sprawl. We were only a block off the Fraser Highway, and the traffic noise was constant as I stepped from the SUV. Years of neglect had grayed the pink stucco of the building, and any attempt at landscaping suffered from the same lack of maintenance. The complex looked as if it hadn't been touched since it had been built in the early eighties.

A well-treed park filled the opposite side of the block. And the surrounding buildings appeared recently renovated. The rundown complex was a holdout from another era, perhaps.

The street was quiet, but it was midday on a Tuesday, so most people would be at work or school. I didn't have an umbrella, which was pretty laughable given the size of my bag and the fact that I spent most of my days off in Seattle.

"Do we have an appointment?" I asked as I followed Kett up the walk to the building's front doors.

The vampire didn't answer, pulling open the door without consulting the list of names above the buzzer. Either he broke the lock so easily that I hadn't seen him do it, or it had already been broken.

I followed him into the entranceway, which smelled distinctly of day-old food with an underlying layer of pervasive mildew.

We took the stairs, rather than the elevator, to the fifth floor in continuing silence. Stale cigarette smoke dominated the stairwell, and I tripped over the puckered berber carpet as we entered the corridor. It was blotchy gray, but I noted that it hadn't originally been that color.

Police tape was crisscrossed over the door of apartment 516. Kett reached for the handle.

"Have you been here before?" I asked.

"I had no previous need to enter the apartment."

I took that to mean he'd simply been in or around the building. The fine details of why there was police tape across the door weren't any of my business, though. "I should go first. You expect magic, yes? And you want me to do a reconstruction? You might leave residual. I'm not sure. I've never worked with a vampire before."

Kett turned his silvered gaze on me. "You wish for me to wait in the hall?"

I couldn't tell by his detached tone, but I had a suspicion that the suggestion was an utter affront to him. "For a moment."

The vampire tipped his chin downward in what I assumed was a nod of acceptance, then he pulled the police tape from the door and popped the lock on the knob. The deadbolt wasn't engaged. He stepped back, and with a formal sweep of his hand, indicated that I should enter before him.

I ignored the gesture, which I took as sarcasm. I had a job to do, so I would do it.

I stepped into the dim apartment and immediately stumbled over a pile of shoes by the door.

Kett grabbed me by the elbow, steadying me. His touch was almost gentle, but it was like being held by a marble statue. The instant I had my footing, he released me and stepped back, standing just inside the doorway to the hall.

I paused to let my eyes adjust to the darkness, focusing on the immediate area for any residual energy spots that might offer enough power for a reconstruction.

The front door opened up onto a living room, with a galley-style kitchen directly to the left. Beyond the kitchen, a hall ran deeper into the apartment. Sun-bleached curtains hung over what I assumed was a small patio at the windowed side of the living room. A well-worn sectional sofa faced a large flat-screen TV on the wall to my far right. Beer cans and take-out food containers were scattered across the coffee table. The air was stale, but not unpleasant.

"No obvious magic here," I whispered.

"No," Kett said agreeably. He hadn't stepped any farther into the apartment, but being taller than me, he must have had a good view of the main room over my shoulders.

"You can see magic?" I asked, willfully forgetting it was impolite to ask after another Adept's magical prowess. If I had to work with the vampire, it only seemed logical for me to know what assets he brought to our professional relationship.

"Some."

That was interesting, and not a noted vampiric talent. At least not in any magical lore I'd studied. I was fairly certain he could see far better in the dark than I could, though.

A trace of light seeped in through the curtains and through the broken Venetian blinds in the kitchen. I gathered we were facing north, which didn't help with illumination on a gray day.

I reached into my bag and pulled out a candle. Green for earth, which I felt the strongest affinity toward. I was a witch and a Virgo, after all. I also grabbed my butane lighter.

"You use a lighter," Kett said, amused.

I lit the candle. "What would you use?"

"I am not a witch."

I glanced back at him. He observed me detachedly, as if he hadn't just implied that my magic was useless if I couldn't even light a candle with it.

"Shall I continue?" I asked snottily.

"Please do." Kett still sounded annoyingly amused.

Ignoring him, I cracked my personal shields just enough that I should have been able to pick up on any residual magic within the circle of light cast by the candle I was holding aloft. Selecting the path of least resistance through the dilapidated furniture, I circled the living room. A broken hockey stick was propped in one corner, sports magazines and discarded flyers were piled under a water-stained side table, and a pizza box was half-tucked between two couch cushions.

I wasn't sure if this was the normal state of the apartment or whether it had been empty for some time. I was looking only for magic, though. Nothing else mattered to the investigation at this point. Not the vampire, nor the disheartening surroundings.

I traversed the hallway, passing the tiny kitchen and refusing to be distracted by the molding mound of dishes in the murky sink.

The next doorway opened into a boy's bedroom—judging by the posters of women in tight or minimal clothing and the black, crumpled sheets on the bed—but no magic.

I kept to the hall, glancing into the oddly clean bathroom, which was barely large enough to hold a toilet, sink, and tub. Even cast deep into shadow by my candlelight, the grout was blackened with mold for about a foot and a half above the tub. The shower curtain appeared to be missing, along with all the towels.

A few more steps took me to the end of the hall and the second bedroom. I hadn't seen a single shred of evidence as to why crime scene tape had been used to seal the front door.

Holding my candle before me, I stepped into the disheveled bedroom. It was larger than the boy's room. A queen-sized mattress lay on the floor, without a frame or a box spring. The dark-green sheets were a crumpled mess, as if someone had been wrestling rather than sleeping on them.

"The killing took place in here." Kett's cool voice sounded out from the hall.

I flinched, almost dropping my candle. I hadn't heard him approach.

"I'd like you to reconstruct this room. And the bathroom. If possible."

"The bathroom? Why? There was no magic there."

"Look again."

The vampire retreated back along the hall toward the living room without further comment.

I stepped into the bedroom, finally feeling a glimmer of magic when I was about two feet away from the bed. I leaned over, scanning as I moved the candle above the pillows tossed every which way across the head of the bed.

A fine mist of blood was sprayed across the back wall, with more possibly streaking the pillows. But as far as I was able to tell, there was nothing magical about the blood itself.

Unsure where the glimmer was manifesting from, I pulled out and placed all four of my candles around the room. I wasn't going to look closer until I had my circle in place. I nudged aside a pile of paint-splattered clothing to place the green candle, and used a stack of *Penthouse* magazines to hold the white pillar.

Calling forth my magic and sealing the circle, I coaxed the glimmer to reveal its origins. The scene before me darkened even more. Whatever was about to be revealed had taken place in the early-morning hours. As far as I could see, the room was empty. Then a dirty-blond teen wearing a set of light-green hospital scrubs walked backward into the room, climbing onto the bed.

I watched as the scene unfolded before me in reverse. The teen pummeled something or someone on the bed. He also appeared to be biting his victim. Feeding, I assumed. And though his eyes whirled with what appeared to be blood and his pale skin marked him as a vampire, his magic was insubstantial. Faded.

The blood splatter disappeared from the far wall. The boy bounced back from the bed and stepped out of my circle. As if he had practically pounced on his victim from the door, biting him without warning.

Had the boy turned into a vampire in the hospital, or perhaps the morgue, then snuck back here to kill his purely human father? Or brother? Was that why I once again couldn't see the victim?

"Now the bathroom."

I flinched, whirling away from the dim magic I was trying to reconstruct. The vampire was standing in the doorway. Light was emanating from down the hall. Apparently, Kett had turned it on.

"Don't you want to see this?" I asked, leaning down to channel what little energy I'd collected into an oyster-shell cube I'd retrieved from my bag.

"Later. I can speculate based on the police report. It's the hint of magic in the bathroom I want to know about."

I gathered my candles, closing the circle. Then I followed Kett into the bathroom. It was so small that we couldn't comfortably stand in it next to each other. A sickeningly yellow, glaringly bright bare bulb was all that remained of the overhead light.

"I don't feel anything in here," I said.

Kett pointed behind me toward the base of the tub, near the wall that held the empty white-plastic towel bar.

I looked closer at the spot he indicated, then shook my head.

"Set your candles. Here, here, here, and here," he said, directing me to two points in the tub and two on the floor.

I complied doubtfully. Lighting the candles, I held my hands over the spot he'd pointed out.

Something flickered in the mold-blackened caulking.

"Why is it clean in here?" I asked. "But nowhere else?"

"I gather the father cleaned after the apparent suicide. But the police didn't get a chance to send in a crew after his murder."

"The lack of blood in the bedroom, or the victim, would have confused them."

"That's taken care of. Now focus."

I swallowed a retort, then attempted to coax the glimmer I could feel on the floor forward.

"Blood," I murmured, understanding why the vampire had sensed the magic when I hadn't.

"The teen's?"

"I don't think so. It's different. It's—"

Intense magic bloomed beside me from outside the circle. I instinctively flinched away from it, almost clambering into the tub to get away.

Kett was holding his hand toward me. A drop of blood dotted the tip of his index finger, then it disappeared without so much as a hint of a scratch or mark left behind. He had cut himself, though I saw no evidence of a blade.

"Like this?" he asked.

I shook my head, struggling to shut my senses down and keep my personal shields in place. I didn't like looking at intense magic outside of a circle. It felt as though the vampire had attacked me, blindsided me, with magic manifested in a single drop of blood. That was utterly disconcerting.

Kett raised an eyebrow.

I was still shaking my head, acting as if I might have lost my mind. I stopped, focusing on the drop of blood in the circle rather than the far-too-powerful vampire crammed into the tight bathroom with me. And blocking the exit.

I took a breath, coaxing the glimmer in the circle forward and attempting to rationally assess it, comparing it to the tenor and feeling of Kett's power. "Much less intense," I finally said. "Same basic makeup, maybe. Perhaps diluted. I'm not a dowser."

"No, you aren't."

Instead of retorting childishly about his completely unprofessional behavior, I continued to focus on the puzzle presented in the circle. The executioner of the Conclave should know better than to cut himself and potentially contaminate the scene and my reconstruction. Which could only mean he'd done it deliberately. Perhaps to test me.

Or perhaps to muddy my findings.

"There's something else," I said. "An image trying to manifest from the magic in the blood."

I squinted at the dim swirl of energy in the circle. "A container? Like the blood was housed in a package of some sort?"

"No. Whatever cleaning solutions were used in here wouldn't be able to destroy the magic. There is only that one drop."

I allowed the glimmer I had coaxed forward to fade away. It was far too insubstantial to manipulate any further, collecting it would be a waste of a cube. Though it did confirm the presence of magic other than that of the fledgling vampire.

Someone else had been in the apartment, leaving a single drop of blood behind.

"Why would a...master vampire leave a fledgling? If this is a drop of his blood? Don't you, I don't know, oversee their rising when you create a...child?"

Kett glanced at me, then turned his head to contemplate the drop of blood without responding.

I straightened, snuffing out my candles. I wasn't surprised that he was unwilling to answer my questions. I wondered if the Conclave specifically forbade discussing the creation of fledgling vampires.

Waiting for the wax to harden so I could pack the candles away, I pulled out my cellphone. "You said there was a police report. Do you know the teen's name?"

"Dennis Bradford."

I texted the name to Jasmine, along with a quick note asking her to see if she could connect him to Colby Hansen.

"Where is the fledgling?" I finally voiced the question I'd been loath to ask since I'd reconstructed the scene in the bedroom. "We should have a team looking for him."

"No need," Kett said, stepping through, then pausing in the doorway. "He's dead."

"You killed him."

"He was rogue, ridiculously weak, and out of control. Incapable of control. Would you have had me attempt to housebreak him?"

I shuddered at the thought. Rogue vampires featured heavily in the cautionary bedtime stories recited to all Adept children. "How many bodies?"

"Three, plus his father. Thankfully, he was easy to track."

"And the police were easy to enthrall."

Kett turned his cold gaze on me. "Would you have had me do differently? It's fortunate that I learned of the killing spree early enough to cover up the murders."

"He rose in the morgue?" I asked. "He was wearing hospital scrubs."

"Clothing pilfered from the morgue attendant. He hadn't taken the time to change. I apprehended him on the way to his mother's. Thankfully, he appeared incapable of operating a vehicle, the early-morning streets were clear of large numbers of potential victims, and she lives over an hour away. I doubt he would have spared the three other children who were in residence."

My chest tightened, but I kept my voice even, attempting to match Kett's dispassion. "Did he dissolve? Like the teen in the graveyard?"

"No. I ripped his head off, then burned the remains rather quickly."

Bile rose in my throat. I quickly gathered my candles, hoping to cover my discomfort. I never got this deeply involved in an investigation. Never had to deal with any aftermath or process anything that might have occurred before the reconstructions I collected as evidence.

Kett was no longer in the hallway when I exited the bathroom. I quickly made my way toward the front door, glancing into Dennis's bedroom as I passed it. An older laptop computer and a headset on the desk caught my attention. I wondered if he'd worked a job after school to pay for the computer, but then I refused to allow myself to think about the teen's life any further.

I wasn't an investigator. I just collected evidence. Getting involved or caught up in the personal minutiae wouldn't be helpful, not for me or to the case.

I stepped into the room. Neat stacks of large playing cards were set on either side of the laptop, along with handwritten notes covered in numbers—some sort of points system, perhaps—and a set of multisided dice. The card on top of the nearest stack was decorated with a drawing of a dark-haired, bearded man wearing a gray cloak, and was titled 'Sorcerer.' Dennis had been playing a game of some sort, possibly about magic. I didn't recognize the cards from anything I'd seen at Jasmine's, but my cousin's interests didn't usually extend to offline gaming.

I pulled out my phone and snapped a picture of Dennis's desk. Then, trying to touch it as briefly as possible, I wrapped the laptop in a discarded Canucks sweatshirt, holding it and the headset at arm's length.

I turned to find Kett waiting for me in the doorway. I was pleased that I managed to not flinch at his sudden, silent appearance.

He raised an eyebrow.

"Colby Hansen was a gamer," I said. "Dennis had a headset, and these cards and dice..."—I gestured toward the desk—"...so maybe he was as well. Jasmine might be able to pull something off the computer. Something to connect the boys."

Kett sneered. "I'm not interested in the humans, reconstructionist. Technology won't catch whoever turned the teens."

I lifted my chin. "I doubt the vampire who's done this has a Facebook page or a Twitter account. But we are dealing with humans, and—"

Kett held out his hand, effectively silencing me and indicating his wish to move forward without so much fuss.

I shut my mouth and passed him the computer. Perhaps I should have felt vindicated, as if I'd won some minor battle. But I didn't.

Kett unwrapped the computer, tossed the sweatshirt back into the room, and tucked the laptop underneath his arm. Apparently, his magic didn't fry technology. Or he was deliberately destroying possible evidence.

I would have sworn the shirt landed in the exact spot I'd picked it up from. So either the vampire had an eidetic memory, or he'd been watching me the entire time without me knowing it.

Neither option was particularly thrilling.

"Odd," I said, glancing around the bedroom a second time. "Shouldn't the police have taken the laptop? Wouldn't that sort of thing be automatic in a murder investigation?"

"Their investigation has concluded."

I settled my gaze on him. "Did they conclude it? Or did you?"

"We'll take the laptop if you wish. Though I cannot imagine how the electronic ramblings of a child's mind will be at all helpful, let alone readable. The cleaners will be here within the hour."

"The cleaners? Your cleaners?"

"Indeed."

I snorted, crossing to rifle through the desk drawers. "I bet you bought the whole damn building."

"And if I did?"

"Well then, might I suggest that some upgrades are in order?"

"Indeed. With a bulldozer."

"The people who live here don't need to be homeless, Kett. But some fresh paint and new carpet might be nice."

He didn't answer. When I turned around, the bedroom was empty. He'd left without a word. That was becoming a pattern with him.

Chapter Five

"So Dennis Bradford's father's body is in the morgue at Surrey Memorial Hospital." Jasmine's rich, almost throaty voice was amplified by the speaker on my cellphone, rather than being thinned.

"It's been taken care of," Kett said, not bothering to take his gaze from the glassed entrance of Sentinel Secondary. We'd been parked in the visitor lot, adjacent to the entrance of the two-storey high school, for about ten minutes.

The drive into West Vancouver had taken us back onto the freeway, over the Second Narrows Bridge, then up the mountain. An hour later, and we were back in the neighborhood where Colby Hansen had lived and been buried, then unburied. Still trying to piece together the events leading up to his final destruction.

"Looks like the guy was a drunk," Jasmine said, ignoring Kett's interruption. "I've found evidence of multiple domestic abuse calls, no charges. The Ministry of Families and Children…you know, social services in Canada…paid regular visits to the apartment."

"How do you know that?" Kett asked.

"I'm a computer hack and Internet diviner in one gorgeous package, vampire." Jasmine laughed at her own personal assessment.

Kett side-eyed the phone sitting on the shelf above the glove box doubtfully. "Divination is not magic that would be compatible with technology."

"She's joking," I said.

"I am not." Jasmine's laughter-filled protest was almost drowned out by the sound of a voice coming over a loudspeaker in the background behind her. My cousin was working while waiting for her flight to Vancouver, which she'd said wouldn't be boarding for an hour or more. "Just give me a few more seconds."

I could hear her fingers tapping overtime on a keyboard. She was always in her element when working her magic, as was I when collecting a reconstruction.

After I'd initially tried to introduce them and been cut off by the vampire, Jasmine had talked Kett through giving her remote access to Dennis Bradford's laptop. The computer was currently open and tethered to the vampire's cellphone in the back seat of the SUV. As far away as it could be from me, since I might fry it with a single touch. Well, a concentrated series of touches, at any rate.

Unlike my magic—and that of most other witches, actually—Jasmine's power was compatible with human technology. Not that technology was a great way to track Adepts—which was usually the main aspect of her job—but her specific skill set made her a highly sought-out freelance investigator. She didn't head her own team, but most lead investigators were a dozen years her senior. Jasmine also wove magical protections—wards against magic—for technology by request at an exceedingly generous hourly rate. Thankfully for my pocketbook, I got her services for free. Otherwise, my phone wouldn't last nearly as long as it did.

Kett had followed through on his promise that we'd speak to Colby's girlfriend after I reconstructed the magic he'd sensed at the Bradford apartment. But now that we were waiting for her to get out of school, I was feeling uneasy, more so than I'd been all day. I wasn't particularly skilled in questioning teenagers, especially nonmagical ones. And even after spending only half a day with Kett, I was fairly certain he wasn't exactly skilled at communicating with anyone. I had a feeling that the vampire ranked humans somewhere around where cows were ranked by meat-eaters, and I wasn't sure that he held Adepts in much higher regard.

"Hell, yeah," Jasmine crowed. "The kid was for sure a gamer. Took me fifteen seconds to crack the password. ElfLord69. Teenaged boys are so predictable."

I had absolutely no idea why the password ElfLord69 was so predictable. But I kept my mouth shut, glancing over my shoulder at the open laptop in the back seat. Windows and programs were being opened and closed remotely, flashing across the screen.

If I hadn't already been feeling like a stalker for sitting outside a high school, watching Dennis's life being excavated in the back seat would have driven it home. People had secrets. People should be allowed to keep secrets. I had secrets that I wasn't interested in anyone knowing, not even Jasmine. Secrets were a fundamental part of being able to function in everyday society.

Of course, I hadn't been turned into a vampire, been abandoned by my maker, and then murdered four people.

And as for stalking a school, generally parents weren't keen on their kids being questioned by a witch, let alone a vampire.

So I was uneasy. People were dead. Innocents. It was past time to get over it.

"Any connection between the deficient fledglings?" Kett asked.

"None that I can find yet," Jasmine said. "But Dennis played a lot of different RPGs, online and off, using different user screen names. I'll see if I can find duplicates among the people he played with, and will try to log on to some of these message boards. I'll get back to you."

"School's out," Kett said, reaching for the phone.

"I'll see you at the airport," I said in a rush, just before the vampire tapped the screen and ended the call.

A bell rang out across the visitor parking lot. Then teenagers began streaming through the glass-and-steel front doors. I had no idea how the vampire had known the bell was about to ring, except maybe he could sense the mass movement within the building. Either that or he'd lied to Pearl about being involved with Colby's death and had previously stalked the teen at his school. I acknowledged both as possibilities, then refused to be intimidated by either.

I'd just keep telling that to myself. At some point, it would be true.

Kett opened my text messages, scrolling through to find the picture Jasmine had sent of Luci.

We both glanced at the picture, then up at the sea of teenagers before us.

"How are we going to spot her in this crowd?"

Kett lifted his hand, pointing toward a group of teens currently exiting the main doors.

On my phone, the teenaged girl appeared average in every way—height, weight, hair. But by the cluster of people that surrounded her like a barrier or a battering ram as she exited the school, she was exceedingly popular.

"Lots of friends," I murmured.

Luci and her companions crossed away from us, toward a parking lot on the side of the wide building.

"Not a concern," Kett said, slipping out of the SUV.

I followed him out of the vehicle and across the short run of grass that separated the visitor lot from the front sidewalk of the school. Teens streamed around us, full of energy and eager chatter, and unaware of anything beyond their friends or their phones.

If the neighborhood, school, and clothing of the students hadn't already proclaimed the affluence of the area, the cars parked in the student lot would have. Used BMWs and older Mercedes occupied most of the spots—apparently, wealthy families bought secondhand as well—but a number of new Audis and a couple of Porsches were also scattered about. Not that I could sneer at such displays of wealth. I was a Fairchild by birth, even if no longer by choice. I'd wanted for nothing as a child, financially. Unfortunately, in my family, personal safety and unconditional love had nothing to do with money.

Luci and her gaggle of friends were chatting in a tight cluster beside an older red BMW, midway across the lot. The friends appeared to be playfully bickering, but Luci laid her brown-eyed gaze on Kett as we approached, then didn't look away. She appeared calmly resolute, so I assumed that the vampire hadn't ensnared her.

"Luci Jennings?" I asked as we stopped a few feet away.

Her gaze flicked to me. She nodded, then looked back at Kett.

Every one of her four friends stopped talking, turning to look at both of us with equally stony gazes. Had I been sixteen years old—and not a Fairchild witch—I would have been terrified.

The boy in the group—a sandy-haired athlete who stood a good two inches taller than Kett—narrowed his eyes at the vampire. "What do you want with Luci?" he spat.

Luci laid her hand on his forearm, stepping forward from the group. "It's okay, guys. Give me a second."

Her friends—all crossed arms and glowering faces—took three measured, oddly choreographed steps to the back of the BMW.

"You're here about Colby," Luci said. "I expected you days ago. And not in the daylight." The brunette cocked her head to the side. She was wearing diamond studs in her ears. "Or is this enough cloud cover?"

Kett was completely motionless beside me. There was something in his lack of movement or response that I found exceedingly menacing. I refused to glance over at him, though, keeping my attention on the teenagers and desperately trying to figure out a way for this conversation to not end in violence, blood, and five teenaged corpses.

Finally, Kett cast his gaze over Luci's head, capturing the attention of the four teens grouped behind her. One by one, their eyes widened in fear.

"Please," the girl whispered, then swallowed. "They were only helping me."

Kett returned his gaze to the teenager directly in front of him. Luci's mouth parted, revealing the perfect teeth that only optimal health and a talented orthodontist were capable of producing. Her expression became blissful. She swayed forward.

I laid my hand on the vampire's arm, pushing past the adrenaline spike that came from touching him without permission, along with the swirl of fear that the corded, hard muscle underneath the soft cashmere of his sweater evoked.

"Don't," I murmured, regretting speaking the second after I did so.

Kett clenched his hand, bending the arm I was touching at the elbow. "You dare, witch," he said, not looking at me.

The teens behind Luci began to shuffle their feet, as if they were concerned and thinking about doing something about it.

"Can you ensnare them all at the same time?" I asked, carefully measuring my tone. "Modify their memories right here and now in this parking lot, with dozens of humans nearby?"

Kett didn't answer.

"Witches can," I said, emboldened by the fact that he hadn't begun rending his way through the crowd. "Without even laying eyes on them."

I lifted my hand from his forearm, reaching over to pluck one perfectly straight strand of hair from Luci's head.

"Ouch," the teenager said.

Kett dropped his arm back to his side.

"Luci?" I spoke quietly, coaxingly. "Who helped you in the graveyard? Who did you tell about Colby?"

"John and Melinda," she said dreamily. "They brought the gasoline and the shovel when I texted."

"Just them, no others?"

"No others," she repeated.

"John. Melinda," Kett said, calling to the other teens.

I shuddered at the seductive power laced through his voice. Two of the teens stepped forward. Their eyes were glazed and their expressions blissful.

The vampire's control was mesmerizing and completely horrifying. What happened when Kettil the executioner stopped playing at 'passing' for human? What happened when the vampire grew fatigued with dampening or limiting his power?

Kett took a single step forward, then appeared on my other side with his pale hand extended before me.

I flinched. Usually, power displays—such as moving quicker than a human eye could track—just irked me. But around Kett, I felt as though I were hanging off the edge of a cliff by my French-manicured fingernails. Continually.

Two different strands of hair were entangled between the vampire's fingers. Plastering a professional smile across my face, I reached into my bag and pulled out my compact. I took the two strands of hair from the vampire, twined them through the strand I'd collected from Luci, then coiled all three strands on the mirror and snapped the compact closed. The hair would be powdered with foundation by the time I handed it over to Pearl, but that wouldn't hinder a witch of her power. The teens would sleep well tonight and wake knowing their friend had tragically committed suicide. And nothing else.

"You were expecting us?" I asked Luci.

She shook her head. "Him. Not you."

"Why is that?"

"Colby got the blood from somewhere, so it made sense that someone...someone who sent the blood...would come to get him."

"What do you mean by 'sent the blood'?"

"Cicely said there was a bucket and bags of blood when she found him in their bathroom," Luci said.

I looked at Kett, now certain that I had been picking up the image of a container of some sort from the drop of blood in the Bradford apartment reconstruction. He nodded in acknowledgement.

"Cicely?" I asked gently.

"Colby's sister." Luci glanced back over her shoulder at the younger girl, around fifteen, standing beside John. "We're making sure she gets to and from school...for a while. That's the right thing to do."

Colby's sister's eyes appeared almost bruised. She hunched her shoulders as we all looked at her, dropping her gaze to the pavement. I shuddered at the idea of finding

Declan or Jasmine dead and believing they'd committed suicide.

Kett was holding a fourth strand of hair before I'd even thought to collect it. I added it to my compact without question. Pearl wouldn't be able to wipe the memory of Colby's death from Cicely's mind, but she could help ease the circumstances.

"How did Colby meet the blood donor?" I carefully avoided using the term 'vampire' in the school parking lot with Kett at my side. Humans weren't stupid. Most people would see magic if you pointed at it and screamed its name. Luci had already come to the illogical conclusion that such magic existed before even seeing an actual vampire. It seemed a safe bet that her friends wouldn't be all that hard to convince.

"I don't know that they met," Luci said.

I glanced at Kett, wondering if he had any idea how a rogue vampire could turn a human without meeting him. Standing stock-still, he resembled a marble statue swathed in cashmere in the middle of a high school parking lot. If not for its curly hair and softer jawline, I would have sworn the statue of Michelangelo's *David* had been modeled after the vampire.

I tore my gaze away from contemplating his chiseled cheekbones and deliciously curved pale lips. Only seriously stupid witches stared at dark magic long enough to let it ensnare them.

"How did you know the pencil would vanquish him?" I avoided the word 'kill.' Pending memory wipe or not, I didn't need the teenager thinking she'd murdered her boyfriend.

"It's wood, right? I guessed."

"He could have killed you."

"I...I couldn't leave him like that. He thought he would be happy, but you can't...grow in darkness."

Well, that was an interesting assessment.

"Did Colby expect someone to come get him that night?" Kett asked.

"I don't know. I don't think so. It was a secret. He left me a note."

"Do you still have it?"

"I burned it, along with all the others." Tears flooded Luci's eyes.

"You loved him," I said.

"I didn't want him to be a monster," she whispered.

"How did Colby communicate with his donor?" Kett asked, blithely ignoring the suffering of the heartbroken girl. "If they never met?"

"Online."

"Where?" I asked. "Facebook? Instagram?" I had no idea what social platforms teens thought were cool.

Luci shook her head. The movement was exaggerated, causing her tears to fan out across her cheeks. "Gaming site," she whispered, pressing her hands to either side of her head.

"Strong," Kett said. "She's fighting my hold."

"Let her go," I said, more sharply than I'd intended. "She'll answer our questions without being ensnared."

Kett turned his silver-blue gaze on me and a chill ran down my arms. I shivered, but I met his stare determinedly.

"What gaming site?" he asked without looking away from me.

"I don't know." Luci started quietly sobbing.

Kett disappeared.

I blinked rapidly, forcing myself to not glance around for the vampire.

Luci brushed the tears from her face, shaking off any residual hold Kett's magic had on her. "Sorry," she said. "What did you say?"

I smiled, hoping for professional but getting a tight grimace instead. "My condolences for your loss."

"Did you know Colby?"

"Not really," I said. "I only saw him once. He's lucky to have had you."

I wasn't sure about that last part, but it sounded good. Colby was dead, after all. Was it better to be dead or to be a vampire?

Luci sucked on her lower lip, then nodded.

I smiled, managing the expression genuinely on my second try. "Thank you for your time."

"Okay." Luci turned back to her friends.

The best thing I could do for all of them—Cicely included—was get the strands of hair back to Pearl as quickly as possible. I had hope that once the elder witch worked her magic, it would ease their confused grief.

I turned, swiftly walking back to the visitor parking lot. It was starting to rain. Again. The vampire was waiting for me by the BMW SUV. The lot was more than half empty, and vehicles were still leaving the school in droves.

Ignoring the drizzle that misted my face, I locked my gaze to Kett's. "I'm an accredited reconstructionist," I said, steady and determined. "I'm also a Fairchild witch and a personal friend of Pearl and Jade Godfrey."

I rarely acknowledge the second claim and was stretching the third, but I continued brashly nonetheless. My constant state of fear was making me reckless.

"We are operating under Conclave jurisdiction," Kett interjected before I could continue.

"No," I said. "You're operating under your own self-defined parameters. If you want my help, you will not harm anyone in the course of this investigation—"

"Even if it is your life they are threatening?"

"There are ways to subdue a suspect or a threat without harming them. Ways I'm sure you're proficient at."

"Fine. I will use no unnecessary force, little witch."

I lifted my chin defiantly at the insult. "I'm at the height of my powers—"

Kett laughed. The short bark of amusement echoed through the practically empty lot. "Not even close," he said. Then without another word, he climbed into the SUV.

I had no idea what the vampire thought he meant. I had no idea whether he'd keep to his promise of minimal force. And I had no idea why he thought my life could possibly be threatened during the course of our investigation. As far as I'd been able to tell so far, he was the biggest threat I faced.

What I did know was that I had to get the hair samples from the four human teenagers to Pearl, then make it to the airport before seven thirty.

I crossed around and climbed into the passenger side of the vehicle.

I was never late if I could help it.

Vampire games or no vampire games.

"I found another dead teen," Jasmine said, dragging her bag out through the international arrivals area at Vancouver International Airport. She was wearing a heathered brown merino-wool cardigan that fell around her knees, over a long-sleeved black V-neck T-shirt and skinny-legged black jeans. Her brown leather boots almost perfectly matched the laptop satchel slung across her shoulders.

"Where?" Kett asked, appearing out of the crowd of travelers and the swarm of family and friends currently greeting each other ecstatically.

My cousin flinched, whipping her head around and sending a rampant cascade of dark-blond curls across her shoulders. She hadn't seen the vampire before he spoke. It was unnerving to have a vampire sneak up on you, even when you were expecting to meet one. I knew. He'd been doing it to me all day.

"Kettil, the executioner and elder of the Conclave," I said formally and as per protocol, introducing them as I had tried to do when they'd spoken on the phone. "Jasmine Fairchild, tech witch and certified investigator. Also, gourmet cook."

Jasmine laughed at the gourmet comment. But compared to me, she was a five-star chef. As long as her short attention span didn't distract her.

"Yes," Kett said, smiling pleasantly. "Wisteria's cousin. Dahlia's daughter. Half-sister of Declan Benoit."

Jasmine thrust her hand toward him, smirking sexily. "Well, you've done your homework."

Kett's smile widened to reveal a hint of white teeth as he shook her hand.

Jasmine laughed again, enjoying the attention. Me, the vampire decided to keep in a heightened state of fear. Jasmine, he decided to flirt with. Perhaps he preferred effervescent, slightly sarcastic personalities. Or perhaps it was Jasmine's curls and bright-blue eyes. My cousin's eyes were a lighter blue than Jade Godfrey's, but a lot of witches shared that coloring—including my entire family.

Except for Declan. But then, he wasn't a blood relative on the Fairchild side. No, Declan's eyes were a golden hazel, and—

"Daydreaming in the middle of a case?" Jasmine folded me into a hug, effectively drawing my attention back to the present day. "That's not like you, Betty-Sue."

I laughed, gratefully accepting the embrace and the distraction. Jasmine was the only person in the world—besides our Aunt Rose—who hugged me. "It's good to see you, Betty-Lou." I whispered the childhood nickname into her mass of pineapple-and-coconut-scented hair. We'd been greeting each other as such since we were nine.

"The dead teen?" Kett prompted, scanning the crowd. The mass of humanity surrounding us hadn't yet thinned out. Vancouver was a highly sought-out all-season tourist destination, so international arrivals was presumably a constant stream of people.

"Suicide," Jasmine said, casting her voice low underneath the constant murmur of nearby conversation. "Same as the others. In Seattle. I found Colby and Dennis on a couple of gaming sites together. I compiled a list of Dennis's user names, then started cross-matching and tracing all the players he interacted with."

"Passports," Kett said, holding his hand out to us.

Jasmine still had her arm linked around my neck. She was holding her laptop bag as far away from me as possible in her other hand. She hated having to replace her computer, so was especially careful with it every time we visited.

"I'll have a flight plan logged," Kett said. "The jet is on standby, but it will still take an hour or so to recall the crew."

Jasmine's jaw dropped, then she wagged her eyebrows. "A private jet, eh?"

I chuckled, shaking my head and digging through my bag for my passport.

Kett's expression was as impassive as always, one hand still extended as he dialed a number on his cellphone with the other.

Jasmine deliberately glanced around the bustling arrival area, letting out an anguished sigh, then dropping her passport into Kett's open hand. "Well, the Vancouver airport seems nice at least."

Indeed, Vancouver International Airport was built out of miles and miles of steel and glass, all tied together by wood accents and well-placed First Nations art. It was one of the prettiest airports I'd ever seen.

"I'll have your possessions brought from your hotel," Kett said to me.

Before I could respond with my room number or offer up my key card, the vampire slipped back through the crowd, speaking to someone quietly on his phone in a language other than English. German, maybe? I didn't have an ear for languages or music.

"I wouldn't have minded some cupcakes," Jasmine said mournfully.

I slipped my arm through hers. "I grabbed a dozen when we stopped by the bakery to drop hair samples to Pearl. They're in the car, along with Dennis's laptop, which I'm assuming Kett will also grab, since I don't have the keys."

"Yes! You completely rock, my friend."

I chuckled, allowing Jasmine's effervescence to buoy me as we meandered in the general direction Kett had gone. I assumed we'd need to go to some private section of the airport, but I had no idea how to get there.

"So…dibs on the vampire," Jasmine said.

"You're joking."

"So…no? You want first crack?"

"Seriously, Jasmine. He's not…not…"

"Powerful? Dangerous? Sexy? Actually, crazy hot. In that 'I might devour your soul, but I could also love you forever' kind of way."

I stopped, pulling her to an abrupt halt, then disentangling our arms so I could look her in the eye. Her three-inch-heeled boots made her the same height as me in my two-inch heels. "Please be joking."

"You can't tell me you haven't noticed. And...it's been twelve years—"

"No."

"No, you haven't noticed? Or no, you aren't ever going to love another human being ever again?"

"I'm not sure vampires are capable of love. Nor do they qualify as human. And I do love. I love you."

"Your devotion is heartwarming. But it doesn't warm your bed."

"Neither would a vampire."

"Fine." My lovely cousin shrugged, then linked her arm through mine again.

We wandered through a section of shops, passing the open seating area of a restaurant, then a bookstore.

"So..." Jasmine said. "You aren't going to go for it?"

I sighed dramatically. "No."

"Good."

"The boy in Seattle played online with Colby and Dennis?" I asked, getting us back on neutral ground. Jasmine and I never agreed about relationships, sexual or otherwise. My cousin was steadfast and openhearted, maintaining relationships with people who'd done us both great harm and had barely apologized for it. She also liked to flirt and fall in love, with Adepts and nonmagicals alike.

I didn't.

Though I was grateful for Jasmine's tenacity when it came to familial relationships. Otherwise, she would have never forced herself back into my life, and I'd have been all alone in the world.

"Gavin Lowell," Jasmine said. "Yes. I found his obituary."

"Suicide?"

"Yes.

"Did he...slaughter anyone?"

"They cremated him." Jasmine smiled sadly. "So if he was going to rise, I guess he didn't get the chance."

A lot of families were losing sons. I was hoping we could track down the rogue vampire quickly.

"Could be a complete coincidence, of course."

"Could be."

"I'm still digging through the message boards. Some are more difficult to crack than others. Gavin didn't bother with clever user names, so he was easy to identify. But there has to be something else that links the teens, besides all of them playing the same online game."

"I guess it depends on who they were playing with."

"You think a vamp would pose as a teenager to ensnare victims online?"

"I don't know. As far as I'm aware, vampires aren't so generous with gifting eternal life. They have rules about turning Adepts, don't they?"

"We hope," Jasmine said quietly. "But the boys were human."

We approached an escalator, pausing to grapple with Jasmine's overly large bag.

"How long did you think you were coming for?" I groused.

"Hey! I was in San Francisco. I did some shopping."

I laughed. And for one blissful moment, I wasn't worried about the mounting body count among teenagers or about the vampire hunting them.

Then Kett appeared beside us, relieving Jasmine of her bag as if it weighed nothing—which, for him, was probably the case.

"This way," he said coolly, slipping off in the opposite direction from where he'd originally gone.

I gazed after him for a moment, then spoke to Jasmine. "Text an update to Pearl?"

"You think someone should know we're flying to Seattle with the executioner of the Conclave?" Jasmine asked teasingly.

I looked over at her. "Yes. Someone powerful definitely needs to know where we are at all times now."

Her smile faded. Nodding, she pulled out her phone, texting as we followed the vampire through the crowd of unsuspecting humans.

The vampire's jet was a sleek, customized, six-seat Learjet 70, replete with white leather seats and all the latest technology. Though Jasmine had teased Kett about his access to something as pretentious as a jet, the Fairchild coven owned an older-but-similar model. Or they had twelve years ago. It seemed likely that they would have upgraded by now. Neither Jasmine nor I availed ourselves of the plane, though. Too many strings.

I took a seat in the middle of the jet, trying to stay equally far away from the engines at the back and the controls in the cockpit, out of force of habit. Though it seemed doubtful that my magic could have any effect on something as large and powerful as a jet engine. Jasmine sat across the aisle from me, immediately pulling out her table and setting up every electronic device she carried with her, plus Dennis's laptop, which had been waiting for us on the jet. I wasn't sure where the box of cupcakes had gotten to, but hoped the steward brought them around later for a snack. Otherwise, Jasmine might riot.

Kett didn't reappear until after we'd taxied down the long runway, then had taken off into the cloudy evening. Perhaps he liked to sit with the pilot. Perhaps he had phone calls to make. Even the executioner of the Conclave had to check in with someone, didn't he? He sat in the seat in front of Jasmine, but didn't bother to swivel his chair around to face us.

"There's cola all over the keyboard," Jasmine said, grumbling cheerfully as she double-checked every file and program, just in case she'd missed anything in her remote pass.

"Sorry," I said. "Just be happy it isn't another fluid. It was owned by a teenaged boy."

"Eww, Wisteria!"

"Do you have Gavin Lowell's address?" Kett asked, almost absentmindedly. I wouldn't have thought that tone possible for him.

"His parents' address, yeah. Some suburb of Seattle." Jasmine's fingers flew across the keyboard of the laptop. Thankfully, despite her earlier comments, vampires didn't seem quite as intriguing to my cousin as technology was. "North, I think. I don't know Seattle well."

"Or compass directions," I added jokingly. Then when Kett actually glanced my way, I immediately wished I hadn't been so informal around him. "Are we just going to show up at the house to ask Gavin's parents about their dead son?"

"You reconstruct," Kett said. "I'll investigate."

"What else would she do?" Jasmine said. "Gargle peanut butter?"

Kett partially swiveled his seat, so that his long legs were in the aisle. "I've heard that expression before. I don't understand its proper usage."

Jasmine laughed, but the vampire wasn't joking. Well, I wasn't sure if he was joking or not.

"If they cremated the boy," I said, ignoring the weird moment, "and if no other incidents took place like with Dennis and Colby, there probably won't be anything to reconstruct. So all we'd be doing is harassing the parents with questions they either can't answer or that will be painful for them."

"Is this what you mean?" Kett asked, placing his phone down beside Jasmine's right wrist.

With her attention still glued to the laptop, she glanced at the phone, then flinched. "Oh, God. No. That's not...no. Where did you find that definition?"

Kett raised one eyebrow. "I used Google. Then consulted the first entry. The urban dictionary. It seemed appropriate."

"No," Jasmine repeated, looking aghast. "That's not what it means. Is it?" She double-tapped Kett's phone screen, closing the web browser, then passed it back to him. "That's not it." Then she looked at me, grimacing. "Never look that up."

"Who is Chuck Norris?" Kett asked. His attention was on his phone again.

Jasmine shook her head, returning her attention to her laptop and not bothering to answer him.

"What about a note?" I asked, trying to get us back on topic. "Don't people who commit suicide leave notes? If Gavin actually committed suicide, maybe he left a Facebook post or said something to a friend. If he did, then we don't need to harass the parents. Can you look for that?"

"Um, sure." Jasmine's tone was remote, as if she was just responding because I'd paused, not because I'd asked a specific question. "Here. I have something better than a note. Or worse, maybe, depending on your perspective."

"Show me," Kett said.

Jasmine swiveled the laptop so the vampire could see her screen. He scanned it, not even bothering to lean forward. I was pretty much the same distance away from Jasmine, or maybe even slightly closer, and I could barely make out that there were words on the screen.

"What?" I asked.

"A conversation between the boys," Jasmine said. "They formed a pact."

"A suicide pact?"

"An immortality pact." Kett sounded as detached as usual as he said it, but the idea of a group of teens seeking immortality seemed like the sort of thing that should have bothered him.

"So one member of the group is actually a vampire?" I asked. "Strong enough to turn the others? Does it work that way? Would they have just needed to ingest or…transfuse the blood? And at what volume? How many pints could the vampire give at one time? And he's all over the place, crossing international borders now."

Kett looked out the window at the dark clouds below us, not answering a single one of my questions.

"How many boys?" I asked Jasmine. "Do you even know they're all boys?"

"No," Jasmine said. "And five as far as I can tell."

"Five. Jesus."

" 'Sent the blood'," Kett murmured. "The human girl said."

"Luci," I said, clarifying for Jasmine.

My cousin nodded, then started typing on her own laptop, which she had opened up on the shelf beside her.

"Sent," I said, following up on Kett's statement. "Implying the vampire mailed the blood? That's impossible. Customs—"

"Courier," Jasmine said, interrupting. "Whether north from Canada or south from the States, it might get through more easily by courier."

"Might? What vampire operates under the 'might' category?"

"A young one," Kett said. "Perhaps without a master. Alone. And unaware of our laws."

"A fledgling that strong?" I wasn't certain how vampires were 'made,' but I was fairly certain it would take a powerful vampire to do so.

Kett eyed me. Adepts didn't like discussing their magic, but he was the one who'd requested my help, so it was within the parameters of my job to ask.

"It's not impossible," he said.

"Okay," Jasmine said. "We have five participants in this convo. We know ElfLord69 is Dennis, because we're logged in as him." Jasmine pointed to the mostly black screen she had open on Dennis's laptop. The conversation she was referring to was a scroll of white that I couldn't read from where I was sitting.

"And Colby and Gavin?" I asked.

"Not sure yet. The user names are different on this site."

"Are you saying that one of those five is a vampire?"

"Not any of the three we've already identified," Kett said mockingly.

I wanted to snap back about being a reconstructionist, not an investigator, and that I hadn't trained as Jasmine had, but I stifled the impulse. It would only come off as whining.

"It could have been Gavin," I said. "He was cremated."

"A vampire would never use the name Gavin," Kett said.

Jasmine snorted, then giggled.

Again, I wasn't certain if he was joking or not, so I simply barreled ahead. "You just said he was a fledgling."

"I said it was possible, but he is certainly not newborn. A newborn would be incapable of...communicating using a messaging board."

"His magic would prevent him?"

"No. His bloodlust would be uncontrollable. He'd be incapable of focusing on even the simplest of tasks. For the first half century, at least."

Jasmine's fingers faltered on the keyboard, then slowly resumed typing.

My mind stuttered over the information Kett had just blithely revealed. The idea that it took fifty years to gain some sort of control made me wonder again about how old Kett actually was, sitting on a jet with two potential meals within easy reach. His distant demeanor suddenly made complete sense.

"So when you said young, you meant young for a vampire," I said.

Kett didn't answer.

And it dawned on me that whenever he didn't answer, it was either because he didn't have anything to contribute to the discussion, or because he considered the question irrelevant or obvious.

"Figure out the user names and find the vampire. Got it," Jasmine said with false cheerfulness. "I'm pretty sure that 18Tennyson92 is Colby. That's pretty obvious. The boy never posted a meme or quote that wasn't from some sort of death-obsessed poet. In fact, are you sure he wasn't the ringleader? He's got vampire written all over his Facebook wall."

"Quite sure," Kett said.

"Who started the conversation?" I asked. "Who brought the subject up?"

"Dennis," Jasmine said. "But like it was picking up a previous conversation, not as if he was floating the idea for the first time."

"So are we bothering Gavin's parents or not?" I asked.

"If the witch finds us an undead gamer, then no," Kett said. "If not, then yes. We will proceed when we land."

"I am a tech wizard," Jasmine said, "but I'm fairly certain that even I can't ascertain someone's undead status from just a user name."

"He meant not recently in the morgue or declared dead," I murmured to my best friend.

"Ah." She glanced over at Kett, then gave me a classic 'oh, whoops' look.

I shrugged, fairly certain that it was impossible for anyone to ruffle Kett, undead jokes or not. Except for Jade. Jade got underneath the vampire's invulnerable skin. But that was because he let her.

A reserved or even offish employer was fine by me. My friends were few and far between, and I had no need to add a vampire to that short list.

I snuggled deeper into my plush seat and closed my eyes. Though Vancouver to Seattle was a short flight, a quick nap would be a good idea. It seemed unlikely that Kett was going to snack on either Jasmine or me while he needed us to track down his rogue vampire. After that, though, all bets were probably off.

I fingered my white-picket-fence bracelet. Kett wouldn't cross Jade though.

"Tell me about this game," Kett said.

Oh, God, no. I could practically see Jasmine's face light up through my eyelids.

"Unseen Arcana? It completely rocks," she said gushingly. "I'm a werewolf, a hundred points away from enforcer class."

"I have no idea what that means."

"It's a relatively new RPG, a role playing game, with an offline component, but mostly played online. Wisteria snapped a picture of the player cards Dennis collected. Here."

I peeked through my eyelashes. Jasmine was holding her phone out for Kett.

"Looks like he was playing a sorcerer, level twenty. That's good. I've never met a sorcerer that powerful myself in real life." She laughed at her own joke.

"Are you saying that nonmagical people are playing a game that directly mirrors or incorporates the magic of the Adept?" Kett's tone was deceptively silky.

Jasmine's laughter died. She didn't answer.

"Jasmine Fairchild? Has an Adept created this game and marketed it to humans?"

Now there was a potentially deadly question. An execution-worthy offense. And not just by the vampires. Witches, sorcerers, shapeshifters—any type of magic user or governing body—would maintain the secrecy of the Adept by any means necessary.

"Of course not," Jasmine finally said. "There are literally thousands of RPGs. This one just happens to be currently popular, and actually well plotted."

"How directly does it parallel the Adept world?"

Jasmine scoffed. "Barely. I mean, there's no mention of dowsers or alchemists or dragons at all. And we all know those exist, right?"

"Yes," Kett said coolly. "We all know. But we three have reason to know." His gaze flicked to me with a hint of disapproval, as if I should have kept my mouth shut about dragons existing or the things I'd helped Jade with in London, then Seattle.

"I'd like to see you try to keep something from Jasmine," I said snottily. "Plus, dragons and guardians aren't exactly a secret. Just rare."

"After we find the vampire we are hunting, we will look into this further." Kett addressed Jasmine as if I hadn't spoken. "I suggest you report it to Pearl Godfrey as well."

Then the vampire turned his gaze out the window again.

Jasmine swallowed, then looked over at me with an exaggerated grimace.

Well, that was another can of worms waiting to explode. And I seriously hoped it was just a coincidence. Because Adept or not, I wouldn't want to be hunted down by Kettil for designing an RPG.

Chapter Six

"Benjamin Vern," Jasmine said.

"What?" I murmured, hoping I was asleep.

"Benjamin Vern. Lives in Seattle as well." Jasmine turned her laptop so I could see a picture she'd pulled up on her screen of a brown-haired teenager with deeply set, darkly hollowed eyes. "He's the fourth player in the immortality pact, and our next stop. I just traced him through the message boards."

"He's not dead?" I straightened in my seat and smoothed my hair.

"No recent hospital records or police reports that I've found yet."

"But is Ben a vampire name?" I asked jokingly.

"Kett thought it might be an assumed identity. For an unregistered fledgling trying to pass as human."

I peered around, then up and down the aisle. All the other seats were empty. Kett had apparently vanished. "How do you wander off in a jet?"

Jasmine shrugged. "He's not in the bathroom. Actually, I'm not sure how long he's been gone. He muttered something about being hungry and having his pilot's license—"

"What?" I cried, struggling out of my seat belt and bolting to my feet.

Jasmine dissolved into a fit of giggles.

"I'm here, witch," a cool voice said from the front galley. "I was making a phone call."

Jasmine stifled her laughter.

"Very professional," I muttered, sitting back down.

"It's fun working with you again." My best friend was completely unabashed about making me believe that Kett had gone to snack on the pilot.

"It is," I said with a smile. I couldn't begrudge her the joke. Having Jasmine around was a balm, even when I didn't know I'd been hurting.

Benjamin Vern lived in a small brown bungalow with an equally small fenced front and back yard, just off the I-90 Express and twenty minutes south of downtown, in a small suburb of Seattle that I hadn't even known existed. Though there was a great coffee roaster, QED, just a few blocks away.

Someone had planted lavender and rosemary along the edges of the front walk, from the sidewalk to the door.

Jasmine—attached to two computers and a phone now—stayed in the SUV that had been waiting for us at a private hangar at King County International Airport five miles south of downtown Seattle. As far as I could tell, the vehicle was identical to the one Kett had driven while in Vancouver. Which made me wonder if the vampire was a bit OCD or simply a massive control freak. It also made me wonder whether or not the Conclave maintained a presence in Seattle, Washington, where I also resided when I wasn't working. Because if so, that was news to me.

Kett and I stepped onto the sidewalk to observe the brown-and-beige rancher. It was deep into the evening, nine thirty or so. The clouds had partially cleared as we'd landed, and the crescent moon was bright. The curtains were drawn in the front windows of the house.

"Magic?" Kett asked.

"I don't see or feel magic just like that," I said. "I have a process, but it would look out of place on the front lawn in a residential neighborhood without a distraction spell for cover."

"You could see all the magic you wanted."

"How would you know?" But as soon as I'd snapped the words, I instantly regretted letting my professionalism slip.

Kett turned his distant gaze on me, observing me as thoroughly as he had the house. The moonlight reflected off his silver-blue eyes. "I know because we share a similar magical ancestry. Similar talents, if you will. Retained from before I was remade."

I wasn't sure how to continue my half of the conversation. Kett unnerved me. If I ever dropped the magical blinders I held carefully and diligently in place and took a peek at him, I had a feeling he'd appear so intimidatingly powerful that I would have been practically incapable of standing at his side without constantly quaking with fear.

And I wasn't interested in spending any second of my life paralyzed by fear. I'd done enough of that as a young teen.

I already knew that Kett was more powerful than he'd appeared in either of the reconstructions I'd collected of him. Just as Jade felt more powerful, even through my personal shields.

Magic was like that. Eager to fill a void, or to strengthen a weakness.

Nonetheless, I wasn't interested in explaining myself or my choices to a vampire. To anyone, really. I'd seen what my family did with great power, and I had no wish to fulfill any sort of inherited familial destiny. Or to indulge in my genetic predisposition toward embracing darkness.

"You would see magic here, then," I said, speaking instead of allowing the strained silence between the vampire and me to stretch out any longer. "If there was any to see."

"Perhaps. Witch magic isn't completely compatible with vampire. But there is a lot a person would give up for immortality."

Some Adepts would have suggested that a vampire gives up his or her soul for that particular gift, but I wasn't about to voice that out loud. Instead, I attempted to change the subject. "If this is the house where the vampire lives—"

"Doubtful. No basement."

"You appear to have no issue with daylight."

Kett chuckled quietly. "A fledgling would."

"There could be a crawl space."

Kett snorted, as if no self-respecting vampire would spend the daylight hours huddled in three feet of cement-walled darkness. Then, without further warning, he strode up the walk, climbed the short steps, and rapped on the front door lightly with his knuckles.

I followed, stopping a step below and to the right of his shoulder.

The vampire lifted his hand to knock a second time.

"Wait a moment," I said quietly. "Humans move slowly."

Kett stretched his arm in front of me, pressing the doorbell nestled beside a traditional brass mailbox.

I almost laughed at his insolent behavior, but satisfied the impulse by smirking behind his back instead as I glanced around. Well-tended flower beds lined the front of the house under the windows. Though they likely boasted daffodils and tulips in the spring, they were currently edged with pansies beneath mostly-spent roses. A bird's nest was tucked into the eaves just above the left side of the door. I stepped nearer, standing on my tiptoes to look inside, involuntarily flinching at the sight of its contents.

"What?" Kett asked, not taking his eyes off the door.

"Nothing…just dead birds that I wasn't expecting to see." I remembered having read somewhere that when baby birds died, the parents were sometimes unable to push them out of the nest, but I brushed the morose thought away and returned my attention to the door. "Is anyone inside?"

"One person," Kett said. "Slowly approaching now."

I eyed the door, waiting for it to open. It appeared to be newer than the house, and the lock looked heavy duty. "That's odd," I murmured. "Is the door reinforced?"

"Yes?" a female voice called from inside.

Kett glanced over his shoulder at me.

"Teresa Vern?" I called, hoping I was speaking loudly enough to be heard without yelling and potentially disturbing the neighbors. "My name is Wisteria Fairchild. I'm here to ask after your boy, Benjamin."

A series of locks clicked open down the length of the door. Teresa was evidently serious about security.

An olive-skinned woman in her early thirties opened the door. She had tousled brown hair and had thrown a Seahawks sweatshirt on over blue scrubs. Spotting Kett standing before her, her welcoming smile faded, and she started to close the door.

"Wait," I said, stepping up beside Kett.

Teresa's deep-brown gaze flicked to me, then back to the vampire on her doorstep. Not that she knew he was a vampire—as far as I could tell, she didn't have a drop of magic in her—but he was an intimidating figure nonetheless. "Fairchild, you said?"

"Yes. Wisteria." I kept my tone light. "I know it's an unusual name. My parents were hippies."

Teresa's eyes narrowed. "In the eighties?"

She was technically correct. My parents weren't of the hippie generation, but no one had ever called me on that fact when I'd used the line before. I couldn't exactly lead with the information that I was a witch, and that witches were traditionally named after colors...or colors and flora, in the case of my family.

I smiled. "They were late bloomers."

Teresa's gaze settled on Kett to my left. "You said you were here to ask about Ben?"

"Is he alive?" Kett asked coolly.

"Of course," Teresa snapped.

"I apologize, Ms. Vern," I said. "We're investigating a series of suicides connected to an online game that we understand your son plays."

Teresa blanched. She was still poised in the process of closing the door, and her grip tightened on its reinforced edge. "Suicides?"

"Yes, ma'am."

"May we speak to Ben?" Kett asked. "Ascertain if he knew the boys or communicated with them?"

Teresa shook her head emphatically. We'd upset her, and her gestures were becoming jerky. "He's not here right now. He's visiting his father."

"But you saw him today?"

"Two hours ago," Teresa said. "How...how many boys are dead?"

Kett turned his back on her, abruptly walking away. Flustered, Teresa stared after him.

I sighed inwardly. I was surprised that the vampire had bothered to address a human in an even remotely polite fashion, but he had no cause to upset her further.

"I'm sorry, Ms. Vern. I'm glad we were mistaken."

Teresa nodded, but her gaze was still on Kett. She hadn't loosened her grip on the door.

"You'll check in with Ben?" I asked. "If he had contact with these boys—"

"I can take care of my own, Ms. Fairchild."

"Yes, of course. Thank you for your time." I stepped awkwardly away from the door and the situation, quickly moving down the walk.

Teresa hadn't turned on any exterior lights when she answered the door, and the moon had gone behind a cloud, forcing me to be careful with my footing. Kett was standing by the rental SUV, gazing up at the darkened sky. He was a pale smudge in the night.

As I neared the sidewalk, I turned to glance back at the house. Teresa Vern was a shadowed figure in the window of what I assumed was a living room off the entrance, watching us depart.

"She was scared," I said tersely, on the unprofessional edge of pissy.

"Her child is alive," Kett said, not at all ruffled by my bluntness. "There is no magic in the immediate vicinity. He is of no consequence."

"Still, we could have spoken to him."

Kett lowered his gaze from the sky. I defiantly met his icy stare.

"Do you think the woman would have granted us access to her boy?"

I didn't. "Teresa Vern," I said, correcting him waspishly.

He smirked. "Do you think Teresa Vern would have granted us leave to speak with her boy, Benjamin?" Every word out of his mouth was deliberately enunciated.

I couldn't tell if he was mocking me or actually attempting to communicate more effectively. "No," I said begrudgingly.

"Would you have had me rip her from her home, coerce the boy's location from her, then alter her memory of the incident?"

"No," I said quietly.

"Who does my behavior remind you of, Wisteria Fairchild?" Kett's silky-smooth tone implied that he already knew every little thing about my life.

I didn't take the bait. "Something is still off. She was too scared."

Kett shrugged. Perhaps he was accustomed to having everyone around him continually quaking with fear. "There is nothing here. We will move forward with the next name."

"The one who was cremated? What are we going to do? Harass his parents? Steal his ashes?"

Kett smiled, his white teeth a bright spot in the darkness around us.

First thing I would do if I ever wanted to move out of the city and into the middle of suburbia would be to petition for more streetlights. But then, I knew all about the monsters that lived among us.

"That sounds like fun." The vampire turned, climbing into the SUV.

I shivered, suddenly aware of the chill settling in with the night. "I was being sarcastic."

My protest went ignored. Grumbling to myself and my lack of professionalism, I crossed around and climbed into the back seat of the vehicle. Who made stupid jokes about stealing the ashes of a teenager around a vampire? Apparently, me.

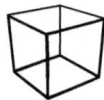

Fuming and feeling useless, I stood tucked into the deep shadows beneath the front eaves of the Memorial Funeral Home on the outskirts of the upscale Capitol Hill area of Seattle. Kett was checking the perimeter while Jasmine compromised the security system.

And I was doing nothing. It served me right for being less than professional, for being flippant with the executioner of the Conclave. And for involving Jasmine. I always had to be the superior reconstructionist, always had to prove I was the best at that one thing. The one thing I could control—

"Sneaky bugger," Jasmine said from the front doors. She was fiddling with her phone and some other electronic device I couldn't see because I wasn't allowed to get close to it. "Just blending into the shadows underneath the security lights like that."

She took a long slurp of a milkshake she had ordered from some drive-through we'd stopped in at, just off the highway. I hadn't ordered anything. Neither had Kett. Obviously.

"He is a vampire," I said.

"Cute, too."

"Don't start."

Jasmine burst into peals of laughter.

"Shush," I said. "We're supposed to be stealthy."

"He's just not your type."

"I don't have a type." And I didn't. I just had one long, large heartbreak. One person who I couldn't have in my life without hurting him—or worse, getting him killed. Thanks to my family. But Jasmine knew all that, upside down and from every angle. She'd been there. And we'd all made our choices in the moment. We'd chosen to save each other and damn our futures in the Fairchild coven.

"You should, Betty-Sue," Jasmine said sadly. "You should have a type."

The security pad that Jasmine was fiddling with beeped once, then appeared to short out. I had lots of experience with things shorting out. I probably could have just held my hand over the device and created the same reaction. Though likely not without setting off the alarm first.

Jasmine grunted with satisfaction, tucking her phone and other gizmos into her satchel, then reaching back to brush her fingers against the back of my hand. Her skin was chilled from the milkshake.

"This is more than crazy, you know." I deliberately changed the subject.

"What? Breaking into a funeral home or working for a vampire?"

"Both."

"You're the one who called."

"You're the one who answered."

Jasmine laughed. "Hell, yeah, I did. You can't do this without me. And I wouldn't miss it for anything."

I brushed my fingers against her hand this time. She shivered, smiling. My magic always did that to her, but she claimed to not mind. I was the witch who was uncomfortable around any magic I couldn't control, not her. I knew that was odd, but it didn't change the reality.

Kett materialized out of the dark night.

I flinched.

Jasmine squeaked, dropping her milkshake.

Kett caught the to-go cup before it was anywhere near the ground, right above Jasmine's knee. He remained stooped there for a moment, smiling up at her. Charmingly.

She smiled back at him coyly.

He straightened, handing the milkshake to her.

"Thank you, sir." She was flirting shamelessly.

I laughed. So very little fazed Jasmine for any length of time. My life was always quieter, and far too serious, when she wasn't around.

She flashed me a smile.

Kett regarded me with a raised eyebrow. Perhaps I was as much of an enigma to him as he was to me. Though it seemed unlikely.

"Are we breaking in to this place or what?" I asked.

"Already broken," Kett said. He stepped away, then paused as if correcting himself. He turned to Jasmine. "Thank you for your assistance."

"Oh, yeah? Cool. It's what I do."

Kett regarded her for a moment more, his expression almost quizzical. Then he melted into the darkness without offering further instructions.

"I guess we're supposed to follow him," I said.

Jasmine tucked her arm through mine, and we stepped into the darkness along the edge of the gray-sided building. The security lights didn't trigger with our passing, and I wondered whether that was due to Jasmine's fiddling or if Kett had turned them off somehow.

"I've never broken into a funeral home before." Jasmine's stage whisper was loud in the dark.

"But you've broken into other places of business?"

"Of course," she said, seemingly affronted by the question.

I laughed quietly. If my branch of the family was mired in tradition, Jasmine's acted as though they'd invented the concept of tradition in the first place. Neither of us was in any way wild, but Jasmine was better at faking it, hence the flirting with a vampire. At least I hoped she was faking.

The back door of the funeral home was still illuminated by an overhead light highlighting the four-foot-square concrete landing and the two steps leading to it, but I couldn't see Kett anywhere. Farther along, a small parking lot was currently occupied by two hearses, with a short paved ramp leading from it to a double set of loading doors. The third parking spot was empty.

The loading door to the far right was slightly ajar.

Jasmine pulled a set of plastic gloves out of her bag and tugged them onto her hands.

"Um, excuse me?"

Jasmine giggled. "Static electricity," she said, as if that would explain anything to me. "Get your mind out of the gutter."

"I hadn't formed any particular opinion," I said. "But thanks for that series of images."

"Something needs to wake you up."

Jasmine was still smiling, so I pretended she wasn't referencing my lack of a sex life, or my lack of any relationship potential at all...sexual or otherwise.

I was content with the small life I'd built, though. It was safe and comfortable, and I contributed to my small circle of Adept society. I opened my mouth to say as much, then shook my head at my dourness. "Whatever...or whoever chooses to wake me for breakfast the next morning better not be wearing those."

Jasmine laughed, allowing the awkward pause to pass unacknowledged.

"Shall we?" I attempted to recapture the lightness I'd felt a moment earlier. "We're following a centuries-old vampire with extensive, unknown powers into a funeral home. What could possibly go wrong?"

"Well, we could lose our accreditation. Then we'd have to resort to running an organic grocery or holistic clinic."

"You've thought this through."

"Extensively." Jasmine tugged the door open further, then stepped inside the dark, wide corridor beyond.

The smell of antiseptic wafted from the shadows ahead. The odor was so pungent that I wouldn't have been surprised to find out the halls were mopped with an industrial-strength cleanser after closing every evening.

I followed my cousin into the building. "You could always become Kettil's blood slave," I whispered.

"Oooo," she whispered back. "Do you think the position is open?"

The door clicked shut behind me, taking with it the wash of light that had been partially illuminating the corridor.

I smacked into Jasmine, who'd abruptly halted in front of me, mashing my teeth against my lips on the back of her hard head.

"Ouch!" she cried dramatically.

"I haven't had the need for a stable," a cool voice said behind us, "for over two hundred years now."

A beam of light slashed through the darkness surrounding us. Jasmine, who was still making a show of rubbing the back of her head, had activated the flashlight on her phone.

"But I would never turn down a willing witch," Kett said.

His breath brushed against the exposed, suddenly-feeling-far-too-vulnerable skin on the back of my neck. All at once, my choice of hairstyle—a smooth, discreetly pinned French twist—seemed utterly foolhardy and unintentionally provocative around a vampire. I didn't move, wary that any reaction on my part might trigger a savage attack.

Jasmine turned her light toward me, angled downward. Kett was standing beside, not behind me.

"Magical blood must be tastier," she said, as if we were having a regular conversation with a regular person, say about whether fries were better with or without gravy.

"Indeed," Kett said.

I slowly turned to look at the vampire. The pale marble statue dressed in decadent cashmere and soft-washed jeans standing beside me. A monster barely trying to pass through the human world. He was smirking at Jasmine, as if he already owned her. As if she were his to take, to destroy.

No one owned Jasmine.

Irrational, rash, and ill-timed anger flooded through me. I raised my right hand toward Kett's shoulder, though I wasn't sure why. I had no chance of holding him back if he went for Jasmine. "Jade Godfrey has more than enough magic for any vampire," I said.

His smile dissolved. He turned his silvered eyes from Jasmine to me, resting his inhuman gaze on the wrist of my right hand, which I was still holding aloft.

I lifted my chin, curling my fingers into a fist. Unwittingly called forth by my anger, magic boiled around my hand, glowing all along the edges of my platinum bracelet, just waiting to be unleashed.

What the hell I thought I might be able to do with that magic to a vampire of Kett's power—even backed by whatever Jade had done to the bracelet—I had no idea.

"Wisteria..." Jasmine whispered, aghast.

"Are you afraid or simply jealous, little witch?" Kett's attention was still glued to my wrist trinket.

Jasmine snorted indelicately. "Wisteria, jealous? Please."

Kett raised his gaze to meet mine. Within the dark corridor and lit only by the downward cast of Jasmine's flashlight, his eyes were soulless mirrors. I could see my own internalized darkness and pain reflected within his silver-blue orbs.

"I thought we were done with dominance games," I said, attempting to rein both myself and the situation in.

"Then stop playing them." The vampire stepped by me, then Jasmine, and melted into the shadows. A moment later, he appeared before a set of swing doors twenty feet down the hall.

Jasmine gasped.

My heart rate spiked, though I tried to fight it. Oddly, it had been slow and steady while I'd been considering ripping the vampire's own husk of a heart out of his cashmere-swathed chest.

Kett glanced back at us. At me. A red glow flashed across his eyes, so quickly that I might have imagined it. Then he exited the hall, leaving us alone.

I lowered my hand, releasing the magic I'd been holding. I'd never called forth my magic like that before. So Jade's bracelet apparently worked, though I had no idea what it actually did and whether or not I had to be really angry to trigger it.

Jasmine was still staring after Kett.

"Just remember he's not human," I said. "Not anymore." My voice was dark with unreleased anger.

"Spoken like a true Fairchild witch," Jasmine said without ire.

"Some prejudices are held for our own protection."

My cousin nodded absentmindedly. Her thoughts were apparently elsewhere.

I touched my platinum bracelet, running my fingers over its tiny house, fence, and tree charms. Then I started up the hall after Kett.

Jasmine wrapped her arm around my neck, tugging me close enough to press her lips against my ear. "Has it occurred to you…"

"That Kett's hired us to investigate his own crimes?" I whispered back, barely moving my lips. "Yes."

"He'd have to be crazy. The Godfreys…"

"We've seen crazier."

"We're related to crazier." Jasmine's words and the reference to our shared childhood settled around us with a stifling weight.

I stepped away from her loose embrace, strengthening my voice. "This isn't that."

I turned away from all the questions that had flooded my mind in the instant she'd vocalized her doubts about Kett, then compared him to our family. I clamped down on everything I wanted to ask—about vampires, this case, and why I was actually involved in any of it—and every can of worms I wanted to open about our family. Then I strode down the hall to do my job.

I was a reconstructionist. Teenaged boys were dying—being murdered, as far as I was concerned. That was my sole focus.

The image of another battered and bruised dark-haired boy in need of rescuing flashed through my mind. But I shoved the thought away, tucking it behind the wall that surrounded my heart.

That was ancient history.

Though not anywhere near as old as the vampire waiting for me to do my job, whether or not my findings exposed him as the perpetrator.

The swing doors led, predictably, to the morgue, or whatever it was called in a funeral home. The antiseptic smell deepened here, so much so that it seemed to coat my nasal passages. I tried to not breathe too deeply. The floor was tiled and slightly angled toward a drain in the center of the main room. Three white fiberglass trays—similar to hospital gurneys, but with a high lip running around their edges—sat empty before a large steel door that I assumed led to the refrigeration unit. Thankfully, the trays weren't holding sheet-covered corpses. Though based on the equipment standing against three of the four walls, it seemed a safe guess that this was where the mortician did his preparation and embalming.

A small administration office stood to the far right of the main doors. Within, a desk lamp illuminated a paper-strewn desk. Either Kett had turned the lamp on or the occupant of the office had left it on all night. I had never understood how people could be so disorganized and still function.

In the office, Kett was scanning a bookshelf. Its shelves held a number of sealed brown cardboard boxes, each approximately six inches by six inches and tagged with white printed labels. Even without entering the room, I could guess that these contained cremated ashes that hadn't been collected by a family member yet.

Kett selected a box, swiveling to set it on the desk.

I pulled the first of my candles out of my bag, closing the space between us. White for air. I placed the pillar to the east of the box, instinctively knowing which direction was which even when surrounded by walls of concrete and wood. I wouldn't need a large circle for this reconstruction.

Jasmine, who'd followed me to the door, glanced around briefly. "I saw another office through the front door, with a computer," she said. "It's always worth a look. I might be able to uncover more information about the autopsy or see if the funeral home has dealt with any similar cases in the last couple of weeks."

Kett nodded, watching me as I carefully placed the other three candles. Jasmine exited back through the swing doors. I wouldn't want to hang out in a morgue either if I were her.

I paused, looking over at Kett expectantly.

"I'd like to watch," he said.

"From behind the window." I indicated the partially glassed door behind me. "And close the door. That should be enough of a barrier with a reconstruction as confined as this."

He nodded, exiting the office and shutting the door behind him.

I had expected him to argue. If I'd known the vampire better, I should have been able to call and manipulate the reconstruction spell with him in the room, and even walk him through it as I did so. But honestly, after glimpsing the glimmer of his magic roll across his eyes only moments before in the corridor, I hoped to never know Kettil that well. Ever.

I rarely saw magic that way outside of a well-constructed circle. And I certainly never saw it with my personal shields locked down as firmly as I held them at all times around Adepts of power. Kett was way too powerful. I wasn't going to be holding his hand through a reconstruction. Ever.

Ignoring the vampire standing at the half-window in the door, I lit the candles as I circled the desk, making quick work of it. Normally, I walked the room, feeling for any other residual, but that wasn't necessary here. If the weakness of the previous reconstructions were anything to judge by, it was unlikely that I'd find even a glimmer of magic among Gavin Lowell's ashes.

Lifting my palms between the two candles nearest me on the desk, I imbued the circle with my magic, snapping it into place around the box. I reached out for any energy contained within the ashes, any residual waiting to be uncovered.

There was nothing. I peered down at the box through the edge of my circle, seeing the printed label that bore Gavin's name. I continued to stare at it, soft-focusing my eyes as if I might look through the cardboard. Pretending I could see within it. Imagining I could sense a spark of magic buried in the ashes.

I sensed nothing.

I lifted my gaze, shaking my head in Kett's direction.

That was a mistake.

I had never looked directly at someone like him through an active circle, with my senses wide open and seeking magic. He pulsed with power. Magic gathered around him like a voluminous cloud…all shadows and smears, streaked with red and black, and—oddly—hints of gold. He raised his hand to the glass between us. Magic streaked after his movement, infinitely echoing his gesture. Twin pulses of red dwelled in the hollows of his eye sockets. A secondary smudge of blue appeared in his palm, then faded. As if he'd triggered some sort of dormant magic.

"Wisteria?" he asked. His voice was muffled by the glass door.

I'd never seen residual collect around an Adept in such a way. Even in the reconstructions I'd done of Kett, he hadn't appeared this way. I'd seen his actions and his own residual magic, but this smear, this dark cloud—

I shook my head, dropping my gaze to my own hands. They pulsed with blue witch magic, just a shade lighter than my own eyes, than Jasmine's eyes. All Fairchild witches had similar coloration. Blue magic in my palms. Blue magic in the vampire's palm.

I squeezed my eyes shut, forcing my focus back within the circle and onto the box. This was my job. Staring at the vampire's magic was just dangerous.

But no matter how carefully I looked or how long I waited, there wasn't even a glimmer of magic among Gavin's ashes. Nothing to reconstruct.

Stymied, I reached over to snuff the candle nearest me, but stopped when I felt a flicker of magic to my left. I reluctantly pivoted to look at the shelves that held the boxes of cremated remains, catching a glimmer on the edge of my vision. A flash of something.

A figure?

I reached for the circle I'd constructed on the desk, coaxing it to move toward the flickering residual.

The office was tiny. I might have unknowingly triggered a reconstruction outside the circle, accidentally brushing a deposit of residual magic with the energy called forth in my casting. It didn't happen often. I kept my circles tight. But I hadn't expected residual energy nearby, other than from Jasmine or Kett. And neither of them had been in the office long enough, nor wielded any magic that could have imprinted this way.

Though based on what I'd seen of the vampire a moment before, perhaps I shouldn't have been so hasty to theorize. Maybe he left residual wherever he walked.

I successfully shifted the circle over to encompass the shelves, lifting it with my hands as if it had actual weight. Not many reconstructionists could move an established circle, which was why they often reached wildly out without a circle for their collections. Actually, not many witches could move a cast circle either. It was a Fairchild ability. I'd tried to teach Jasmine the technique when we were young and I was still casting standard witch spells, but her magic hadn't cooperated.

The flickering reconstruction on the shelves took form.

A blond boy, who appeared to be around fifteen, was lying across the shelf, suspended in midair. I could still see the other boxes of remains through his faded image.

"That doesn't make any sense," I murmured.

The boy appeared to be sleeping, though he was clad in a cheap navy-blue suit that was tight across his shoulders, rather than pajamas.

Then, without a warning or so much as a single breath, he woke up.

His eyes whirled with blood-red magic.

"I see the boy," I called, assuming that Kett could hear me through the door. "He's a vampire."

I reached out to the manifested energy within the circle, hoping to pause the faded image and capture it within one of my cubes.

The boy reared up, smacking his head on something above him. He cradled his head for a moment, confused. Then he pressed his hands above his head and to the sides.

I couldn't see what he was touching. The residual magic was simply too weak. It was also playing out in real time from beginning to end, which confirmed that I'd triggered the reconstruction process when I'd first cast. I really needed to be more careful.

"This is odd," I said, speaking out loud for Kett's benefit. "He's acting as if he's been buried—"

The boy started screaming. Horrible shrieks of unspeakable pain. Fire sprang up alongside him, then spread across his body. His suit ignited, instantly aflame.

"No," I whispered. "No. No…"

I reached for the residual magic. I tried to grab it, control it. To disconnect myself from Gavin's terrible second death.

The boy screamed and screamed.

I couldn't disconnect. I couldn't stop it. I watched with utter, frozen horror as he burned, fully aware of every moment of his tortuous cremation.

Cool fingers touched my outstretched arms, wrapping around my wrists and trying to pull me away from the reconstruction.

I was the one screaming.

I couldn't stop screaming.

Gavin's skin melted, then curled into ash. His shrieking faded. My own voice became louder as his died.

Cool hands pressed over my eyes, shutting out the vision.

The magic tying me to the reconstruction snapped.

My legs gave out. I fell, collapsing against what felt like a marble pillar with arms. The statue of stone that was Kett. He held me upright, slumped against him.

"They mislabeled the box," I said, sobbing. "They burned the boy. He woke up. He woke up right before they burned him."

Kett still held his hand across my face, blocking my sight.

"Death vision," Jasmine said. She'd entered the office without me knowing, perhaps when I was in the thrall of the reconstruction. "Not being at the actual site of the boy's death, she wouldn't have expected it. She's caught in the echo."

Kett lifted me, cradling me while still managing to hold his hand over my eyes. He was carrying me with one arm as if I weighed nothing, which I most certainly did not.

Air stirred around me. My hair had fallen out of its French twist, the pins tangled within it. We were moving. The vampire's footfalls crunched on something.

"Glass," I murmured, trying to focus on the now and not on what had been.

"You broke the windows," Jasmine said. "Every bloody piece of glass in the bloody place."

I didn't remember doing anything of the sort.

"With your magic, witch," Kett said. "I assume you were trying to break free from the reconstruction."

"My magic doesn't work like that," I said. But my protest sounded lame, even to me.

No one answered me. Or, rather, everything went quiet all around me. Then I couldn't see or hear or feel anymore.

I woke to the sound of Jasmine's fingernails clicking on a keyboard, the familiar noise instantly comforting. Then I realized I was crammed into the back seat of Kett's SUV.

I opened my eyes. Lights blurred past the window. It was still late evening, and we were still in the city.

A magic hangover hit me like a sledgehammer to the center of my forehead. I groaned, squeezing my eyes shut.

"Good morning, sunshine." Jasmine sounded far too cheerful in the front passenger seat.

"I hope you're taking me home," I said.

"You will be useless until you sleep." Kett's cool voice emanated from the driver's seat next to my left shoulder. "Jasmine explained that you'd be more comfortable in your own bed."

"I didn't know I'd see—" I cut myself off before I started sobbing again. The recollection of Gavin's suffering was still fresh in my mind.

"We were in a funeral home," Kett said without obvious inflection or condemnation. "You should have expected such a thing."

"It doesn't happen like that," I retorted, attempting to sit up. I was rewarded for my effort with another blistering pulse of pain behind my eyes.

"Normally, a reconstructionist needs to be at the actual site of the death, or murder, or whatever," Jasmine said, defending me. "The trauma of Gavin's death must have somehow imprinted on the residual magic in his ashes—"

"A rare but not impossible occurrence," Kett said dismissively.

"Maybe," I said edgily. "When reconstructing the death of a newly turned vampire. You can't expect me to have a solid frame of reference for that."

"You need to collect more than one rising to learn a lesson?" Kett asked, completely rhetorically. "What about two?"

"I guess I'm a slow learner."

"Obviously."

"Well, it's good to get that cleared up." Jasmine turned to offer me a sliver of a smile when the vampire didn't respond to her snark. "Okay, Betty-Sue?"

I nodded, braving a second attempt at sitting up. Kett was correct, though. I'd been sloppy. I'd gone in with preconceived expectations, then had been thrown when I saw Kett's magic through the lens of my circle.

"It won't happen again," I said.

Jasmine reached back and squeezed my knee.

Kett didn't respond, which was fine. Because I was already working on figuring out how to extricate myself and Jasmine from working with him.

As best as I could tell, the vampire's magic was completely volatile. He was an unstoppable, destructive force. I didn't want to be anywhere near him a moment longer than I needed to be.

Except...the echo of Gavin's death haunted me.

The SUV glided along the slick streets. Rain beaded on my window, Seattle's lights flaring within the relentless droplets as through a prism. It was hard to think beyond the magic hangover, but the scene of the teen's death replayed in my mind as certainly as if I'd collected it in one of my oyster-shell containers.

"Three boys confirms a pattern," I murmured.

"Two was rather definitive," Kett said. His tone was as disengaged as ever, but I got the sense he was mad at me. But for what, exactly, I didn't know. A blown reconstruction seemed like a tiny complication within the scope of his everlasting life.

"Wisteria is right," Jasmine said. "Two, however improbable, might have been coincidence, but three confirms that the boys acted on their immortality pact."

"Not Benjamin Vern, though," I said.

"He just wasn't as stupid as the others," Kett said.

"Or the vampire hasn't gotten to him yet." My statement hung in the dark air between Kett and me.

Jasmine's fingers didn't falter on her keyboard.

Kett had to be aware that we suspected him despite his declarations of innocence. Who wouldn't?

He spun the steering wheel smoothly in his pale hands, guided toward my apartment by the map on the GPS. Jasmine must have punched in my address.

"It must be a powerful vampire," I said, pushing my luck and phrasing my question as a statement, "to turn so many in such a short period of time."

Kett lifted his gaze to the rearview mirror, but he didn't answer.

How vampire magic actually worked was little more than a series of guesses cobbled together by the rest of the Adept community. I couldn't be sure I actually knew what I was asking.

"Would you know the maker in that case?" I rubbed my aching eyes. Referring to the murder of the boys as 'making' irked me, but it seemed proper.

"Had the teenagers been fully transformed, then yes," Kett said. "I would know any vampire capable of transforming the nonmagical. However, I do not know the vampire who is committing these transgressions."

"How do you know for sure?" Jasmine asked.

Kett didn't answer.

I hazarded a guess. "The boy in Surrey. Dennis. You...tasted him, didn't you? That's how you identified the drop of blood in the bathroom. That's why you wanted me to compare its magic to your own?"

Kett stayed silent.

"The one who went rogue," Jasmine said, as if it justified Kett killing Dennis. And maybe it did. I'd never been faced with a rogue vampire before. But according to what I knew of the history the witches had accumulated on vampires, a body count of four was blessedly low.

"You would have known Dennis's maker, then?" I asked again.

"Yes," Kett said, finally condescending to join the brainstorming session.

"Would you be able to raise so many in such a short time?"

Jasmine's fingers paused their incessant tapping.

Kett rolled the SUV to a stop in the roundabout before the entrance of my apartment building. I lived—when I was in town—two blocks from Pike Place Market.

"I wouldn't have thought so," Kett said, lifting his eyes to the rearview mirror. "As little as two years ago."

"And now?"

"Now I have died by a blade created by the alchemist, who is one of the most powerful Adepts currently walking the earth. I have been reborn through the blood of my grandsire, who hadn't divided his power for more centuries than I've claimed since I became a vampire. Then I consumed blood that should have driven me insane or destroyed me from the inside out, like liquid sunshine. And finally, I stood before magic that caused most of the others at my side to falter, coming away burned but ultimately unharmed."

My head swam. I'd been holding my breath, my gaze locked to Kett's in the rearview mirror. He couldn't ensnare me through the mirror, could he? No. It was his confession that caused my heart to pound in my chest. It was too much information, too much to share with witches he barely knew.

"But you knew all that," he said softly. "Didn't you, Wisteria, friend of Jade Godfrey?"

"No." My voice squeaked. I cleared my throat. "Just the first part."

"And I have shared the rest. Shall we bond through trading secrets? Will you trust me, then? Do you have anything as damning to contribute?"

"Don't we all?"

Kett's lips quirked in the mirror, doubtful.

I laughed quietly. For two days, he'd been dropping hints regarding the depth of his knowledge of my past and family. But I understood now that he knew nothing. Because not even a vampire would sneer at my darkest deeds.

"Pax Johnson," Jasmine said, blithely interrupting us before I tried to one-up the vampire. Not that I would have. It wasn't just my secret to tell. "I thought his first name was just a user name, and then he deleted his profile, which threw me. Pax is the fifth boy in the pact."

"Where?" Kett asked, still holding my gaze in the mirror.

"Tacoma," Jasmine said.

"Alive?"

"As far as I've been able to find out."

"Keep looking." Kett dropped his gaze from the mirror. "I'll pick you up midmorning."

And just like that, we were dismissed from the SUV.

Jasmine swiftly packed up her satchel, then helped me out of the back seat.

Kett pulled away, circling out of the drop-off area before we'd made it up the four shallow steps underneath the glass-fronted atrium of my apartment building.

I groaned again, remembering the broken glass at the funeral home. "We need to call a cleanup crew. There's someone in town, isn't there?"

"Already done. Plus, I placed a short-term distraction spell out front that should hold for a couple of hours. Until sunrise at least." Jasmine paused, still holding me upright by the waist, as I dug into my bag for my keys.

"Thank you," I murmured. I was completely unaccustomed to being the one who needed to be cleaned up after, let alone looked after.

"I don't think he did it," Jasmine said, watching Kett drive away.

"You didn't see his magic. It haunts him."

"So does yours."

I glanced at my best friend, surprised. She met my gaze, then lifted her eyebrows expectantly. But I had no idea what she meant.

Jasmine sighed, taking my keys from me and passing the fob over the reader to unlock the door.

We didn't speak as we crossed through the entrance, then rode the elevator all the way to the top floor. Which was always okay. The comfortable silence between Jasmine and me was filled with history, inevitability, and love.

Chapter Seven

"I expect you to stay attached to the executioner of the Conclave like an overzealous binding spell, Wisteria Fairchild." Pearl Godfrey's tone was crisp over the speaker on my cellphone. "You and Jasmine represent the Convocation in this matter. You will not give him any grounds to supersede us."

I stood in my pristinely clean kitchen, my bare feet neatly situated within the grout lines of the white porcelain two-by-three tile. A sliver of sunlight broke through the clouds that obscured my view of Elliott Bay and the inner harbor through the window over the stainless steel double sink. The errant rays warmed my peach-pedicured toes while I listened to Pearl's instructions.

Since it was only just after sunrise, Jasmine was still asleep on the Murphy bed in my second bedroom, on the opposite side of the penthouse apartment. The bedroom functioned as a guest room when my cousin was in town, but normally the only piece of actual furniture in it—that didn't fold up into the wall—was my Pilates reformer.

Even though I was as far away as I could be in the twelve-hundred-square-foot apartment, I'd closed her door before I'd made the call to Pearl.

The freshly squeezed orange juice I'd left in the behemoth stainless steel refrigerator before going to Vancouver hadn't gone bad yet. But the fruit I'd left out on the counter was wrinkled. I also needed to compost the remains of all the take-out containers in the fridge before I left the city again.

"Are you still there?" Pearl asked, her voice just as commanding over the phone as it was in person. Though I did find her easier to talk to when I wasn't being constantly exposed to her intense magic.

I briefly contemplated pretending that my phone had died, which it did every three or four months. But this one was brand new, and I had a strong suspicion that the chair of the Convocation would know the instant I lied.

"Yes, ma'am."

"Don't bother with the ma'ams, Wisteria Fairchild," Pearl snapped.

By calling this early in the morning, I'd really been hoping to simply leave a voice message. Unfortunately, Pearl was apparently an early riser with call display.

"I could send Jade," she said.

"No," I said, too quickly. Then I attempted to cover my bluntness. "I'd be concerned that my reconstructions might fail around her magic."

"She could clear the area while you were casting," Pearl said sourly.

"Yes, ma'am. But not really the point."

"Never mind." Pearl sighed. "It was a stray thought. Jade is…overkill. By your own admission, Jasmine doesn't need any help charming the vampire. Otherwise, I'd send Scarlett. You're not afraid of him, are you?"

I opened my mouth, ready to declare myself utterly terrified of the ancient being who'd been chauffeuring me from site to site. But then I hesitated. A Fairchild didn't admit fear or lack of ability to a Godfrey. Pearl wasn't going to be the head of the Convocation forever, though witches were long-lived, and any elders who hadn't gone dark were particularly powerful. Usually, I didn't care about witch politics, or about aligning myself with the Fairchild philosophy. But I didn't like the idea of appearing weak or inefficient either.

"I'll do my job," I said instead.

"You always do," Pearl said. "And very well. I know he is difficult to be around...but I'm not sure we'd all be alive right now, especially after Tofino, if he hadn't joined us. The Convocation, as well as the shapeshifters of the pack, owe him some consideration."

'Thanks to Jade' was the unspoken ending to that statement. Once again, I opened my mouth to ask all the questions that Pearl had placed so conveniently before me. And then once again, I shut it. I didn't need to know any more secrets, and I already knew too much about the vampire.

Secrets were a commodity in the Adept world if you knew how to use them, but I was already playing that game with one powerful witch family. My own. I didn't need leverage against the Godfreys or the Conclave. And even if I wanted to, I also didn't have the backing needed to make any sort of power play.

"He's different than he was..." I said, but then I corrected myself midthought. "An echo of what he was in London." I hadn't actually met Kett in London. I'd just collected the residual magic around what had appeared to be his final destruction.

"Yes," Pearl said, but she didn't bother to elaborate. "He's not a danger to you, though. He won't incur Jade's wrath. I believe he loves her in some way."

I nodded, then verbalized my response for the phone. "Yes."

I'd seen Kett take a killing blow for Jade in London. That had to be some sort of love. But I wasn't completely sure that a centuries-old immortal being beholden to the Conclave would completely mitigate his behavior just because he didn't want to upset a dowser in her midtwenties.

"All the victims have been human?" Pearl asked.

"Yes."

I knew it was prejudice that made her want that clarification, not any issue of whether or not the Convocation had jurisdiction. For all the sneering that Adepts did at humankind, and at other Adepts they saw as less than them—or as dangerous to them, like the vampires—they very carefully kept themselves hidden from human eyes. Being massively outnumbered by beings you saw as little more than worker bees was still perilously outnumbered.

I would have assumed that Pearl might have been more concerned about exposure. But vampires died rather tidily if fire was involved, and their rogue kills were often written off as savage animal attacks by human authorities. Humans who didn't want to see magic or bogeymen on top of the everyday horror of their lives.

"You will duplicate any relevant reconstructions."

"I will."

"Thank you, Wisteria."

"As always, Ms. Godfrey."

"Have a good day."

"You too."

Pearl ended the call.

I sighed, noting that the stovetop clock read 2:14 because I could never be bothered to set it properly. It was just after 8:00 A.M. I wanted to snuggle into bed with Jasmine, as we'd done as kids before Declan had turned our duo into a trio, before we'd been apprenticed to our uncle, before everything had eroded into nothing.

Well, the walls had always been tarnished and crumbling, but we just hadn't known it.

If I stood around in the quiet apartment any longer, the death-vision loop of Gavin's cremation would reassert itself in my mind. The continual remembrance of his horrendous death had already disturbed my sleep so much that I'd been up with the dawn. I needed to keep moving, to help Jasmine and Kett solve the case, and to hope that the reconstructions of the dead teens didn't haunt me forever after.

I grabbed my phone and my navy-blue trench coat, texting Jasmine as I left the apartment.

Going for coffee and breakfast sandwiches.

I knew she'd check her phone the moment she woke.

As I walked, I calculated that if I killed some time grabbing coffee, I could be in line when Beecher's Handmade Cheese opened. I adored their grilled sandwiches, and saw no reason why bread and cheese shouldn't have been considered a reasonable breakfast.

"I've been thinking about how Teresa Vern opened the door for me, specifically after I gave her my name."

I was sitting cross-legged on the blond-oak hardwood floor of my second bedroom, resting my back against my Pilates machine. Jasmine was snuggled underneath a cashmere throw and a white cotton sheet on the Murphy bed, with only her hands and face uncovered. I had just finished the second half of my basil, tomato, and Beecher's Flagship cheese grilled sandwich. The fragrant basil flawlessly complimented the nutty flavor of the aged cheddar. And the perfectly cooked tomatoes had drizzled across my fingertips while I ate, so I licked them clean. Jasmine didn't care about proper etiquette, and it wasn't as if I was going to lick the parchment wrapping as well.

"What about her?" Jasmine asked around a full mouth of smoked turkey paired with Flagship and Just Jack cheeses. She'd woken immediately at the waft of coffee steam I'd deliberately blown in her face. It was a ritual we traded—depending on who woke first—whenever we visited each other.

"She knew my name. That's why she opened the door."

"Did she say she knew you? Fairchild is a common surname among humans too."

"Don't say that within my mother's hearing."

"I'm very careful to stay way, way out of your mother's reach."

"I know you are."

Silence fell between us. I savored my dark brew. Seattle boasted a multitude of fantastic coffee roasters, many of which were within walking distance of my apartment. I was an equal opportunist when it came to which cafes I frequented and what drinks I ordered. Today, I'd opted for a dark roast from Ethiopia, no frills. Jasmine hadn't even sipped her triple-shot latte yet. Food was her foremost focus at all times, while I was pretty sure I could live on coffee if it ever came down to it.

Unfortunately, that was a trait I shared with my mother, Violet Fairchild, the potion master of the Fairchild coven.

When I was growing up, our backyard had been a jungle of plants that—when prepared in perfect combinations—could kill without a trace. Of course, the

Convocation frowned upon such things, especially since poisons were notoriously difficult to counter with magic. So my mother channeled her skills into more benign, highly sought-after brews. Cosmetic enhancements were probably still her bestselling products, but a lot of witches bought ready-made spells from her, either because those spells were beyond their own skill level to brew, or because they contained elements that were rare and difficult to obtain or store.

Jasmine's perfect curls and clear complexion were due to an exceedingly pricey shampoo and skin cream sold by a witch based out of San Francisco. I purchased the peach-scented twelve-hour lip gloss I favored through the esthetician I saw every three weeks in order to maintain my French manicures. She also happened to be a half-witch who had a special set of wares she sold to Adept clientele only.

I took another sip of coffee, letting the perfectly dark-roasted brew drag my thoughts away from my family as Jasmine reached for her second sandwich, a sinfully simple grilled cheese.

I wasn't fully Academy trained like most reconstructionists. Some investigators held that against me—though always privately, never to my face. I hadn't taken interrogation or investigative training, then specialized. Rather, I had challenged the exams after my first year of courses. I hadn't been granted the right to do so before, though I'd requested it.

The Academy didn't typically certify reconstructionists at the tender age of sixteen. However, they had given me my accreditation in a private ceremony a week before my seventeenth birthday. Jasmine, who joined me a month after I'd entered the Academy, had taken three more years to graduate. But I'd been training with a former instructor since the age of nine, and Jasmine had chosen to focus on tech, a branch of magic the Fairchilds sneered at.

"Teresa Vern acted like she knew you?" Jasmine said, as if she'd just processed my earlier observation.

"Not exactly. She was smiling when she opened the door, then she saw Kett."

My cousin excavated her arm from the cashmere blanket, extending her hand, then beckoning toward the second brown-paper bag resting on the hardwood floor beside me. "Gimme."

"They're for later."

"Gimme, gimme." Her dark blond curls danced around her face as she leaned toward me, but she couldn't quite reach the bag.

I sighed, deliberately nudging it with my elbow just enough that she could snatch it, chortling gleefully to herself over scoring her bounty.

"So...she knows someone else named Wisteria." Jasmine freed a chocolate pastry from the bag, inhaling its scent deeply and with great satisfaction.

I smiled. "It's just a niggling idea."

"Pain au chocolat." Jasmine murmured the French to herself as if speaking to a lover. She took a bite of the pastry. "No magic though," she said around her mouthful. "If Teresa or someone else in the house were magical, you would have known. Or Kett would have, for sure."

I shook my head, but not in disagreement. Jasmine was right, but something still felt off. Adepts instinctively knew each other, even if they couldn't feel or see magic, or even not knowing what type of power the other Adept wielded. For me, meeting a person of unknown magical persuasion was like the feeling of eyes boring into the back of my neck or nails on a chalkboard.

That spoke volumes about how I viewed the Adept community.

Jasmine shivered whenever an unknown Adept was near. A light shiver, like after a well-earned sneeze.

"I'll dig deeper into the Verns," she said.

"How's that guy?" I asked, changing the subject clumsily.

"Which one?" Jasmine laughed. "The sorcerer or the werewolf?"

I inadvertently swallowed my coffee wrong, then had to cough it out. "I thought he was a witch," I wheezed.

"Nah. Old news."

"That was only three months—"

A vampire was standing at the base of the Murphy bed. Completely startled, I dropped my coffee. Jasmine started choking on her half-eaten pastry.

I glared at Kett.

He stared back.

Jasmine continued to cough. My best friend was going to choke to death because I'd been startled. I scrambled forward to pound on her back, but she cleared her throat enough to gasp.

"Jesus, buddy."

The vampire—his cashmere sweater was royal blue today, but otherwise identical to yesterday's—raised an eyebrow at Jasmine. Then he leaned down to retrieve my travel coffee mug. It had come to a rest against his black leather brogues. Thankfully, it had been almost empty.

"How..." I started to say, then stopped myself.

"...the hell did you get in here?" Jasmine finished my thought. She waved her hand toward her own coffee, and I handed it to her.

"The apartment is not warded against me."

"What?" Jasmine hissed, giving me a look.

"Why should it be?" I asked, disgruntled. "How many vampires live in Seattle?"

"Two," Kett replied.

"What?!" Jasmine screeched.

"He's joking." I stood and walked to the linen cupboard built in beside the Murphy bed. Retrieving a gray hand towel from the upper shelf, I crossed back to mop up my spilled coffee.

Jasmine stared at Kett.

He smirked at her.

She glared back.

His smile turned charming.

Her glower turned flirtatious.

I stopped myself from groaning out loud.

"A cleaning spell would be more effective," Kett said as I wiped the last of the coffee up from beside his foot.

"So would knocking," I snapped.

"On the contrary. This way, I get to see you in your natural habitat, unfiltered."

Jasmine laughed, but she sounded a little unsure of herself.

It hadn't struck me as a joke either. I also wasn't a fan of big bad vampires scaring my best friend. "I can get the apartment warded."

"Not quickly," Kett said. "You are the only witch of note in the immediate area."

I smiled at him.

He narrowed his eyes at me.

I deliberately widened my grin. "You should get your records updated."

Two could play the 'I know more than you' game. Kett thought he could goad me into using magic, or admitting I was incapable of even basic witch spells. Well, not incapable. Just out of practice and happy to stay that way. It was simpler and safer to keep my magic functioning as it currently did.

"A name would be helpful," Kett said.

I laughed quietly. A number of witches—though most of them were half-blood or less—did call Seattle home. I didn't actually know whether any of them were capable of creating wards of a level that could keep a vampire of Kett's power out of my apartment. But as soon as we finished our investigation, I was going to be giving Pearl Godfrey a call. She'd know who to talk to, even if I had to pay to fly someone in.

"Pax Johnson," Kett said, letting the subject drop.

Jasmine untucked her bare legs from underneath the bedding, reaching for her laptop. She'd slept in a T-shirt and panties, though Kett didn't seem in any way affected by the amount of skin flashed his way. I'd known my cousin was a flirt, and that she liked to follow through with the occasional tryst, but I had no idea Jasmine had such a death wish. Though I suppose a human psychologist wouldn't have been surprised, even knowing only the gist of our shared childhood.

"I got an address for Pax last night," Jasmine said, her fingers dancing across her keyboard. "And this is interesting…Ben Vern was logged in until three in the morning playing Unseen Arcana. His IP address indicates that he went back to his mother's, or was within a few blocks of the house while playing. Should I friend him?"

"I have no idea what that means," Kett said dismissively. Then he turned and left the room.

"I guess we'll meet him in the car," I muttered.

Jasmine snorted.

I left her to get ready, gathering my own things. We were off to Tacoma, the land of blown glass and Almond Roca. Poor Pax Johnson. Though I wanted out of the investigation as soon as possible, I hoped he wasn't the vampire behind the other boys' deaths. If that turned out to be the case, it was unlikely that Kett would let him live another night. Though maybe that was a good thing. I doubted very much whether there was any rehab for vampires.

Not that I had any say in the matter, nor any power to stop the executioner of the Conclave.

Though that wasn't exactly a revelation. Still, in this situation with the boys, my powerlessness irked me in a way it rarely did.

Technically, Tacoma was only an hour and fifteen minutes from Seattle—or from my apartment, specifically—but in traffic, the trip could easily take upwards of two hours. Apparently, Kett had timed our drive directly between the morning and lunch rush, though. I wouldn't have expected anything less of him.

The vampire didn't mention my unprofessional behavior from the previous night, or my getting caught in the echo of a death vision like a complete beginner. So I didn't offer up any more apologies.

Jasmine chatted away from the front passenger seat while her fingers flew over the keys of her laptop. Kett's and my reticent responses didn't faze her one bit. She was still gathering information on all five of the boys, sifting through their messaging and other online activity and looking for leads beyond Tacoma.

She was also looking further into Teresa Vern at my behest—though we didn't bother mentioning that to the vampire, who would have just sneered at us paying extra attention to a nonmagical he'd already dismissed.

Relegated into the back seat again—the farthest away I could get from the electronics in the dash and Jasmine's devices while still having a seatbelt—I was more than happy to have my cousin take the lead. She was trained for it. I would just get underfoot, or I might even hamper an investigation into nonmagicals if I touched the wrong thing.

"Are you sure we shouldn't go by his school?" Jasmine asked.

"No," I said sharply, the single word immediately undermining my own determination to stay as uninvolved as possible.

"The reconstructionist is wary of my presence around schoolyards," Kett said. His indifferent tone betrayed no emotion.

"Yeah? I get that," Jasmine said.

I stifled a laugh. Trust Jasmine to back me without question, and trust her to do so out loud whether or not it was rude.

"We will drive by his home while his parents are at work and his siblings are at school," Kett said. "It will give the reconstructionist time to walk the site, as she prefers."

I didn't answer. Kett didn't need constant confirmation about whether or not he was correct in his assumptions.

"If there is nothing there," he said. "Then we will proceed to the school."

"Got it covered," Jasmine said. "He attends a high school a few blocks from his house."

"It's amazing that all this information is so easy to access," I said.

"Facebook is my friend," Jasmine said. "Plus, having Dennis's computer helped. After I broke the main password, everything else was just digging."

Pax's family lived in a neighborhood a few minutes east of downtown Tacoma, where a series of housing developments appeared to have been built in the early- to mid-nineties. Beige siding, cream trims, terra cotta-colored garage doors, and low fenced backyards dominated.

It was just after noon when we pulled up across from Pax's. The well-maintained two-storey house practically occupied the entire lot. I likely could have touched the neighboring houses to either side if I stood between them. A large development was being built across the street, and the painted plywood wall encircling it ran the entire block. Concrete was in the process of being poured, but no framing had gone up yet.

"No hedge," I said, eyeing the flat green lawn and treeless front yard. "The neighbors and any construction workers are sure to notice me wandering around in broad daylight."

"Looks quiet on either side," Jasmine said.

I glanced around the neighborhood. Other than the construction at my back, the entire block was comprised of ten- to fifteen-year-old matching homes with more fences than trees.

"It's not raining," Kett said. "But there are no children's toys scattered in the yards and no people walking dogs. Everyone is at school or work."

"Fine. If I get arrested, I expect to be immediately bailed out." I opened my door.

"I'm sure the investigating mundane could be convinced of the merits of your trespassing," Kett said dryly. "Without the use of handcuffs."

I shook my head, hoping the vampire wasn't suggesting that I spell a police officer—or worse, that he'd be pleased to get involved himself. The Convocation frowned heavily and judgementally on magic used anywhere near humans.

I closed the door of the SUV, strolling across the street. But before I could reach the opposite sidewalk, a floppy-haired teenager pedaled around the corner and nearly mowed me down on his bike, which he then dumped on the lawn of the house I was just about to check for residual magic.

I paused, awkwardly aware that I was sticking out like a sore thumb in the otherwise empty neighborhood.

The teen jogged up the few concrete steps to the front door, tilting a couple of evergreen-filled terra cotta pots on the landing until he found a key. He was completely oblivious to the fact that I was standing frozen at the edge of the street.

I pivoted away, casually crossing back to the SUV.

Jasmine stepped out with her laptop in hand as I approached. "That's Pax. See?" She raised the computer in front of me, holding the screen as close to my face as she dared. "Same Mariners T-shirt."

"Wouldn't he have a key to his own house?" I glanced back over my shoulder. Pax had gained entrance and disappeared within. "And he's obviously not a fledgling vampire."

Kett, now wearing an unbranded baseball cap pulled low over dark sunglasses, climbed out of the driver's-side door.

Jasmine had returned her attention to her computer without answering me.

"Shall we?" Kett sauntered across the road without waiting for me.

I immediately hustled after him.

"He has a free period after lunch today," Jasmine called from behind us.

I glanced back at my best friend in disbelief. That sort of information really shouldn't have been so readily accessible. She settled back into the passenger seat without acknowledging me.

I tripped over the curb, managing to not fall face first on the sidewalk. Kett was halfway up the driveway and heading around the side of the house.

"Wait," I hissed after him. "Think about what you look like."

He paused.

I joined him, casting my voice low. "We should knock. You can't go skulking around the side and back of the house looking like that."

"Looking like what, witch?"

"Like a...well, like a grown man stalking a teenaged boy."

Kett stiffened his shoulders and stared at me. His sunglasses were so dark that I couldn't see his eyes. "You are suggesting I look like a pederast."

"Well, you're not a salesman."

Kett quirked his lips.

Perhaps the idea of selling things door to door amused him. But I wasn't laughing. I was so out of my comfort zone that it was making me antsy. I didn't like being less than composed, ever. It gave people ideas about how easy I was to manipulate or distract.

"The front door, then?" He lifted one pale eyebrow high enough that it cleared the top of his glasses.

I nodded, becoming aware that I was inadvertently clutching my bag with one arm crossed protectively across my chest. I dropped both arms, stepping up to the front entrance with the vampire by my side.

It still unnerved me that Kett could walk around under the sun unscathed. Being under cloudy skies in Vancouver was one thing, but this was full daylight with only a hat and sunglasses for protection.

"Why would he answer?" Kett asked as I reached for the doorbell.

"Why wouldn't he?" I pressed the bell, hearing it chime a sweet tune inside the house. "It's his home. His neighborhood. He feels safe here."

Kett didn't respond.

Heavy footfalls approached the door from inside. Pax opened the door, half a slice of pizza crammed in his mouth.

He narrowed his eyes, looking at me, then glancing at Kett, then back to me. He was taller than Kett, but gawky.

Before I could speak, the boy said, "Already Christian here," and swung the door closed.

Kett stopped it with the flat of his hand.

Pax glared at him.

"We aren't here to sell you anything," I said.

"Let go of the door, buddy," Pax said, ignoring me.

"Tell me about the immortality pact." Kett's voice was flat but demanding.

Pax's mouth went slack. The hunk of pizza dropped from his suddenly limp hand. He had tomato sauce smeared on the side of his face.

"Don't," I said, assuming that Kett was exerting his influence on the teen. But Pax's gaze flicked to me when I spoke. He was just surprised, not ensnared.

"Don't know what you're talking about," he said. Then he retrieved the piece of pizza from the floor and crammed it into his mouth.

"Your concern for humans is almost admirable," Kett said, speaking to me but looking at the teen. "Or would be, if I intended any harm."

"No one should ever be made to do anything against their will," I said stiffly.

Kett looked at me. I didn't bother meeting his gaze.

Pax's eyes had widened, ping-ponging between us. He wasn't stupid enough to miss the veiled threat in Kett's words.

And I wasn't interested in playing games. "Your friends are dead," I said.

The teen shifted his feet. He was still holding the door with one hand, blocking our entrance to the house with his body. I wondered if Kett could cross the threshold uninvited, or if that was another myth about to be blown to pieces as well.

For Pax's sake, I really hoped not.

Technically, the vampire had entered my apartment without issue, though I suspected that my working with him might have been invitation enough. Or maybe it was that I spent so little time in the apartment, and invested so little of myself into it, that it wasn't actually considered my home. It was highly unlikely that any vampire, including Kett, would be able to cross any of the thresholds held by a Fairchild in Connecticut. For good or evil, the coven had owned and occupied those properties for hundreds of years.

"I didn't have anything to do with it," the teen said with utter sincerity. "You guys cops?"

"Not in the sense you mean," I said with a glance at Kett.

The vampire had reverted to staring at Pax.

"I knew it was stupid," the teen said. "Vampires don't exist. Neither does immortality."

Kett stilled. Actually, Kett was oddly still all the time. It was his magic that shifted, as if moving inward somehow. I really didn't want to feel his magic. I shouldn't have been able to inadvertently feel his magic.

I fought a sudden sharp desire—an almost overwhelming need—to step to one side, forcing more space between me and the vampire. I didn't want to affect the dynamic of the conversation. I didn't want to jeopardize Pax.

Because vampires most certainly existed.

"You said no to the others?" My question caught in my throat, but the teen didn't seem to recognize the death threat standing at my side. Colby's girlfriend, Luci, had been much more aware of her surroundings. But then, she'd slain her vampire boyfriend only a couple of days before meeting Kett.

Pax shrugged.

"We've tracked down five of you. Are any more of you going to die?"

"Don't think so."

"Helpful," Kett said.

"Listen, Pax." I was anxious to move forward without violence or magic or biting. "My name is Wisteria—"

"Like the flower?"

"Yes."

"Your parents were weird, then."

"Yes. My parents were more than weird."

"I don't game with Ben anymore." The teen abruptly changed the subject. "I deleted my Unseen Arcana profile and everything. Well, the one I was using before."

"And everyone else in your group?"

He shrugged. "You said they were dead."

"Do you know differently? A sixth member perhaps?"

Pax shook his head.

"Did they kick you out of the group when you said no?"

Pax looked uncomfortable, but then shook his head.

"You didn't actually tell them no." Kett pressed his fingertips to the door, pushing it back until it hit the teen's shoulder.

Pax swallowed. "They're my friends…they were my friends. I won't talk against them."

"Did Ben say no as well?" I asked.

Pax shook his head.

"Did someone send you a package?" Kett asked, taking one step toward the teen as he did.

I laid a hand on the vampire's shoulder, though I was loath to touch him. "Do you still have the package?" I asked quietly.

Pax nodded, his eyes suddenly huge and fixed on Kett. He was white-knuckling the edge of the door, pressing back against Kett's deceptively light touch and unable to move it an inch.

"Go get it for us," I said, quietly commanding the teen. I didn't want to frighten him further.

Pax finally looked at me.

I smiled encouragingly. I thought about promising him that everything would be all right, but I didn't make promises I had no hope of being able to keep. If Kett went for the teen, I had no way of stopping him. No one did, except maybe one of the Godfreys.

The vampire took a step back, allowing his arm to drop back to his side.

Pax let go of the door, stumbling away from it as if it had been holding all his weight, though he kept looking at me.

"Please," I prompted.

"It's in the garage fridge," he said.

"We'll meet you outside." Then I reached across the threshold and closed the door.

After a moment, the bolt slid into place, locking us out.

"He's not even remotely telling us the truth," Kett said.

"And you know that how?" I descended the steps, turning toward the driveway. "By his heartbeat? He's scared."

"I could make him not scared," Kett whispered against my right ear, though he'd been nowhere near me a second before.

I flinched away. But when I rounded on him indignantly, he was still standing by the front door.

The vampire raised an eyebrow over his sunglasses. Again.

Smug bastard.

I turned away, deliberately walking to the center of the driveway and standing before the garage door. Kett appeared beside me. I tried to not flinch a second time. I was unsuccessful.

"This is it," I said, more than ready to articulate the 'I've fulfilled my contract' speech that I'd been practicing since Vancouver. "We get the package—"

"If he actually has a package," Kett said. "If he isn't inside calling the police."

"—and Jasmine and I are done." I ignored his interruption. "The package will lead you to the killer. Only five boys were involved, according to both Jasmine and Pax. You won't need any more reconstructions."

"I have no objections," Kett said. "I'm more efficient alone."

"Fine," I said. "We agree."

A motor triggered from within the garage, lifting the door upward.

I suppressed a smirk. Professionals didn't need to be smug.

Feet shod in shiny white sneakers, then legs clad in worn jeans appeared as the door lifted. Pax was waiting for us a few feet away, holding a square box about a foot-and-a-half on each side. When the door cleared his head, he stepped forward.

"I don't want to get anyone in trouble," the teen said.

"I know," I said. "But your friends are dead."

Pax nodded mournfully, then handed the parcel to me. It was still sealed, addressed to him, and shipped from Astoria, Oregon. The labels were handwritten, and the box had been stamped and delivered by the US postal service. I wondered whether the Canadian packages had gotten through customs and into Colby's and Dennis's hands through sheer dumb luck. Deadly, wasteful luck.

"Astoria," I said, glancing at Kett. "I thought you said there were only five of you in the immortality pact?"

"There was," Pax said. "It killed the others, hey?"

"You didn't open it."

"Obviously."

"They killed themselves," Kett said smoothly.

Pax shoved his hands into his pockets. "Yeah? I got that part of the instructions. But why would you care about the package, then? If it was just a bunch of stupid suicides?"

"Who sent this?" I passed the package to Kett in the hope that holding it would make it more difficult for him to strangle the teen.

Pax shrugged. "Not me, obviously."

"But one of the five?"

He shrugged again. Apparently, he'd talked himself out of his fear somewhere between the front door and the garage. "Don't know exactly."

"Who started the conversation?"

"I already said I didn't know. I was invited last."

"By who?"

"18Tennyson92. I don't know his real name, so don't bother asking."

"Why aren't you playing with Ben anymore?" I asked, following up on what the teen had said earlier.

"He's weird, okay? And, like, sick a lot. So he doesn't always keep up. His characters aren't skilled enough."

"Recently sick?"

"Nah. He's got cancer. Or he did. A couple of times. Instead of playing, all he and the other three did was talk about death. And the game is boring if you can't get past a certain level."

Kett turned away, box in hand as he headed back toward the SUV. Apparently, the interrogation was concluded.

"Thank you, Pax."

"Whatever. Just leave me out of it."

"I'll try."

"Right." He walked back into the garage, slapping the door switch before he entered the house.

I waited until the garage door was fully closed, keeping myself between Kett and Pax. Though I knew that no door would stop the vampire if he wanted in.

I climbed into the back seat of the SUV. Jasmine was leaning across the front seat, taking a picture of the package in Kett's lap. The second she turned back to her computer, Kett sliced open the packing tape with a fingernail—a fingernail that slid through the tape like an exceedingly sharp knife.

"I thought you were done with the investigation," he said without looking at me.

I tore my gaze away from his hands, looking back at the house across the street. I'd had no idea his fingernails were that sharp, and the revelation did nothing to settle my discomfort.

"I'm not a bigot," I blurted.

"Excuse me?" Kett paused with the package half opened.

"It's not just because you're a vampire. I don't like anyone having access to the power you have at your fingertips."

"It's not the power you should be worried about, witch," Kett said coolly, "but the person who wields it."

"Same thing."

"If Pearl Godfrey had been standing beside you on the doorstep, would you have feared for the boy's safety?"

"Of course not." I answered automatically, without thinking about it.

A smile spread across the vampire's pale face. I knew that if I'd dared to look, I would have seen a seething cloud of magic cloaking him, following him. But when I focused instead on his gaze in the rearview mirror, he appeared almost human.

"Astoria checks out," Jasmine said. "I don't think the label has been forged. The shipping number tracks."

"And the return address?" I asked. "What are the chances it leads to our vampire's lair?"

Jasmine laughed, though with no humor. "Slim. It's a dud. The street address is mistakenly or deliberately incorrect. So I can't tie anything together yet. I don't know if all the packages were sent from the same post office, or even at the same time."

"But someone walked into a post office in Astoria and mailed that package," I said.

"It appears so."

Kett glanced down at the box in his lap. "No vampire of power lives in Astoria, or in Oregon at all."

"Yeah?" Jasmine asked. "Vamps aren't a fan of wine country or open ocean?"

"Indeed," Kett said. "Too much sun, perhaps."

Though I didn't vocalize the thought, I felt quite certain it was more a matter of Oregon being too close to the Godfreys, and the territory of the shifters of the West Coast North American Pack, which was based out of Portland.

"What about a regular vampire?" I asked instead. Kett's wording had been quite specific. "Or a vampire traveling to Astoria to ship this package from there, trying to cover his or her tracks?"

"We've already discussed the limitations of fledgling abilities." Kett pulled open the flaps of the corrugated box, pushing aside some bubble wrap to reveal a bag of blood.

At least it looked like blood. In an IV bag.

"Blood?" Jasmine asked.

"Yes," Kett said. "Three units. Not enough."

"It's not like we didn't expect blood to be involved," I said, setting aside his 'not enough' comment for a moment. "Did any of the coroners' reports mention a transfusion?"

"No," Jasmine said. "But maybe the families didn't request autopsies? When cause of death was so obviously suicide? I'm not sure what's standard among humans."

Kett pierced the bag of blood with his thumbnail, then licked the blood off his thumb.

I momentarily envisioned Jasmine and me being slaughtered where we sat.

Kett shuddered, grimacing. "Old. And cold."

"TMI," Jasmine said.

"I have no idea what that means," Kett said haughtily.

"Too much information," I said. "So? Vampire blood?"

"Yes." Kett didn't elaborate.

"So some vampire is befriending teenaged boys online and mailing them bags of his blood?"

"So it appears." Kett's voice was distant as he contemplated the box in his hands.

"How does that make any sense?"

"It doesn't."

"If the boys aren't injecting or transfusing the blood," I said, putting some of the pieces together, "then they must be drinking it."

"I'm not sure how quickly vampire blood would be absorbed by a human." Kett acknowledged my supposition without actually acknowledging it. "Perhaps there wouldn't have been any for the medical examiner to find."

"Are we heading into Astoria?" Jasmine asked. "I've got the address of the post office. That'll give us a starting point, at least, and I'll have some time to see if I can somehow link the packages, or figure out if the return address is just a typo."

Kett nodded, passing the box back to me, then starting the SUV. Jasmine typed an address into the GPS.

"Should you have known this other vampire by taste?" I finally asked, since apparently Kett wasn't going to offer up any more information.

"Yes. Or his maker. Or any of his line." He sounded peeved.

"Should you know who this vampire's maker is?"

"We are not a numerous species. The Conclave will not be pleased."

"Once we find the fledgling, you'll need to find his maker?"

A slow grin bloomed across Kett's face. "Indeed."

"What did you mean by not enough? When you saw the three bags of blood?"

Kett's smile faded. "I'd been wondering why the boys were rising sickly and weak."

"Not enough blood?"

"Specifically, not enough magic in the blood. But there should be enough for you to attempt a reconstruction."

"What? In the back seat of a moving vehicle?"

"Certainly. That's why you are here, isn't it? The only reason. To do your job. You're capable of pulling an impression, at minimum."

Jasmine stopped typing, shifting slightly away from the vampire until her right shoulder was pressing against the door of the SUV. Reacting to the feeling of his magic rising with his cold indignation, perhaps.

Either that or she was clearing my line of fire.

I gathered my magic around me tightly, resolutely blocking out whatever might be emanating off Kett. I wasn't as easy to rattle as I had been as a teenager. I wasn't going to explode.

At least not yet.

"Yes. I'm still here to do my job." I retrieved an oyster-shell cube from my bag, setting it on top of the box on the plush, white leather seat beside me.

Kett smirked.

He was totally manipulating me. And he'd been doing so since even before I'd laid eyes on him in Bishop's. But that wasn't why I was obligated to see the investigation through.

Even with my speech outside the garage, I couldn't ignore the fact that the dead boys still needed someone with no bias to speak for them. Plus, I knew without asking that the new lead provided by the box meant that Jasmine wasn't going anywhere until we actually solved the case. And there was no way in hell I'd leave her alone with Kett.

Gavin's fiery death was seared into my mind, possibly imprinted on my soul. Someone had to pay for his pain and suffering. I might not be the person who brought criminal Adepts to justice. But I could still believe in retribution.

Chapter Eight

We followed the package's origins to Astoria, Oregon—now fairly certain we were hunting a vampire who'd used one of the dead teens as a mouthpiece or figurehead.

By car, we could drive to Astoria two ways. Either crossing to the coast from Olympia, then entering the town over a massive bridge that spanned the mouth of the Columbia River. Or we could take the I-5 and cross directly west on the I-30. Naturally, Kett selected the latter, more direct route. Though with all the traffic on the highway, the two-hour-and-forty-minute trip wasn't much quicker in the end.

Jasmine was continuing to compile files on all the teens we'd discovered so far. Still following up on their other online contacts, real life friends, family, jobs, parents—anything that might give us another lead.

While Kett drove, I managed to pull an image from the vampire blood. It was fuzzy, as if not particularly well lit. But based on the slight, tall build and the dark hair of the male figure I reconstructed, I was fairly certain it wasn't any of the teens we knew to be involved in the immortality pact.

The vampire pulled over at a rest stop near Castle Rock, just north of the Washington–Oregon border, to obsess over the image I'd captured in the cube. While he did, Jasmine and I popped into the washroom.

We returned to the SUV, and before I'd even shut the back passenger-side door, Kett rounded on me from the front seat. "The image is barely discernible. Can't you sharpen or lighten it?"

"I'm not a camera or some computer imaging program."

Jasmine snorted, opening her laptop and settling back into work. I had no idea how she spent so many hours attached to a screen and keyboard. She was currently playing the Unseen Arcana RPG with a group of players that included a user who she thought was Benjamin Vern. Though the teenager was using a new username, he was still playing the game as a necromancer. We weren't exactly legally investigating the suicides or murders of the boys, but I still wasn't sure about the ethical implications of Jasmine befriending one of the possible suspects—or victims.

Kett held the cube on the tips of his steepled fingers, looking back at me. "I understood you to be a more skilled reconstructionist."

"Hey!" Jasmine protested.

"Try again," Kett said, ignoring my cousin. Then he tossed the cube over his shoulder and into the back seat as if it were a piece of garbage.

Angry, I caught the oyster-shell cube before it bounced on the leather seat a second time. Its magic slapped against my palms, reverberating within the container.

"Whoa," Jasmine said, swaying forward as if something had hit her from behind.

Kett smirked at me in the rearview mirror.

I wanted to strike him so badly that I actually caught myself raising my right hand. More magic reverberated around the car again—my magic, untethered by my anger.

"Try it now," the vampire said.

"Wild magic is less than useless," I spat. "Reconstructions are delicate, focused—"

Jasmine tapped the space bar on her laptop a few times. Then she sighed dramatically, hammering the keyboard with exaggerated vigor.

I peered over the back of the passenger seat. The laptop's screen was black.

"Damn it," she said, somewhat theatrically and seemingly intent on dispelling the tension between Kett and me.

It didn't work.

I clenched my teeth. My involuntary, reactionary casting had broken her laptop. Excellent. Now even more angry that the vampire had caused me to fry Jasmine's computer, I slammed the cube down on top of the box holding the blood. Not bothering to relight my candles—which had been dangerous enough while driving during the first reconstruction anyway—I simply recalled in my mind the boundary I'd previously established. Then I pulled residual magic from the blood through the plastic and cardboard that surrounded it.

No. I ripped that residual magic, channeling it into the cube.

"I'm going to be useless without my computer." Jasmine eyed the vampire pissily.

All Fairchilds always knew where to direct their anger—at the outsider.

Kett leaned across her, pulling an iPad out of the glove box and handing it to my cousin.

"An iPad mini," she said doubtfully. "Despite popular opinion, this is not, and never shall be, a proper replacement for a laptop."

"It will hold you until we find a store," Kett said, speaking to Jasmine though he was watching me in the rearview mirror.

"If it even starts," she grumbled to herself. "And Apple stores don't grow on trees."

I glanced down at the cube still sitting on the box beside me. It glowed with magic, though I had no idea what new image or images it contained. I'd been too angry, too keen on proving Kett wrong, too determined to show that I'd already done my best, so that I hadn't taken any notice of what had flashed through my mind as I grabbed the residual magic.

"You don't put enough of yourself into your reconstructions," Kett said, his tone cold. But no longer judgemental.

"A reconstruction isn't about the caster," I said. "This is probably contaminated."

The vampire arched a single eyebrow.

Jasmine glanced back through the seats, eyeing the cube. "Pretty," she said. "It better be worth frying my computer." She glared at Kett, then turned her attention to the iPad, which appeared to have successfully started.

I ran my fingers across the edges of the cube. An image of a dark-haired man appeared on its top surface. "Same slim build," I said. "Tall."

I positioned my fingers solidly on the top edges, coaxing the reconstruction to project just above the cube, as I did when testifying during a tribunal. Even miniaturized, the reconstruction was startlingly substantial. Almost real, as if I might reach out and stroke the vampire's cheek. If I was ever insane enough to go around caressing a vampire's face.

The man in the image turned his head, squeezing his eyes shut and grimacing in pain. When he reopened them, his eyes were whirling with blood.

I flinched, nearly knocking over the cube.

"More detail than before," Kett said. "Good." He didn't sound smug, though. "Is this the moment the blood was separated from his body?"

"Would that hurt him?"

"No."

"He appears to be in pain."

Kett didn't respond, so I continued. "Reconstruction doesn't work like that. 'Yes' would be the easy answer to give you. This could be an imprint of that moment, but there might be a stronger magical influence, greater than the moment of bloodletting that's depicted here."

"I thought you might pull more. A scene perhaps."

"There might not have been other magic or action taking place at the time."

Kett nodded. Then he turned back around to start the SUV, pulling out of the rest stop parking lot.

"He looks human," I said without thinking.

"He's young. Not very powerful," Kett said, seemingly unfazed by the inference that I found him inhuman.

We pulled into the traffic streaming along I-5, Kett perfectly matching the speed of the vehicles surrounding us. He wasn't a reckless driver.

I played with the magic of the reconstruction, spinning it underneath my fingers, trying to catch a glimpse of the background or even the foreground of the moment. Replaying the vampire's grimace over and over again, looking for clues.

"He's...I think he's actually lying down," I murmured. "I don't think he's standing."

No one answered me. I really did wish reconstructions had a zoom function. While capturing them, I could move closer to certain aspects of the scene I discovered in the residual magic, piecing together clues. But not afterward, not once events were stored within the cube.

"So this is weird," Jasmine said. "You asked me to look into Teresa Vern..."

Kett glanced up at me in the rearview mirror, but he didn't bother asking why I was interested in Ben's mother.

"And?"

"Well, her Social Security number is only twenty-two years old."

"Maybe she remarried. She's divorced, yes?"

"Or she only became a US citizen twenty-two years ago. Or she was a victim of identity theft. Lots of possible reasons, but interesting anyway. If I had my laptop, I could dig deeper, quicker. She's totally legit, though. Name, address, work history, taxes. And, yeah, Ben has been battling leukemia since he was about eleven. But his mother's online footprint only goes back twenty-two years or so."

"I doubt it's anything of interest to us," Kett said.

"She is, after all, only human," I said snarkily.

The vampire ignored me, which was fine. I was making a point, not looking for a response.

"Will you keep looking?" I asked Jasmine.

"I will. Right after we stop in Longview and get me a new computer." She leaned forward and typed a new address into the SUV's GPS. According to the map, we were nineteen minutes away from our new destination.

Jasmine eyed Kett. "You're buying."

"Of course," he said stiffly.

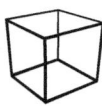

The entire picturesque town of Astoria sloped gently up from the river's edge. After a couple of blocks of historic buildings that had been converted into various businesses, hotels, and restaurants, the landscape gave way to mostly older homes on good-sized lots. The residential neighborhood just up from the river was comprised mostly of Craftsman-inspired architecture, but a few random Victorian, Tudor, and converted Georgian duplexes were mixed throughout.

We arrived at the post office that Jasmine had identified as the point of origin for Pax's blood shipment, a massive building that occupied half its block. It looked to have been built sometime in the 1930s, and was capped by a red tile roof. Knowing that we couldn't exactly interrogate the postmaster about whether or not a vampire had mailed a bunch of boxes filled with packets of blood a couple of weeks ago, it was meant only as a starting point for our hunt.

Kett parked in a half-empty lot behind the post office, then slipped from the SUV without a word.

I followed slowly. A breeze off the river caught the front ties of my navy-blue silk blouse, flicking them up over my shoulder as I scanned the neighborhood. I shivered, reaching back into the SUV for my navy-blue trench coat and teal pashmina stole. Autumn had taken hold as the afternoon waned, though it was still a couple of hours from sunset.

I didn't know Astoria at all except as a place to drive through, and for the delicious Bowpicker Fish and Chips food truck—or food boat, in this case. No Adepts of note that I was aware of made their homes here, or anywhere else on the coast of Oregon, so there was no one we could consult about suspicious activity. As long as he wasn't leaving bodies drained of blood in his wake, a vampire might have been living and hunting in Astoria for decades.

The area around us was pretty but worn around the edges, almost sun bleached. Kett was standing on the sidewalk—a strikingly pale marble statue in the gray late-afternoon light. He turned his head, listening for things I knew I would never be able to hear. He stood out against the background of the historic riverside town, and the contrast was startling to note. As ancient as he was, he was utterly alien in this environment. Even if he'd been wearing a suit and tie instead of cashmere and jeans, he still would have been too vital, too dreadfully beautiful to traverse Astoria's streets.

As if he could hear my thoughts, the vampire glanced over at me. His eyes appeared to be a deeper blue in the low light, but I knew they turned red when he was hungry or angry. I knew his chiseled features and smooth demeanor hid a vicious, immortal monster. Kett's gaze dropped to my hands. I was cupping my left hand over my right wrist, unintentionally covering my white-picket-fence bracelet from the vampire's view.

For a moment, I swore that the platinum trinkets warmed underneath my grasp.

Kett turned his attention back to our surroundings.

"What the hell are we doing?" I whispered.

Jasmine stepped into my peripheral vision, her gaze also glued to Kett. "Hunting a vampire with the executioner of the Conclave."

"Right," I said shakily. "Thanks for the clarification. So...um...are you going to try to cast a seek spell?"

Because we had the blood of the vampire we were hunting, a seek spell should have been an easy working. Except Jasmine's castings weren't terribly reliable, and I'd probably destroy any magic contained in the blood if I tried to manipulate it outside of a reconstruction.

"If necessary." She held her phone up. "Or we could just look for the nearest hermit."

I laughed, assuming she was joking. She wasn't. "I don't know what you mean."

"Well, it's a leap in logic full of what-ifs, like what if the vampire just used this post office as a decoy. But we're here with no other viable leads, so we might as well look around."

"Right. I meant how can you possibly tell someone is a hermit without…living next to them?"

"Only eleven houses in the immediate area haven't changed hands—you know, been sold or transferred—in the last thirty years. So then, concentrating on those addresses, I know that Ms. Smith, Ms. Jones, and Ms. Wilson regularly attend a knitting, bridge, and kayaking club. Fred Mason is on the reserve fire brigade. Not a great job for a vampire. Sue Byrd runs a daycare, and so on and so forth."

I was staring at my cousin with my mouth hanging open. "So on and so forth? You…you are exceedingly scary."

Jasmine threw her head back and laughed. Her peals of joy rang throughout the parking lot, drawing Kett back to us.

"How many houses are there to investigate, witch?" Kett asked Jasmine.

"I can narrow it down further if you give me a bit more—"

"How many?" Kett's tone was stiff and steely. Though he would take what help we could offer, it was obvious the vampire would prefer that we weren't tagging along.

"Five."

"Show me on a map."

Jasmine obligingly stepped up beside Kett, practically leaning against him while showing him the screen of her phone.

Kett pointed to the screen. "You take these two. I'll take the three farthest out. If you find something of note, text me."

"And if you find…" I started to ask.

Kett had disappeared.

I was talking to empty air. "...anything of note?"

Jasmine smirked at me. "I don't think he can hear you."

"Oh, he can hear us," I grumbled, tugging my stole tighter around my neck and setting the weight of my bag more securely on my shoulder.

Jasmine chuckled as she zoomed in on her screen. "It's this place anyway," she whispered. "Three blocks up and two over. As far as I've been able to figure out so far, the guy who owns it doesn't work, doesn't maintain any social media accounts, doesn't belong to any organizations, but he still pays bills, including his property tax and utilities."

I looked at her, shocked.

She shrugged, exaggerating the gesture. "Kett didn't ask."

"He did ask!"

Jasmine giggled. "He didn't ask nicely. And I could be wrong. It's not like the guy has a subscription to Martha Stewart Vampire Living or anything."

"But let's head there first?"

"Yeah, let's do that."

Jasmine was wearing a brown suede coat, which perfectly complimented all her curves, over low-slung distressed jeans. When she lifted her arm to swing her brown leather satchel on, I caught sight of the tattoo on her belly—an intricately drawn letter B with a superscript number three. B cubed. For Betty-Sue, Betty-Lou, and Bubba—our two childhood alter egos, and Declan's.

I looked away. We all carried our past with us in some way. Or at least Jasmine and I did. Me with my bracelet, and her with her self-designed tattoo.

She settled the strap of her satchel over the shoulder nearest to me, so that the brand-new laptop we'd picked up in Longview—and which she'd gotten back to work on surprisingly fast with her cloud backup data—was slung as far away from me as possible.

She tucked her phone into her far jacket pocket for the same reason as we headed up Eighth Street.

The converted historic buildings and apartment complexes around the post office gave way to regular homes after two blocks. We turned right on Franklin Avenue, passing a small park. The fire hydrants we passed were painted yellow, and I could smell at least a few people barbecuing as we followed Jasmine's map. Though it wasn't near sunset yet, the gray sky was darkening with rain-heavy clouds. Streetlights began to flicker on after another block, though people hadn't begun to pull their curtains yet.

I felt like a voyeur, soaking in all the signs of normal life. Cataloging every toy, or basketball hoop, or RV in every front driveway. Every rose and lilac bush. Every snippet of conversation tumbling out of open kitchen windows.

"Betty-Lou." I sighed. This was the life Jasmine and I had visualized for ourselves when we were still young enough to dream of parents who actually loved us more than they loved power.

"I see, Betty-Sue. I see."

I looked away from the homes, concentrating on the hard, eroded pavement underneath my feet, and scanning the interior of each occasional car slipping down the street beside us for a dark-haired, too-pale face.

"Wisteria…" Jasmine said.

"It's okay, Jasmine."

"No." She nodded emphatically up ahead and to the left with her chin, rather than pointing. "There. On the corner."

High laurel hedges hid the first floor of what appeared to be a decrepit Victorian manor. The cream paint of the wraparound front patio was faded, and the steeply pitched red roof needed new shingles. One of the windows in the upper floor of the house's garret tower was broken.

By unspoken agreement, Jasmine and I crossed between two parked cars, darting diagonally across the street and approaching the house from the side. Up close, I couldn't see anything beyond the hedge, which was neatly trimmed back from the sidewalk.

"Someone maintains the yard," I murmured.

"Someone doesn't want to draw the attention of the city ordinance people," Jasmine said.

We turned left, casually glancing through the black-painted, wrought-iron gate wedged into an archway cut through the middle of the hedge. A fairly new, unusually large mailbox hung off the middle of the gate—a box in which a mail carrier could deposit all but the largest of packages without setting foot on the property. The front patio was bare of furniture, as was the grassed front yard. Decorative window moldings encased stained glass above and on either side of the front door.

We kept walking, as if we might have been out for an after-work or before-dinner stroll. The basement windows I caught a glimpse of while passing were bricked over.

"Basement," I said.

"Yep. Magic?"

I shook my head, but I hadn't been looking for magic on the first pass.

"It's a little too typical, isn't it?" Jasmine said. "Run-down Victorian manor in the middle of a family-friendly neighborhood. Hermit lifestyle? You want to bet that the neighborhood kids dare each other to open the gate or ring the doorbell?"

"I don't imagine the doorbell works," I muttered as we turned the corner, then doubled back for our next pass.

"I mean, how have the neighbors not armed themselves with stakes and pitchforks by now?"

"Would you prefer he worked the night shift at the local Walmart?"

Jasmine chuckled. "I just mean, he could have anything, right? He's a vampire."

"A fledgling, according to Kett."

"So? Stay out of the sun and he's immortal, invulnerable, with all those mind-control abilities…I'd have a penthouse in the tallest tower in San Francisco, looking west over the bridge."

"With some heavy-duty blackout curtains."

Jasmine continued, seemingly lost in the fantasy she was spinning in her head. "I'd rob banks. With that shadow trick Kett has going on, plus my tech skills? I'd be brilliant at it." She sounded almost wistful.

I stopped short.

My cousin took a few more steps, then turned to look back at me.

"You've been playing that game too much," I said. "Unseen Arcana."

"Maybe."

"Jasmine…" The tinge of sorrow I heard in her voice physically hurt me to hear. "You could have all those things now. I wouldn't recommend robbing banks. But if you were really good at it, you might get sanctioned by the Convocation."

She nodded, casting her gaze around my feet.

"What's wrong?" I whispered, shivering now. The chill in the air was deepening with the onset of the evening, but it was the conversation that was making me cold. Normally, Jasmine was the warm breeze that held me aloft.

"Nothing," she said, casting her gaze aside and blatantly lying.

"What's wrong?" I asked again, more insistent this time.

My cousin raised her brilliant blue gaze to meet mine. "What's always wrong? Our vile, soul-destroying past."

We stood in silence. Warm light was radiating from the family homes surrounding us. Quiet traffic purred on the main street a few blocks away. The first of the autumn leaves rustled in the light breeze along the sidewalk, drifting past our ankles.

"I can't fix that," I finally said, ignoring the tears welling up in my eyes.

Jasmine plastered on a smile, stepping back to wrap her arm through mine. "And that is why we're skulking the streets of Astoria, hunting a rogue vampire."

I forced myself to laugh. It came out strained, but I managed to push away the tears that had been evoked by our conversation. "Right."

We traversed the next block in silence, though Jasmine's grip on my arm was firmer than it usually was.

Her phone pinged with a text message.

"Kett," she said, glancing at the screen. "He wants an update."

I shrugged, focusing my attention on the high laurel hedge and the windowed tower as we approached the house again.

Jasmine texted back some emoticon that I didn't get a good look at.

"What are the chances he knows what that is?"

Jasmine's phone pinged. She tapped the screen, then giggled. "He got it."

Lovely. My cousin was flirting with a centuries-old vampire via text messaging now. What was next? Snapchat?

"Magic time," I murmured.

Jasmine dropped my arm as we came abreast of the laurel hedge for the second time. I slowed my pace, carefully reaching out with my witch senses for traces of residual magic.

Jasmine stepped past me. "Garage with a side gate. Or maybe it was a carriage house at one time. So he might use either entrance."

"I imagine he could also go over the hedge," I said, eyeing the large branches of a pair of trees in the backyard. "What's that? An elm?"

"Oak," Jasmine said. "Look at the shape of the leaves."

"What am I? A botanist?"

"You asked."

"Looks climbable."

"Magic?"

"None I can sense from here. But there's something around the corner."

We stepped around the hedge. I kept my gaze on the sidewalk and greenery so I didn't get distracted.

"Vampire magic," Jasmine said.

"Really? Where?"

She pointed ahead of us.

I looked up.

Kett was standing by the front gate. He didn't look happy. I could tell because his arms were crossed.

Jasmine smiled at him sunnily. "I was just going to text you."

He shook his head almost imperceptibly as he reached over and opened the gate. "Wait here." Then he disappeared into the front yard.

Evidently, I'd been wasting my time casing the Victorian manor subtly.

We stepped up to the gate. Deep shadows loomed over the first floor and patio. The evening was taking hold of the cloudy day quickly. Kett was nowhere to be seen.

"Loitering out here isn't going to seem suspicious to the neighbors at all," I muttered.

Jasmine stepped through the gate.

"Hey!"

She glanced back at me over her shoulder. "It was your idea."

I followed her just far enough to latch the gate behind us and scan the front walk, noting that it was crumbling at the edges.

"I was just going to suggest a barrier spell or something," I grumbled.

Jasmine shrugged. "I don't have many. Why waste them when the hedge does a better job?"

Kett appeared on the front patio, turning to glance back at us. "As far as I can tell, the house is devoid of life. Wait two minutes, then follow."

He snapped the lock on the front door, opened it, and entered the house.

Jasmine sucked in her breath through her teeth. "I could have picked that."

"Devoid of life?" I echoed. "I'm not sure that rules out a vampire, does it?"

We crossed to the red-painted front stairs, which felt firmer underneath my feet than they looked. The solid, dark-stained wooden double door still stood partially open. As far as I could tell, it was a newer addition to the manor, though it might still have been twenty years old or more. I couldn't hear anything inside.

"Who owns the house?" I asked Jasmine.

"Nigel," she said, consulting the notes on her phone. "Nigel Farris."

"How long has it been in his name?"

Jasmine shook her head. "Longer than I can access the records. The city hasn't digitized everything yet."

"Nigel isn't much of a name for a vampire."

Jasmine snorted.

Kett appeared in the doorway. "I said follow."

"In two minutes," Jasmine said indignantly.

"And it's been two minutes. Downstairs. Through the kitchen at the back." The vampire disappeared into the house again.

Jasmine looked at me. "Did he sound…grim?"

"Yes."

"Great." She rolled the 'r' of the word for as long as she could make it last.

Then we followed a vampire into the house of a rogue vampire.

Unless, of course, this had all been some sort of massive setup from the beginning, and we were about to be sacrificed to some sort of vampire deity or something. Fairchild witches were highly sought after.

On the inside, the Victorian manor was surprisingly immaculate. A winding wooden staircase led to the second floor almost immediately inside the front door, with the living room to the left and the dining room beyond an open set of dark wood sliding doors. Fourteen-foot ceilings and inlaid hardwood ran throughout the first floor. The furniture was older but untarnished, and there was still enough light from outside to negotiate the corridor between the open stairwell and the living room, leading us to the kitchen at the rear of the house.

Based on the appearance of the appliances, I estimated that the place hadn't been remodeled since the early sixties.

The kitchen counters were devoid of small appliances or dishes, and again, everything was pristinely clean.

A white-painted, heavy wooden door opening into the space beneath the upper stairwell stood half open. Open-tread wooden stairs led steeply into a deep darkness.

"Well, that's not creepy at all," Jasmine drawled. She clicked the flashlight on her phone on, pointing it just ahead of our feet.

I glanced at her uneasily. Neither of us was a fan of basements, or the dark deeds that too often unfolded beneath the ground. Witches in general—and Fairchilds specifically—were fans of dirt-floored basements, though. Access to the earth made casting spells easier. I swallowed my irrational fear and headed down.

Jasmine was practically glued to my back as we descended. More illumination bloomed when we were halfway down the stairs. Someone—hopefully Kett—had turned on a light.

Plush wall-to-wall carpet spread out from the base of the stairs, rather than the dirt cellar floor that I'd expected. I paused, turning to carefully observe the large room. The mostly below-grade basement took up about half the footprint of the house. The walls were drywall, rather than plaster covered in multiple layers of paint as they were upstairs. The brick that covered the high windows looked fairly new as well. Obviously, renovations had been done much more recently here than upstairs.

A king-sized bed was neatly made and tucked into the far left corner of the room. A tiffany lamp on the bedside table was the only light source, but it managed to illuminate all but the deepest shadows in the basement. Except for a large fridge in the corner opposite the bed, every other wall was covered in bookshelves, which in turn were covered with endless rows of books of all shapes, sizes, and bindings.

"Jesus," Jasmine muttered, stepping down beside me. Her head was craned to our far right.

I followed her gaze. A man was strapped to a steel hospital gurney that sat near the rightmost wall of bookshelves. The top of his dark-haired head was angled toward us. His feet pointed toward the fridge.

Even from the base of the stairs, I could tell he was dead. And that he had been so for some time. His skin was shrunken and hollowed, every bone in his body standing out in sharp relief. He was dressed in jeans and a black T-shirt.

Kett opened the door of the fridge. It was half-full of what appeared to be bags of blood.

"Jesus," Jasmine muttered again. Then she squared her shoulders and strode farther into the basement, snapping pictures with her phone as she crossed to the fridge.

I dutifully trailed after her, but I couldn't tear my eyes from the corpse on the gurney. Four empty IV bags were strung from poles mounted to the gurney's frame, with all four lines attached to his arms, which were strapped down.

"He…he was a vampire?" I asked.

Kett tossed a bag of blood back into the fridge, though I hadn't seen him take one out. He ignored my question.

"Someone killed him by draining his blood?" I asked, stepping closer to the corpse. "And storing it in the fridge? Why?"

Jasmine was taking pictures of the bagged blood.

"The blood in the fridge is human." Kett spoke at last, appearing beside me to peer down at the corpse. "It's his stash. His sustenance."

Baffled, I just stared at him. He met my gaze, his expression stony. I wasn't sure if he was angry that the vampire had been killed, or if he was just pissed off at the situation in general. Specifically, that our trail had abruptly gone cold.

"A mixture of blood in here," Jasmine said, consulting her phone. "All different types, all originating from a blood bank in Seattle."

"I want you to walk me through the reconstruction as you trigger it," Kett said.

I opened my mouth to protest, but the vampire curled his lip at me. I nodded instead.

"Make your circle wide, witch." Kett eyed the IV bags still attached to the corpse. "Then we will revive him." His voice was cold with fury.

"What do you mean?" I whispered. "He's still alive?"

"Jesus," Jasmine said a third time.

Kett turned back to the fridge. "Set up your candles."

I locked my gaze to Jasmine's. Her eyes were as wide as mine felt.

I had no idea what was happening, or what could have happened. All I could do was my job. I clutched onto the thread of stability that thought provided for my suddenly overwhelmed mind.

I would do the reconstruction, and then everything would get sorted. Somehow.

Chapter Nine

Walking another Adept through a reconstruction while commanding the residual magic was difficult—and uncomfortably intimate. I had to balance the residual magic alongside whatever the witness brought with them into the circle, while maintaining physical contact with that Adept at all times.

Holding Kett's cool hand was like gripping a piece of moldable marble. Or maybe a sentient stone capable of randomly deciding that crushing every bone in my hand was a good idea. But though touching him was distracting, the vampire kept his magic well contained, so that I didn't need to struggle to reconstruct the events that had occurred in Nigel's basement over the last few weeks.

Of course, the ease with which I picked up a brown-haired boy in his late teens draining every last ounce of the vampire's blood might have also had something to do with the brutality of the attack.

Jasmine had gone back to collect the SUV at the post office, removing herself from the house so the magic of the reconstruction didn't fry her devices. I had closed the circle I'd paced out to encompass the bulk of the basement, leaving Kett and myself about a foot of room to move alongside the bookshelves at the farthest point away from the immobilized vampire on the gurney.

The residual captured within the circle was strong. It responded immediately to my magic, no coaxing needed. We watched the scene that sprang forth in silence—the events playing out backwards, from the point where the boy hauled the boxes of blood up the stairs to the moment of him initially confronting Nigel while the vampire was reading on the bed.

"Benjamin Vern," Kett said, identifying the teenager. His grip on my hand didn't intensify, but his tone was dark.

I nodded. Thanks to Jasmine, we'd seen enough pictures of all the teens involved to know on sight who it was that had attacked and stolen Nigel's blood, then mailed it to the others.

"He's not fully human," I said. "Otherwise, we might see the results of his actions, like with Luci in the graveyard, but not him."

"He's not fully vampire, either," Kett said. "Play the reconstruction back."

I hesitated, analyzing the streaks of residual magic shifting around within the wide circle before us. "There's something underneath." I glanced over at Kett. "Another layer."

He nodded stiffly. "Please continue with your first reconstruction in that case. Collect it within one of your cubes. Then we'll uncover what lies beneath."

I nodded. "I need both hands, but you need to maintain contact with me, skin to skin—"

The vampire slipped his hand within my trench coat and up the back of my silk shirt. He placed his cool palm lightly against my lower rib cage, just above the top of my navy-blue wool crepe pants.

Right. I'd been about to offer him my forearm.

Swallowing down on my amped-up discomfort, I spread both hands toward the circle, drawing the magic to me a second time.

The reconstructed scene played from beginning to end.

Benjamin Vern—an unruly-haired eighteen-year-old standing five-foot-nine in scuffed sneakers, artfully torn jeans, and a too-large black leather jacket—jogged down the wooden staircase to our right.

Nigel, who appeared to have been in his early thirties when he was turned into a vampire, had been reading a book on the bed at the beginning of the reconstruction. But at Benjamin's entrance, he stepped to the center of the room so quickly that the reconstructed magic blurred around him. He was lanky and pale, though not as pale as Kett, standing over six feet tall with dark, unkempt hair. Definitely a vampire, but one who could likely have passed among humans without issue.

"Weak," Kett spat.

"Benjamin or Nigel?"

"Both carry only the magic of the blood with which they were reborn."

"They were both human, you mean? Before they were turned?"

"The boy isn't a vampire. Merely enhanced. Continue."

I had paused the collection when Kett spoke, taking the opportunity to glance around the circle and make sure I was capturing all the residual elements. I had to see them at least once to collect them within the cube.

Though two weeks had passed since this incident, at least by my best estimation, the room looked strikingly similar. The bed, the fridge, and the metal gurney each all stood in the same places. But the IV poles attached to the gurney were empty.

"Who are you?" Nigel asked, though it sounded as if he already knew the answer.

"You can call me Garrick." Benjamin paused a couple of steps from the base of the stairs, scuffing his feet nervously.

Nigel tilted his head. "Or I can call you by your name, Benjamin."

The teen clenched his hands, then stuffed them into the pockets of his oversized jacket. "I want you to turn me."

"I will not." Nigel answered without hesitation. "I've done all I can."

"It's not enough," Benjamin shouted. Then he gritted his teeth at his own outburst.

"You shouldn't be here." Nigel softened his tone. "Does your mother know?"

"Of course not," Benjamin spat.

"Go home."

The teen lifted his head, glaring at Nigel. "I'll make you."

"You cannot possibly force me to turn you. It is not as simple as a transfusion."

Benjamin stiffened his shoulders. "I get that I have to die to trigger the transformation. I know more than you think."

Nigel narrowed his eyes at the sullen teen. Then he turned away, completely rebuffing him.

That was a mistake. Or maybe Benjamin had just been waiting for an opening.

The teen charged across the room, pulling something out of his pocket. Nigel spun to face him, more annoyed than surprised.

"The boy is too fast," I said. "Faster than a human."

Kett didn't respond.

As Nigel lifted his arm to bat the teen away, Benjamin slammed a Taser into the palm of the vampire's hand.

The shock jolted him but he remained upright, managing to wrap a hand around Benjamin's neck.

The teen gurgled in pain, but the vampire didn't immediately press his advantage. That was Nigel's second mistake.

Benjamin wrestled another Taser out of his other pocket, hitting Nigel with it and the first Taser at the same time.

They went down in a tangle of limbs.

Benjamin managed to crawl free of the pile, hacking and coughing. Still on his hands and knees, he pivoted back, slamming the vampire twice more with fifty thousand volts. This time, he applied the Tasers directly to Nigel's temples.

"Weak," Kett said again. His voice was cool and distant.

We continued to watch the reconstruction play through while I gathered the residual magic underneath my hands.

Benjamin managed to drag Nigel to the gurney. With a great deal of struggle, he lifted him onto it, then strapped him down.

Moaning as he woke, then shaking his head, the vampire became aware of his surroundings as the teen inserted the first IV needle into his arm.

"Even his skin is too easily pierced," Kett said dismissively. But despite his underlying ire, he kept his hand gently pressed to my back and his gaze glued to the scene I was collecting.

"Could be a tender spot. Repeatedly used," I said, not sure why I felt the need to defend Nigel. "Maybe from the blood in the fridge? Maybe he doesn't drink it?"

Benjamin inserted a third and fourth empty IV bag, positioning them so they drained downward to the floor.

"He drinks it," Kett said. "He'd have to. If only to survive in this weakened state."

"But the gurney and the IV stands—"

"Are apparently here for another reason."

Nigel began to struggle against the bonds that held him to the metal table. "Stop this, Ben. You're just going to end up killing yourself—"

The teen slammed the Taser against the vampire's neck.

Nigel's scream was short-lived, but his convulsions ripped out two of the IVs. Benjamin hastily grabbed one, then became suddenly mesmerized by the blood dripping from it. He put the tube directly into his mouth, moaning as he sucked on it.

Kett's hand flexed against my back, then instantly relaxed.

The boy reached down with his free hand to briefly hold his now-bulging erection. Then he continued to suck on the IV tube while continually checking the three other blood bags he was filling.

"Vampire blood…is addictive?" I asked quietly.

"The power is addictive," Kett said. "The teen's ecstasy is self-generated. Nigel's venom, even if he doesn't possess the talent to cloud his donor's mind while drinking, is the narcotic."

I absorbed that piece of information. Then while we watched, Benjamin drained every last ounce of blood from Nigel, carefully packing the full bags in boxes and storing them in the upper shelves in the fridge.

When he was done, he retrieved four bags of human blood from the fridge, placed them on the IV stands, and began giving Nigel a transfusion.

"He didn't mean to kill him," I said.

"Why would he? Four bags of human blood isn't enough to revive him," Kett said. "But I'm sure the boy planned to come back."

"If the transformations didn't work?"

Kett was silent as we watched Benjamin pack up the boxes, carefully balancing them atop each other. He was stronger than a teen his size should have been.

"There is more to being a vampire than blood," Kett said. "The teen appears to be well organized. Foolhardy but not stupid. We also don't know what information he's gathered about the vampiric relationship between master and child. Perhaps he believes that killing Nigel would kill his offspring as well."

Balancing his boxes, Benjamin crossed to the stairs and climbed out of the reconstruction. His eyes were bright, fevered. His skin was ruddy with exertion, and a painful-looking grin was plastered across his face.

"He's about to kill all his friends," I whispered. "Or try to."

"Yes." Kett removed his hand from my back, tilting his head as if listening. "Jasmine has returned. Please finish your collection and begin the next one. Don't go near the vampire."

He disappeared, then reappeared at the top of the stairs, quickly passing out of my line of sight.

I shook my head as if that might help clear it. Perhaps I should give Kett the benefit of the doubt. Perhaps he had no idea he was moving too fast for regular witches to track. But he had slowed at the door, presumably so Jasmine wasn't too startled when he suddenly appeared in the kitchen.

I allowed the circle to go dormant while I shifted the magic of the reconstruction I'd collected in my hands, directing it down to the oyster-shell cube on the carpet by my feet.

If things kept up at this pace, I was going to need to construct more cubes or get my hands on some inferior containers. I had used crystals when pressed in the past, but they were notoriously unreliable.

As I channeled the magic into the container, I kept a wary eye on Nigel's corpse on the metal gurney across the room.

Kett returned to the basement as silently as he'd left. He crossed to the fridge, retrieved four bags of blood, and quickly swapped out the empty bags Ben had left hanging from the IV poles around the bed.

I pulled a second cube out of my bag, eyeing him questioningly.

"Apparently, it will take more than four bags to revive him." Something caustic underlay the vampire's words, and I briefly wondered whether Nigel was going to be revived just to be executed after questioning. That was Kett's job title, after all.

But it wasn't any of my business.

In fact, the more evidence we gathered, the more obvious it became that the Convocation had absolutely no jurisdiction in this matter at all.

Kett appeared beside me, slid his hand into my trench coat and up the back of my blouse again without asking, and turned his stoic gaze to the center of the inactive circle.

I willed my magic out along the edges of the circle, touching each of the anchoring candles in turn and closing it a second time. The residual magic rose up eagerly, as it had before, but I brushed the most prevalent pathways away, reaching deeper for the energy I'd felt bubbling just underneath.

A whirl of sunset-tinted magic rose before me, resolving into an image of two people. One dark-haired and on his knees—Nigel—and one with brown wavy hair brushing her shoulders. This second figure stood over the kneeling vampire with a silver stake raised high in her right hand.

"Teresa Vern," I said, more shocked than I probably should have been.

"Teresa Garrick," Kett said grimly. "I became suspicious when Ben used the name, and had Jasmine start looking into it."

I glanced at him, allowing the reconstruction to run its course backward in the circle. Ben had called himself Garrick right before he'd attacked Nigel. And apparently, the vampire had access to information that allowed him to connect that name to Ben's mother, Teresa.

"And the silver stake?"

"Useful, in the right hands."

"Such as a vampire hunter?" I'd had no idea that such a person actually existed, other than Kettil the executioner himself.

Kett turned his cool gaze on me. "Such as a necromancer of power from a family of vampire hunters thought to have been…eradicated."

I nodded thoughtfully, trying unsuccessfully to match his detachment. He had years of experience over me, and no fear of knowing too much about xenophobic vampires. Such knowledge got witches like me killed. As well as entire families of necromancers, apparently.

The magic I held within the circle flickered, threatening to deconstruct. I focused, then attempted to prolong the conversation.

"Twenty or so years ago?" I asked, basing my guess on the records Jasmine had cobbled together on the Verns.

"Approximately," Kett said. "Apparently, the information held within the Conclave is incomplete, and a child survived the unsanctioned slaughter."

A pulse of relief ran through my limbs. "Unsanctioned?"

"A group of rogue vampires banded together. Otherwise, they would have failed. The Garricks had successfully kept the rogue numbers low enough that the Conclave had no need of a presence in the American territories."

"Then what happened?" I whispered the question as the reconstruction faded away, ready to be replayed. I was fairly certain I already knew the answer.

"Then I was appointed executioner of the Conclave."

"And you...took care of the rogue vampire issue."

"Do you doubt it?"

"No."

"Show me the conversation between the necromancer and the weakling vampire."

I nodded, refocusing on the circle. When the reconstruction was of a conversation, I often tried to ignore the first glimpses of the scene, as I'd done in this case. Following dialogue backward was disorienting. And when I wielded magic, I preferred to be focused and precise.

I took a deep breath, drawing all the magic before me toward my raised palms. The edges of the candlelit circle pulsed with power once, then I exhaled and retriggered the sequence I'd uncovered.

Teresa Vern stood over Nigel, silver stake in hand. The vampire was kneeling on the carpet, his head bowed as if in defeat.

"You will do this for me, vampire." Teresa's steely voice sounded nothing like the woman who'd greeted us at her door less than twenty-four hours ago. "Or I will end you."

Nigel shook his head. "I will not subject another to my curse."

"I've tried everything else. Your blood is my last hope."

"Then you have no hope, necromancer," Nigel said, raising his blood-red eyes. "I am death."

Teresa snorted.

Nigel suddenly reared toward her. He got within inches—and then froze with his arms outstretched.

"Jesus!" I exclaimed, involuntarily. "She...she's...controlling him."

"Yes," Kett said tersely. "A trait the Garricks were known for. The ability to control the undead. Few necromancers are capable of wielding such magic."

Nigel's eyes shifted from side to side, as if he were fighting Teresa's hold. But with a fierce, painful-looking grimace, she somehow forced him back onto his knees.

"You will do this," she panted. "I absolve you of any complications."

"Such as your son dying?" Nigel snarled.

"He's already dying, vampire."

"Take him to a healer."

I glanced over at Kett. "But Ben isn't magical. Unless his father was. Necromancy is traditionally only inherited by the female line."

Kett nodded at my hasty, uncharacteristic assessment, keeping his gaze trained on the reconstruction.

"No healer or witch can help my boy," Teresa said, choking back tears. "He doesn't possess a single drop of magic. Like I said, you are my last resort."

Nigel shook his head, but the gesture was weaker, less determined.

"I work in a hospital. I'll bring you quadruple the blood you give me."

"Why don't I just tear your son's throat out and be done with it?"

Teresa didn't appear to be even remotely fazed by Nigel's posturing. "Because I've been watching you. And you don't kill humans."

"I have killed."

"But you choose not to."

The dark-haired vampire fell silent.

Teresa straightened, tucking her silver stake in her pocket as she turned away from the vampire. "I'll have some medical supplies delivered tomorrow."

"You'll kill him," Nigel whispered.

"I know what I'm doing."

Nigel nodded dejectedly.

The magic of the reconstruction faded away.

With dozens of questions whirling around in my head, I leaned down to channel the residual I had collected and reformed into an oyster-shell cube.

Kett's hand slid from my back as I moved, but he remained rooted to the carpet beside me.

"Benjamin Vern had leukemia," I said, speaking to myself more than to the vampire at my side.

"Has," Kett said. "He has cancer."

"But Teresa seemed to think Nigel's blood would heal him."

"Not heal. But perhaps counter the virus. Overwhelm it..."

"But?"

"But the transfusions would need to be weekly. Daily, perhaps. Tiny doses, if the necromancer wanted to be careful."

"Careful not to turn Benjamin, but just to heal him."

"Not heal," Kett said again, his tone icy. "Maintain."

I straightened, slinging my bag over my shoulder and tucking the reconstructions I'd collected within its depths. I'd make duplicates for the Convocation just as soon as I was out of the vampire's abode.

Kett was standing so still that I realized he wasn't breathing. Then I found myself wondering whether he even needed to breathe, except to speak. But I shoved the thought away quickly, reminding myself that cataloguing the ins and outs of being a vampire was not my job. It was another thing that might potentially put me into the category of 'knowing too much.'

Kett abruptly broke his fugue-like state, striding across the basement to the fridge, retrieving more blood and changing out the now-empty bags attached to Nigel on the gurney.

The vampire appeared as corpse-like as ever. Just a long length of withered skin and hollowed-out eyes strapped down to cold, hard metal. But beating heart or no beating heart, he'd absorbed the first bags of blood somehow.

I snuffed out the candle closest to me, leaving it so the wax would cool as I moved on to the next. "But then Benjamin must have figured it out," I said, picking up the thread of the conversation as though it hadn't lapsed.

Kett didn't answer, though. His gaze was on Nigel, watching him for signs of revival perhaps.

"You can see how a boy who'd been sick his entire life would think immortality was a…" But I trailed off, thinking better of my intended wording.

"A gift?" Kett finished my thought coolly.

"Well, better than constantly dying."

"And bringing his friends with him? Will you justify the immortality pact as well?"

I hesitated. "I guess no one wants to be alone."

Kett eyed me.

I dropped my gaze. I was way out of my depth. I collected my candles, tucking them away in my bag.

Then Nigel opened his eyes, revealing two whirling red pools of blood. He spotted Kett standing over him and began to scream, straining against his bonds. I slammed my hands over my ears, the volume was seemingly loud enough to shatter my eardrums.

Kett locked his gaze to the panicked vampire's. Nigel immediately relaxed.

Jasmine slammed open the door at the top of the stairs, running halfway down before spotting me at the base of the stairwell.

"What the hell?" she cried.

I dropped my hands, watching as Kett crossed to the fridge to retrieve still more blood. Nigel remained in his docile state. Evidently, the executioner didn't have to maintain eye contact to control his mind.

The implications of that were stomach churning.

"Wisteria?" Jasmine prompted.

I shook my head.

"Go," Kett said without looking at me. "Thank you for your service. You've performed adequately. I'll pay your fee through the Convocation."

Relief flooded through me. He was officially dismissing us. I could walk away unscathed, taking Jasmine out of Kett's sphere of influence.

And then Nigel and Benjamin would die.

And Teresa Vern...Teresa Vern was a necromancer.

I looked up at Jasmine.

As if instantly gleaning my thoughts, she nodded once in agreement.

"We won't be leaving," I said, putting as much steel as I could muster into the statement. "This is a Convocation matter."

Kett pinned me with his gaze. I looked resolutely at his left shoulder.

"How do you figure that, witch?"

"Teresa Vern...Teresa Garrick is a necromancer. A necromancer within the jurisdiction of the Godfrey coven."

"I won't argue with you," Kett said.

"You don't need to argue with me," I said calmly. "I don't make or enforce the rules. The Convocation does."

I turned to climb the stairs, and Kett was beside me before my foot fell on the second step. His fingers were a steel band around my upper left arm.

I swallowed my shriek of terror, deliberately turning my head to look him in the eye. "When was the last time you texted with Pearl Godfrey, Jasmine?" My voice was shaky and thin.

"Fifteen minutes ago," my cousin said.

"And you informed her that we'd found Teresa Garrick?"

"Yes. She said you were to call her as soon as you had finished the reconstructions."

Kett's painful grip on my arm was going to leave a deep, dark bruise. I called up all the magic I had at my disposal, slowly raising and gathering my right hand into a fist.

"Unhand me, vampire."

A smile ghosted across Kett's face. Then he was standing back beside the fridge.

I stumbled, almost falling off the stairs. I hadn't realized that he'd effectively been holding me upright.

"What the hell?" Jasmine muttered. Then she flapped her hands in my direction, urging me toward her.

Kett was back beside Nigel in a flash, pouring blood down the immobile vampire's throat, forcing him to drink. I was fairly certain Nigel was sobbing as he choked on it.

I wondered if he had been hoping he was finally dead when Benjamin drained him. Finally free of what he called his curse. But if that was the case, I wondered why he'd screamed at the sight of Kett, as if fearful for his immortal life. Or maybe the executioner of the Conclave was just as terrifying to other vampires as he was to everyone else.

I looked resolutely away. And, seriously hoping that we hadn't just bluffed an elder of the Conclave, I steadily climbed the stairs, placing one foot in front of the other to safety.

Assuming that anywhere could be safe in a world that Kettil walked.

"You will ascertain the whereabouts of Teresa Garrick and her son," Pearl Godfrey said over the speaker of my cellphone. "You will verify the reconstructions, and a tribunal will be called."

Jasmine hadn't actually been bluffing about texting with Pearl, so the first thing I'd done—after firmly shutting the kitchen door between me and the vampires in the basement—was to call the chair of the Convocation. My cousin and I were crammed around a tiny table beneath the corner kitchen window, which would have offered a pretty view of the backyard foliage during the day. A view the vampire who owned the house would never see.

The overhead light in the kitchen was on, having been triggered by a timer as anachronistic as the rest of the dated furniture. Nigel, like Kett, was obviously trying to pass as human for the benefit of his neighbors. I wondered whether he'd forget to turn on any lights at night without the timers.

"At least she didn't kill him," Jasmine said to the phone, which she cradled in her hand as far away from me as she could hold it and still be at the same table.

"It wouldn't matter if she had," Pearl said aloofly. "As long as she could prove he was a threat to someone. And unaffiliated vampires are always a threat."

"What matters is her dosing the boy with vampire blood," I said. Ironically, Teresa Garrick would most likely be held accountable for trying to save her nonmagical son's life, but not for assaulting Nigel in the process.

"What matters," Pearl said steely, "is that Teresa Garrick was hidden by the Convocation for her own protection. She was to set aside her necromancer powers and live a normal life. By her own request. It took considerable resources to ensure and enforce that protection."

"Watching someone you love dying and not acting isn't easy for most of us, Pearl," I said, instantly wishing the words back as soon as I had uttered them.

Silence fell on the other side of the line.

Jasmine gave me a wide-eyed look, then wrinkled her nose in a grimace.

Pearl picked up the conversation as if I hadn't spoken. "We're on the edge of a major incident here with the Conclave if the vampire is already insisting on jurisdiction. Normally, I'd send in a team to take over your investigation at this point. But I trust you two to help mitigate, not exacerbate, this situation."

"Of course," I said, not at all convinced that we could 'mitigate' anything when it came to Kett. But, even knowing as little as I did of the vampire, it was easy to agree that an escalation in the Convocation's involvement would unbalance the tension-filled circumstances even more.

"To that end, you will inform the executioner that Teresa Garrick will be assessed and sentenced by the Convocation. He is to leave her to us. She is under our protection. Under your protection."

"Well, that's easy to say," Jasmine muttered.

I interjected before Pearl could rip Jasmine's head off. "And Benjamin Garrick? If he's turned like the others?"

"Whether or not the boy is a vampire, he is none of our concern."

My heart sank. I'd expected that answer, but it was difficult to hear nonetheless.

"What?" Jasmine said. "So we just let the...we just let Kett kill him?"

"How the Conclave chooses to deal with its own is not your concern, Jasmine Fairchild. You will not attempt to intervene."

"That's going to be a hard line to sell to Teresa," I said, trying to appeal to Pearl on a practical level.

"If the necromancer refuses your jurisdiction, you will leave the area and inform me immediately," Pearl said. "I've already formed an extraction team."

I locked gazes with Jasmine. I had never heard of such a thing. But then I'd never been on this side of an investigation before.

Jasmine nodded.

"We understand," I said.

"Teresa owes the Convocation her life. She will be reasonable."

Jasmine and I exchanged doubtful looks. Any necromancer who walked into a vampire's lair and demanded his blood had already crossed so many lines that I wasn't sure reasonable behavior was a reasonable expectation. But Pearl knew Teresa, and I didn't. I also didn't have much say in the matter. I too owed the Convocation. Not my life. I'd bargained for that myself. But definitely my comfortable existence.

"Did the charm really foil the vampire?" Pearl asked. "He stood before her and sensed nothing? No magic at all?"

"None of us did," I said.

"I have no doubt that your senses didn't penetrate Scarlett's casting," Pearl said. "But the vampire is an elder and another matter altogether."

"Teresa never crossed her threshold," I said, feeling the need to justify my competence. "We never entered her home."

"She wears the charm." Pearl's tone was laced with pride.

"It's mobile?" Jasmine asked, exceedingly impressed. "Not tied to wards?"

"I would have felt wards," I said.

"Exactly," Pearl said. "I expect to hear from you on the hour."

"Of course," I said. "But perhaps you should…"

Pearl ended the call before I could ask any more questions or make any more demands.

I finished my thought anyway. "…speak to Kett directly."

I looked at Jasmine, twisting my face wryly. "Happy you answered my call now?"

She laughed. "Hell, yeah. When was the last time you hunted a vampire, only to uncover a necromancer in Convocation witness protection who's dosing her son with vampire blood to keep him alive? Add a hot executioner and the hefty paycheck to follow? Cha-ching!"

I laughed. I couldn't help it. Jasmine had a way of looking at life that lightened my own outlook. She was fearless, though never stupidly so.

Jasmine flinched, then glowered.

Kett had appeared in the kitchen, standing just behind my shoulder. "I've questioned Nigel. He knows little of consequence."

"We've just gotten off the phone with Pearl," I said.

"I heard."

"Oh."

That was my brilliant response as I ran through the entire conversation with Pearl in my head.

"Wicked hearing, man," Jasmine said. "Through concrete and everything."

Kett snorted derisively. "The door is wood, witch." He turned away into the hall.

"Right." Jasmine rolled her eyes at his back, packing up her gear.

I stood, leaning over for my own bag. And as I did, a pale, viciously clawed monster smashed through the aforementioned door. Shards of wood exploded throughout the kitchen. I caught a flash of blood-red eyes and wicked fangs, and then the creature was grabbing me.

Jasmine screamed.

"Stop!" Kett shouted.

The unhinged vampire froze. Its claws were pressed against my neck, jaw, and collarbone, as if it had been about to rip my head off and bathe in my blood.

I managed to breathe, willing my heart to stop thrashing in my chest, but to no avail.

The vampire whimpered, withdrawing its trembling hands.

"Step back," Kett commanded.

The creature complied, shuddering. It curled its claws against its chest, and they slowly transformed into long, almost-delicate fingers. Its fangs disappeared, though its eyes continued to whirl with blood.

"I understood you could walk amongst humans," Kett said. "You stood before the boy without attacking him."

Nigel.

The pale, dreadfully thin monster was Nigel. I hadn't recognized him in vampiric mode with his skin only partly fleshed out.

Nigel squeezed his eyes shut. "I can. But the witches..."

Kett glanced at me. "You'll have to go on ahead. I thought he'd consumed enough blood."

"All right," I said shakily.

"I assume he has a licensed vehicle?" Kett asked Jasmine.

She nodded. "Garage. Out back."

"I'm sorry," Nigel moaned.

"Go back downstairs," Kett commanded.

Nigel's body jerked but he didn't immediately comply. "I won't do it. I won't go with you. I must stay in the house."

Kett stepped forward. He was actually shorter than Nigel, but the junior vampire cringed at his proximity. "You will take responsibility."

"Just kill me," Nigel whispered. "Please, please…just kill me."

My heart pinched.

Jasmine covered her mouth and looked away.

"Your punishment will be meted out once we've neutralized the necromancer and her son." Kett glanced at Jasmine and me, twisting his mouth. "Unfortunately, if we are to avoid an incident…"—his uncharacteristic emphasis on the word 'incident' confirmed that he'd heard every part of our conversation with Pearl—"…the Convocation will require your testimony before they hand the other guilty parties over to me." He turned his attention back to the vampire. "Go. Gather more blood. We'll travel separately from the witches."

Nigel glanced at us, then shuddered again.

Jasmine stepped shoulder to shoulder with me.

The miserable vampire turned away. Passing through the ruined door, he descended into the basement.

"My apologies," Kett said smoothly. "Human blood isn't as…invigorating as Adept. And he is completely unworthy of my own."

"He…he's suicidal," I said, swallowing my own fear over almost being killed. "He doesn't want to be a vampire."

"He made that choice a long time ago," Kett said. "And now he must endure."

"Do you want us to take the SUV?" Jasmine asked, keeping us on task.

Thank goodness for her cool head. I didn't want to get mired in Conclave politics any more than I wanted to be involved in witch business.

"Nigel's," Kett said. "If it won't start, we'll need to know."

Jasmine nodded, crossing through the kitchen.

"Wait," I said. "Don't we need keys?"

My cousin snorted, not even pausing. "Keys? Please."

"Keep your distance from the necromancer," Kett said. "Ascertain that she is in residence, then wait for me. I shouldn't be more than a few minutes behind you."

Neither of us answered him. Jasmine because she was already out of earshot, and me because I wasn't about to take his orders over Pearl Godfrey's, and I wasn't interested in fighting about it.

I hefted my bag onto my shoulder under Kett's watchful gaze. I wasn't sure what he was looking for. Perhaps for me to fall apart? Or lash out?

He leaned into me as I stepped past him. "He could have walked into the sun at any time, Wisteria Fairchild. The blood that fuels him is weak, and he brings no natural talent to his incarnation. Never allow a predator to play at being a sheep."

I nodded, then continued down the long hall to the front door.

"No one walks away from immortality."

I glanced back at this pronouncement, but Kett had disappeared.

Chapter Ten

Jasmine and I drove into Seattle in Nigel's older green Honda Accord in silence. For once, my cousin wasn't attached to her keyboard, because she was driving. I wasn't sure anything else needed to be verified at this point. But then, I wasn't the accredited investigator. If Teresa Garrick was going to be brought before a tribunal, Jasmine's paperwork was going to be massive. Every scrap of background information for all five of the boys and Nigel was going to be combed over and ripped apart. Making my reconstructions had been easy compared to what Jasmine now faced in the aftermath of it all.

I risked sitting in the front passenger seat for the trip. On short drives, I didn't have much of an effect on a vehicle's electronics. It was just under four hours back to Seattle, but if we broke down, Kett was somewhere on I-5 behind us.

Though it was past midnight when we showed up at her house, Teresa Vern, nee Garrick, opened the door before we were halfway up the front walk of the tidy brown bungalow.

She looked weary, drained. It was more than simply her skin being yellowed by the overhead exterior light. She was wearing a red angora turtleneck sweater over jeans, not scrubs as before.

Once again, I couldn't sense a single drop of magic around the house or yard. Not even when I cracked my personal shields and actually sensed for it, as I would if I was prepping to do a reconstruction.

Teresa eyed Jasmine for a moment, then looked at me. Jasmine and I paused on the bottom concrete step, staying out of reach but also physically blocking any exit. From the front of the house, at any rate.

"Did the Convocation send you?" Teresa asked, dropping all pretense.

"Yes," I said.

"How much do you know?"

"Who you are," Jasmine said. "What you've done, and then what Ben did."

Teresa scrubbed her hand across her face, opening her mouth to say something, perhaps to justify her actions. Then she shook her head. "And the vampire?"

"Right behind us," I said. "Both of them."

Teresa's eyes flicked to the dark, quiet street behind us. Even the moon and stars were swathed in dark-gray clouds. The only other exterior light came from the widely spaced streetlights and the occasional security light on her neighbors' homes. As if everyone else in the immediate area was asleep, cozy in their beds.

Except us. We were about to tear a teenaged vampire from the arms of his necromancer mother, whether or not Ben was even fully turned. Remade, as Kett called it.

"We need to see Benjamin," I said quietly. "And we'd like to confirm the events of the reconstructions."

"But you aren't obligated to talk to us," Jasmine added.

"Has a tribunal been called?" Teresa asked.

"It will be," I said.

"And are you authorized to take us by force?"

I glanced at Jasmine. She didn't take her gaze off Teresa.

"Not us," I said.

"Are you a Fairchild too?" Teresa asked Jasmine.

My cousin nodded. "Yes, Jasmine. You knew who Wisteria was when she first showed up."

"The Garricks and the Fairchilds were…known to each other. Allies of necessity. I wouldn't have thought the Convocation would need to send more than you two."

I laughed quietly. "We aren't that type of Fairchild."

Teresa snorted. "And I wasn't that type of Garrick."

"Then Benjamin got sick."

"And he has no magic." Teresa's voice cracked with all the emotion she was holding at bay. "Not a drop of magic."

"So the witches, the healers, couldn't do anything," Jasmine whispered.

Teresa lifted her hands helplessly. "I have all of this magic, all that I don't even want, and Ben didn't get a drop. Not even latent power that could be triggered in order to heal him."

My heart twisted at the anguish in her voice.

But when Jasmine spoke, she was harsh. Unforgiving. "So you assaulted a vampire and turned your boy into a monster."

Teresa dropped her hands. "Yes." She turned away, retreating into the house. "I guess you might as well come in."

Jasmine and I climbed the four steps to the front landing in unison. The house beyond the open door was dark, unlit. Though Teresa must have been watching for us from the living room.

As Jasmine palmed something out of her bag, magic tickled my senses. A defensive spell, maybe. I wondered what else she carried along with her laptop, her phone, and her other gadgets. Also, I hadn't realized her bag was spelled, warded to cloak the magic it held. I wondered if she'd be able to do the same for my bag, though it wasn't like I ever carried anything but reconstructions.

The front-hall closet stood before us. The living room was to the immediate right. Teresa settled down on the couch underneath the front windows. The blinds were open. Sitting sideways, she could watch the street without turning her head.

Jasmine and I stepped into the living room, standing shoulder to shoulder.

"What else do you need to know?" Teresa asked tonelessly.

"Why didn't you run?" Jasmine asked. "If you knew who Wisteria was when she showed up at your door?"

"Where could I go with Ben without the Convocation's protection? I was just hoping..." She didn't finish her thought.

"We need to see Ben," I said. "Then we'll text Pearl Godfrey and let her know that you don't dispute the charges—"

Teresa laughed harshly. "How could I? You said you had reconstructions. I might be untrained, but I know what those are."

Through the living room window, I saw a white SUV pull up, parking behind Nigel's Honda. Kett stepped out, glancing up at the house. I had no doubt he could see us in the front window, even without any interior lights on. Surrounded by the darkness of the neighborhood, the streetlamps lightened his hair and skin even more.

For a brief moment, he looked like an angel. An avenging angel.

I shivered.

"That's it then," Teresa whispered. "He's here to kill Ben."

"We don't know that," I said quickly, not wanting the situation to unravel while we stood like useless idiots in the living room.

On the sidewalk, Nigel stepped out of the SUV's passenger-side front door. Then, in response to a look from Kett, he leaned back against the vehicle and crossed his arms.

"What else would he do?" Teresa said. "There's nothing special about my boy."

"He has rules," I said lamely. "Vampires are rare."

Teresa turned her dark-eyed gaze on me.

I shut up.

Kett was standing in the living room, directly across from Teresa. He'd entered the house and crossed by Jasmine and me without even stirring a breeze.

My cousin flinched.

Teresa slowly shifted her gaze from me to Kett.

"May I introduce Kettil, an elder and executioner of the Conclave," I said.

Teresa swallowed.

Kett turned his attention on me. "Where is the deficient fledgling?"

"Not here," Jasmine said, lifting her hand. She was holding a small rock in her palm. A magical detector.

Kett raised an eyebrow at her. "I already knew that, witch."

So apparently, I was the only one in the dark.

We all looked at Teresa, who stared steadily at the floor.

"Have you killed him?" Kett asked her.

"No."

"Shall I tear the house apart?"

"Why? You already know he's not here."

"He is a danger to any human in the vicinity, Teresa Garrick. I've already witnessed the incomplete transformation of two of his friends. Rabid fiends that had to be put down."

One of those had been put down thanks to Luci, though the vampire didn't mention that part.

"He hasn't hurt anyone," Teresa said, tugging nervously at the turtleneck of her angora sweater.

"Except his friends," Jasmine said. Her tone was once again far harsher than I would have expected from her. "And Nigel."

"I didn't know about that. Not until it was done."

"There are many ways for me to force the truth from you, necromancer," Kett said. "Shall I list your options?"

I opened my mouth to protest. To insist on the jurisdiction of the Convocation, but Jasmine interrupted me.

"Was Nigel supposed to stay by the car?"

I glanced out the front window. The sidewalk was bare of loitering vampires. Teresa barked out a laugh.

Kett was gone. Then he reappeared outside beside the SUV, glancing around.

I wondered if Nigel had fled, or if he was looking for Ben. I wondered whether master vampires could sense their children.

Kett disappeared from beside the SUV again.

"Well," Teresa said. "He's annoyingly powerful. Tea?" She unfolded her legs from the couch.

"We're good," Jasmine said.

"Fine." Teresa sighed. "We'll just get to it, then."

With no warning, dozens upon dozens of dead birds burst out from the fireplace, even as more exploded through the door that I had assumed led to the kitchen.

The reanimated creatures—crows, jays, sparrows, and juncos—attacked Jasmine and me, clawing and pecking us mercilessly.

I screamed, throwing my arms around my head to protect my face. Jasmine hunched down beside me.

"I'm sorry," Teresa said, speaking from beyond the whirlwind of birds. "But if you can't protect Ben, I'll have to do it myself."

Talons and beaks were tangled in my hair, in my clothing, tearing my skin. I couldn't move against the whirling storm of feathered fiends. But I could feel Jasmine digging through her bag beside me, hopefully looking for one of the premade spells she kept on hand.

Heedless of the pain, I wrapped myself over her, covering her head and shoulders with my body while still trying to protect my own face and neck, sheltering her from the undead storm raging around us.

Jasmine found whatever she was looking for. "Cover your eyes," she shrieked. Then she flicked what looked like a pillbox before her.

I squeezed my eyes shut as a wickedly bright light ignited. All the air in the room compressed against us, boxing my ears and taking all sound and light with it.

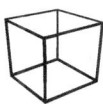

I woke up covered in dead crows, cradled around Jasmine. A deadly blond vampire was standing over us, unmistakably pissed off.

I shut my eyes again, completely prepared to ignore him until he went away.

"Don't make me pick you up, witch," Kett said. "You won't like the toll I exact."

I sat up.

Jasmine groaned. "Did you have to fall on me?"

"I was protecting you."

"Well, I was protecting us."

I lifted my arms. Every exposed inch of my limbs was scratched and peck marked. I was smeared with blood. I glanced up at Kett, smiling uneasily. "So...she can control dead animals too."

He frowned at my observation. Apparently, I was just stating the obvious again.

"How long do you think she collected them?" Jasmine asked. Then she shrieked and pulled a dead chickadee out of her ample cleavage.

"The necromancer is gone," Kett said. "Find her, or I will. Nigel is looking for the boy." He left the room.

"He's not as cute when he's being an asshole," Jasmine said.

I snorted, scrambling to my feet, then helping her up. The living room was covered in dozens and dozens of dead birds.

"What did you throw at them?"

"Just a disruption charge." Jasmine attempted to straighten her torn clothing. Her suede jacket was probably salvageable, but I wasn't sure I could say the same about my trench coat. "If Teresa had still been around, she could probably have animated them again."

"I'm glad you had it."

"It was my last one. And they're damn expensive. I'm adding a handling charge to my bill."

I smoothed my hands over my hair, which was in utter disarray all around my head and shoulders.

"Stop," Jasmine said. "You're just smearing blood all over. We'd better wash. And find some disinfectant. We don't want to catch some zombie virus."

"I don't think it works like that."

"Yeah? You want to risk it?"

I didn't.

So after turning on some lights and skulking around the house, we found the bathroom, dug through Teresa's well-stocked cupboards, and patched ourselves up.

Kett and Nigel were waiting for us in the living room. The dark-haired vampire was seated on the couch with his head cradled in his hands. Kett stood by the fireplace, gazing out at the sporadically lit street. Every last dead bird had been removed from the room, and I wondered whether Kett had forced the cleanup duties onto Nigel. Such a task seemed beneath the executioner of the Conclave. I also wondered where they'd piled the dead birds, but then I shook off the creepy thought.

Kett cast a dispassionate gaze over our patched arms and faces. "I assume one of you can track the necromancer?"

"You can't?" Jasmine asked, heavy on the snark.

"She moves as though human." The vampire's voice was edged with barely concealed fury. "So no, not without systematically entering each and every house in the vicinity where anyone is awake."

"The charm Teresa wears is powerful," I said. "Even Pearl was impressed."

"Yes, a delightful piece of magic." Kett didn't sound all that delighted, though. "I'll thank the Godfreys next time I see them."

"She left her purse," Nigel said, gesturing toward the contents of a bag strewn across the oak coffee table. "And her car."

"Credit cards?" Jasmine reached for the wallet nestled in among keys, a miniature Kleenex package, various lip balms, and a hairbrush.

Nigel hunched his shoulders as she drew near, but he didn't attempt to rip her throat out. So that was a bonus.

"That'll take too long," I said. "We need to find her quickly, or call in Pearl's extraction team."

"A tracking spell?" Nigel asked. "There is loose hair in the brush." He gestured a long-fingered hand toward the table. He was still too skinny for his frame. Almost gaunt. His movements were wooden, as if he were still learning how to be in his own body.

I shook my head. "I imagine the charm blocks magic detection as well. Though someone more skilled at tracking could probably break it."

"I'm not handing this issue over to the Convocation, witch," Kett said. "If the boy is loose, his body count will eventually lead me to him."

I glared at him.

He stared back at me coolly, then transferred his ire to Nigel's bowed head. "If his master was at all useful, he would know exactly where his child was at all times."

"I tried to find him," Nigel said quietly and without looking up. "But I can't sense him. Not in the least."

"Perhaps the boy isn't fully transformed." Kett's tone softened. "It's possible he is more difficult to track in his only partially realized form." He turned his gaze on me, raising an eyebrow. "Shall we go with my plan, then?"

I jutted my chin out at his threat of pillaging the neighbors. "If you want to find an Adept, you just need to think like that Adept."

"You are endlessly helpful, Ms. Fairchild."

I glanced over at Jasmine, who'd arranged every card in Teresa's wallet and was taking pictures of them with her phone. "If you were a necromancer, where would you go to hide?" I asked.

She glanced over her shoulder at me. Then she laughed, opening up the browser on her phone.

"Where?" Nigel asked.

"A cemetery," I said. "That's where her power will be the most concentrated. Though how exactly a necromancer fights witches...or vampires, for that matter, I don't know."

Jasmine held up her phone, looking grim. A map with a blue dot was displayed on it. Apparently, Teresa lived two blocks from Pleasant View Cemetery.

"But I guess we're about to find out," I said.

Chapter Eleven

We walked, circling the far side of the house in the opposite direction to how we'd driven in both times before. Not having passed through that part of the neighborhood, we had completely missed the presence of a cemetery. Living near such a site made complete sense for a wielder of death magic, especially one who was supposed to be in hiding and might have foreseen a need for a fallback location that was amenable to her power. But we hadn't known Teresa Garrick was a necromancer the first time we knocked on her door.

We split up to circle the stone wall that skirted the two-block radius of the cemetery site. Jasmine was with me, Nigel with Kett, just in case we picked up hints of Teresa, Benjamin, or any residual magic.

We didn't find anything.

Thankfully, the neighborhood was locked down and deeply asleep. If any of Teresa's neighbors worked nights, they were already gone for the evening. I didn't even see a single cat prowling the shadows.

We met up again at the cemetery's gated entrance. It was locked, of course, but Kett wrenched it open with a single tug, bending the metal as if it might be toffee rather than thick wrought iron.

Jasmine was hunched over, digging through her bag. "I've got a mixture of distraction spells," she muttered. "Nothing that's going to cloak a massive magical surge, but enough to turn away any stray late-night pedestrians. Oh! And some sound mufflers."

"How do we even know she's in there?" Nigel stood off to the side, his hands buried so deeply in his pockets that it seemed as though he was afraid to let them loose.

"She's in there," Kett murmured. "The Garricks have a historic connection to cemeteries and graveyards, often making their living owning and running them."

"Teresa was maybe ten or eleven years old when her parents...her entire family was slaughtered," I said. "Her connection to them, to her own history, must be tenuous."

"What were you doing at ten, Wisteria?" Kett asked pointedly.

Jasmine glanced over at me.

I didn't answer.

I had seen my family wield magic my entire life. If pressed, I could probably call upon any or all of those workings. I'd be unsuccessful at casting them, of course. But that wasn't Kett's point.

"Jasmine," he said, continuing as if he hadn't been needling me a moment before. "Please place whatever spells or charms you have at the perimeter of the graveyard, keeping them off the property itself."

"I'm not a moron," Jasmine muttered.

"Why off the property?" Nigel asked.

"Ownership," I said. "Even if Teresa doesn't legally own this graveyard, she's most likely claimed it for herself.

That might have implications on the effectiveness of the spells."

"She'll have claimed it," Kett said. "She's not stupid."

Jasmine counted the collection of buttons, rocks, and other little bits that she'd laid out on the sidewalk before her feet. Each held a single spell. "Twelve," she said. "It will be a thin spread."

"Concentrate on the entrance and this block specifically," Kett said. "Then spread them as evenly as possible. Wisteria, Nigel, and I will enter the property."

"It'll take me a while to trigger them all."

Kett glanced at my cousin. "Best get started then."

Jasmine looked over at me for confirmation.

"Don't enter the graveyard," I said. "If you make it back around to here and we're still inside, text Pearl with an update."

"But—"

"Triggering that many spells will drain your magic," I said brusquely.

Jasmine frowned. "Hardly."

I stared her down. She dropped her gaze, gathering the collection of spells into the various pockets of her jacket, jeans, and satchel. I assumed she was grouping them by specific charm.

Kett was watching our exchange too closely for my liking, but there was nothing I could do about it. Jasmine was a strong tech witch. Possibly the best in North America. But she wasn't fantastic at wielding other magic, hence the robust collection of spells that she traded or outright purchased. Her defensive capabilities were limited.

Of course, mine were nonexistent.

I twisted my white-picket-fence bracelet on my right wrist.

Jasmine straightened. I grasped her hand briefly before she stepped to one side of the gate to set, then trigger, the first deflection spell.

"I'm not going," Nigel said abruptly. "I'm just a liability. I'll watch the entrance. I can text you if someone comes or goes. And...if I see Benjamin, I can try to hold him."

"He is your progeny," Kett said wryly. "You should hold sway over him."

Nigel nodded doubtfully.

"Stay in the shadows," Kett said. Then he stepped through the gate.

"I assume you'll be okay out here alone with my cousin?" I asked Nigel pointedly.

"I have myself under control, witch," he said stiffly.

I met Jasmine's worried gaze, offering her a smile I didn't feel. Then I stepped through the gate and followed a vampire into a graveyard way after dark.

That wasn't intensely worrisome at all.

I took a deep breath, forcing myself to keep calm.

The sound of iron scraping on iron came from behind me. I glanced back, barely able to see my cousin as she sealed the entrance behind me. My heart rate spiked.

"I'll see you soon," she called quietly. Then she set off down the block to place the remainder of the spells.

Well-trimmed grass spread out on either side of me. I would have imagined it as a lush green by day, but could barely distinguish any color at all beneath the dark, cloudy sky. Headstones of various shapes and sizes jutted out of the grass, row upon organized row. I glanced around the wide paved pathway I was traversing, wishing for a flashlight with every step I moved away from the streetlights that ringed the cemetery. Or to have the ability to snap my fingers and call up a light spell—a bit of magic I had learned before I was four years old.

But I didn't do that sort of magic anymore.

Kett appeared at my side. His pale skin was practically reflective, and I could see him without effort. "I've done a circuit," he whispered. "But she's well hidden."

A circuit? Of the entire two-block radius? In what? Five minutes?

"I'll lead you to the center where the paths cross," Kett said. "You'll reach out for magic from there, then point me in the correct direction."

I opened my mouth to mention that if he couldn't feel any magic, it was unlikely that I could, but Kett had swept me into his arms and was dashing deeper into the graveyard before I could even speak.

So apparently, 'lead you' was a euphemism for 'carry you without permission.'

The swiftness of our passage forced all the air from my lungs, pressing me so harshly against Kett—whose entire body felt as though it was constructed out of granite—that my ribs threatened to crack.

Moments later, I was back on my feet and gasping for air. My head swam. We were standing deep within the night-shrouded graveyard now.

"Hold me tighter next time," Kett said. His tone was edged in judgement, though he kept a steadying hand on my back.

I stepped away from him, carefully planting my feet on the pavement and inhaling deeply. There wasn't going to be a 'next time' for the vampire and me, not even if Pearl Godfrey personally requested I work with him. I was just a magical device to him. A tool to be used—and now even physically manipulated—by his will.

"You're angry," Kett said.

I didn't answer, because I was just as capable of ignoring stupid statements as he was. Instead, I closed my eyes and reached out my hands, seeking shimmers of residual magic within the darkness.

"Your magic rolls off you when you're angry," he said. "You control all the wrong emotions, Wisteria Fairchild."

"You're in my way," I snapped. "Stand at my back."

Kett slipped in behind me. It was like being backed by a stone wall, though he didn't touch me.

I began to rotate slowly, and the vampire moved with me. If the necromancer was hidden behind the witch-crafted charm, I wouldn't be able to pick up her magic, the same as Kett couldn't.

But I could look for older layers of residual, similar to what I would use to reconstruct a historical magical event. Perhaps of another time Teresa had passed through the graveyard without her charm, or...

"There," I murmured. I stepped onto the grass and slowly crossed through two rows of headstones until I was standing before a small white stone crypt. "What's that?"

I leaned down to cup my hand around the shimmer of residual magic I'd found at the edge of the tomb. "Can you see this?" I asked Kett over my shoulder. "It's old. I'm not sure it's connected—"

"No matter," he said.

A dark-winged form appeared out of the night, swooping low over our heads and landing on the edge of the crypt. Once there, the reanimated crow peered down at us with white, lifeless eyes.

I shuddered.

"She's found us," Kett said.

Something shifted in the air around me, stirring the strands of hair that had loosened from my French twist. It wasn't magic. Or, rather, it wasn't magic I'd ever felt before.

I straightened, following Kett's gaze back toward the main path. "What do you mean?"

"Apparently, Garrick blood runs true."

The grass to my immediate right heaved upward, dirt churning and wooden shards thrust to the surface as the occupant of the grave wrenched itself free of its earthy confines.

I stumbled back, slamming against Kett and bruising my left shoulder.

The corpse pulling itself free of the grave was fresh enough that it still had hair and sinew attached to its graying skeleton. Then the sod and soil churned to our left. A thick-boned arm thrust free of the ground, clawing forward as it dragged a head and upper body into the night air.

Both zombies homed in on us. With the crypt behind us, our only clear route was back toward the main path.

"Oh, Jesus," I whispered. "Oh, mother of God. Please, Lord."

Nothing like a zombie rising to convert a witch to Christianity.

"Don't fret," Kett said, patting my shoulder awkwardly. "I doubt she can raise more than two or three at a time."

Jesus Christ. I was cowering against a vampire like some damsel in bloody distress.

I pushed away from Kett. He let me go.

I was a witch. Witches didn't cower in the face of magic. I was a Fairchild—whether I wanted to be or not. Fairchilds didn't hide from the darkness—

The earth churned above four more graves. And those were only the ones I could see in the intermittent moonlight.

I sidestepped the nearest zombie to my right, zigzagging through the corpses freeing themselves from their graves all around us as I ran for the main path.

Kett moved with me.

We were past the last row of headstones, four or so feet from the pavement, when something grabbed my ankle.

I shrieked despite my resolve as I almost went down. Kett caught me. I twisted to look behind me. I was held fast by a rotting arm. A zombie had grabbed me even before wrenching itself free from its grave.

Looking back was a mistake. Dozens of zombies had freed themselves from the earth and were shuffling their way toward us. Still more corpses in various stages of decay were pulling themselves from their final resting places.

Kett snapped the arm holding my ankle in two, then flicked the severed limb back behind us. It slammed into the bony forehead of the walking corpse nearest us. The zombie's head snapped back with the force of the blow, bone splintered. The vampire had broken its neck with a flick of his wrist.

The zombie stumbled, but it kept moving in our direction.

Kett was smiling. Actually smiling. Not smirking, not curling his lip, but a full-on, joyful, thrilled smile.

"Stop smiling!" I shouted.

He laughed. A breathy, rushed, eager laugh. He sounded human. Specifically, he sounded like a human who was about to do something incredibly stupid.

The sound chilled me through. "Smiling and laughing isn't appropriate in this situation!" I yelled, completely losing my own connection to what was appropriate.

Kett picked up a headstone as if it weighed nothing to him. He tossed it up in the air.

I cranked my head up, unable to do anything but watch as the vampire went mad in a graveyard teeming with zombies.

The stone flew straight up, appeared to hang in the air above us, then spiraled down straight for my head.

"Hang on," Kett murmured against my craned neck.

I threw my arms around his shoulders. He spun, taking me with him. Outstretched bony fingers brushed my cheek.

We stopped spinning.

The headstone crushed the zombie that had been about to grab me.

Kett threw his head back and laughed again.

Jesus. It was a game. The vampire was…playing.

I was going to die.

I had fought, then bargained for my life at the tender age of sixteen. I'd earned my emancipation, protecting myself from anything or anyone who could possibly have hurt me in any way since then.

And now I was going to die in the arms of a deranged centuries-old vampire, eaten alive by zombies.

I wrenched myself free from Kett. Again, he let me go. I scrambled back, making it to the pavement.

The vampire covered my retreat by drop-kicking two more headstones, one of which took the head off one zombie and the other of which cut a second walking corpse in half.

The other side of the cemetery was also teeming with the dead.

"That's more than two," I screamed. "Goddamn you, Kett! That's more than two or three. It's the entire goddamn cemetery!"

The vampire appeared at my side. "Adroit observation, witch." His tone was filled with warmth and sarcasm. "I take it you'd like to go?"

"Go? Go? Go?" I was shouting. I was aware I was shouting, but I couldn't seem to do anything but shout. "We need to find where she's casting and shut her down!"

"Risky." Kett flashed me a grin. "I like it."

I closed my eyes in utter frustration, attempting to regain control of my emotions and tone. "Jasmine's deflectors can't hold against an assault of this magnitude."

Kett darted to the side, took out three more zombies, then returned. "The necromancer won't let her horde beyond the gates. She just needs me neutralized."

I held my hands to my face, holding them like blinders. I was shaking. I hated that I was shaking.

"She has to be here, near the middle of the site, in order to cast the widest circle." I spun, trying to look beyond the horde advancing on us. "She can't wield this much magic behind the witch charm that cloaks her necromancy power, so she'd need to take it off." I caught the blur of something in the dark—a smear of sunset-tinted energy that I didn't recognize. "There!"

I darted forward, sticking to the path for as long as I could. Kett plowed ahead of me, clearing any zombies that attempted to block our way like a linebacker amped on illegal stimulants.

"Left," I screamed, darting off the path and barreling straight toward the source of the magic. I had no idea what the hell I would do if I reached Teresa Garrick. I just knew that allowing a zombie horde to get loose in the middle of Seattle was going to be a serious black mark on my flawless record. Assuming I survived.

Kett spun around me, flashing in and out of my peripheral vision. I tried to ignore him. I didn't need to be even more disoriented.

I went down without warning, tumbling through the darkness without any understanding of why I was suddenly on the ground and not running. Hands grabbed me, scratching, pinching, and dragging me across the churned earth.

I kicked and punched back, ignoring the rotting flesh ripping off underneath my hands and the dankness threatening to smother me.

"Wisteria!" Kett shouted from nearby.

"Here. Here. Here. I'm here."

I was wrenched off the ground, the force snapping my neck back painfully. I was still in the clutches of a decrepit zombie, but that zombie was now being carried by Kett.

Feeling somewhat insane myself, I kicked the zombie's head, over and over and over again.

It dropped me.

Kett caught me before I hit the ground, swinging me up in his arms and running again. We were surrounded by zombies. Utterly, completely surrounded.

And Kett was running the wrong way, heading toward the front gate.

At least, he was trying to run, but the zombies hanging off him were slowing him down. It was mind-boggling. How could beings composed of flesh and bone slow a vampire of Kett's power?

He set me down on the pavement. "Go."

"Go?"

"They want me, not you," Kett said as he stepped back.

No, he stumbled back. Then, moving faster than I could see, he freed himself of the zombies holding him.

"Go, Wisteria. Text Pearl."

I stared at him stupidly. "That's not the plan—"

"Saving you is slowing me down, witch."

I snapped my mouth shut, spinning away and immediately breaking into a run for the gates. We would regroup at the entrance.

The zombies weren't following me.

I glanced back.

Kett was being swarmed by dozens upon dozens of the undead.

I slowed my pace.

The vampire went down. His silver-blue eyes met my terrified gaze. He snarled. "Run!" Then he was gone. Buried beneath a swarming, seething mass of zombies.

I faltered only a dozen steps away from the entrance, turning back to face a horde I had no power to defend myself or the vampire against.

They ignored me. The heaving pile of rotten flesh, rancid clothing, and dead eyes slowly rolled back toward where I had sensed Teresa casting.

The vampire was firmly held within the roiling mass of walking corpses.

I had to get out of the graveyard. I had to warn Jasmine and text Pearl. I had to clear the area for an extraction team and...

I wasn't going to be able to rescue Kett. I was incapable of such a feat.

So he would die.

And the relationship between the Conclave and the Convocation would crumble.

Then Teresa and Benjamin would be executed.

I glanced around, already running back toward the teeming mass of zombies tearing the vampire apart. I'd been in the same situation only moments before. I could still feel those bony hands gripping me, scratching, trying to disable me, even kill me. Kett was fighting against dozens of them. There had to be some weapon I could fashion, something that would be effective against a rampant horde of necromancer-controlled undead.

Honestly, the Academy really needed to teach a course about what to do when your all-powerful vampire partner was overrun by a—

Something slammed against me, shoulder to waist, throwing me sideways into a gravestone. I tumbled, smacking my head against a second stone. Pain shot down my spine.

Then everything went black.

Chapter Twelve

I woke in utter darkness.

Someone was moaning and muttering near me. A male voice. But young, unsure, talking himself into something. Excited but wary.

I blinked. I could see stars above me. I was sprawled across a lawn.

No, not just grass.

A graveyard.

Zombies.

Kett.

I sat up abruptly. A pulse of pain shot through my head.

Someone lunged out of the darkness, pinning me back against a gravestone. Clawed fingers dug into my upper arms as teeth flashed toward my neck. I got my left arm up, blocking my attacker, but he clamped down on my wrist, hard. Blood spurted.

I screamed, grabbing the back of his head with my right arm and yanking him off me with a strength I didn't know I had.

My attacker shrieked in pain.

I hung on.

He dragged me to my feet, trying to flee, but he wasn't reacting to my hold. He was trying to get away from my bracelet, whose magic was burning the hair on his head, searing into his flesh.

Shocked, I let him go. He scrambled away, whimpering as he tried to hide in the nearby darkness.

I caught a glimpse of him—brown hair, long limbs, and sickly skin. Forever eighteen.

"Benjamin?" I asked.

"Don't call me that," the teenager said. Then his voice deepened, sharpened with need. "I can still taste your blood, witch."

I wrapped the bottom of my blouse around my bleeding wrist. The wound stung, but at least I wasn't losing gallons of blood.

I glanced around. All the graves surrounding us were churned up and empty. I could see the main path that led to the cemetery entrance, but not the gate itself. Benjamin had thrown me farther than I would have thought. Or he'd dragged me deeper into the graveyard while I was unconscious.

Even in the filtered moonlight, I could clearly make out the nauseating pile of zombies maybe seventy-five feet away, still churning and seething. Occasionally, one or more walking corpses would fly into the air—often with fewer limbs. But then it and its limbs would crawl back into the fray.

Kett was still fighting.

Pain shot through my head again, reverberating down my spine. My stomach revolted, though I didn't vomit. But I was concussed—possibly badly—which was probably why I was ignoring the teenaged vampire stalking me from behind the gravestones.

I picked up a sound. A voice in the distance. Someone calling out. I glanced back to where I thought the front gate was, unsteady on my feet. I didn't want Jasmine entering the cemetery.

"Ignore her," Ben growled.

Then I heard the voice more clearly. A woman, calling for someone. Teresa was looking for her son. I opened my mouth to call out to her, to expose our location and hopefully end this mess, but Ben lunged out of the shadows, slamming his fist into my stomach.

I collapsed forward, but managed to kick back at the side of his knee as I did.

He went down. He hadn't expected me to fight back.

Big mistake. He was about to learn exactly who I was.

Pushing away the pain radiating through my gut and my head, I gained my feet. Ben did the same, snarling and on the edge of rabid. I widened my stance, steadying myself. Then I raised my fists, leading with my left and protecting my face with my right. I kept my elbows tight and rolled my shoulders slightly forward, settling naturally into the posture that had been drilled into me time and time again by a long line of self-defense instructors.

Running was always the first line of defense. If you could run, then run. Fast. But if you couldn't run, the second line of defense was to go for the knees of your attacker.

Third, balls.

Fourth, eyes.

And I apparently had a fifth option that no one else wielded. A platinum trinket armed against vampires by the dowser herself. Still the only white picket fence I would ever own, my bracelet glowed with power on my right wrist.

"No one touches me without permission," I said. "Let alone a weakling of a vampire."

Mouthing off to your attacker hadn't been on any of my instructors' to-do lists, but I was seriously pissed off.

"What are you going to do about it, witch?" Benjamin spat. "I'm immortal. You're just a sack of blood."

"Come get your dinner, then."

As he lunged for me, I faked left, then smashed my right fist and all the magic backing it into his nose. Cartilage shattered under my assault. Pain exploded within my hand.

Ben shrieked, stumbling back as he pressed his hands over his face. Unfortunately, he recovered quickly.

Moving faster than I would have thought possible—though being concussed wasn't helping with my perception—he slammed into me, using his greater strength to take me down. We rolled, each struggling for a hold.

If he hadn't been obsessed with biting me, the teenaged vampire would have easily won the fight. He was the stronger one.

Instead, I managed to wrap my right arm around his neck, touching my bracelet to his bare skin so that it seared him. Then, when he tried to twist away, I curled my legs around him, forcing him to drag me as I shifted my hold to end up on his back.

I got Ben into a chokehold, then yanked him backward and gained my feet. I kept him pressed against me—him kneeling, with his back to my front.

All the while, the magic of my bracelet burned him.

He'd been struggling to contain his cries, but once I had him pinned against me, he began to shriek. Even as I tried to catch my breath, Teresa stepped out of the shadows before us. Her dark gaze took in her struggling son, his neck covered in a mass of red blisters.

"Stop it," she whispered.

"I won't." I tightened my hold, momentarily choking off Ben's frantic cries.

Four zombies broke off from the seething horde covering the vampire, scrambling toward us.

"You know who I am, necromancer." I shifted my grip to grab Ben on either side of his head, burning the flesh of his right ear and his face wherever my bracelet came into contact with his skin. "You know what a Fairchild witch is capable of."

Benjamin screamed again.

I blocked out his terror. I had to in order to continue torturing him. Kett and I would die if I didn't. And Ben would heal either way.

"Stop it!" Teresa shouted. The zombies were at her back now.

"I'll kill him," I said. "Even if your horde tears me apart afterward. I'll kill him, then I'll take you with me. I've already prepared my death curse."

In truth, I had no idea how to craft or even phrase such a curse. But the Fairchild reputation would back my bluff.

I cranked Ben's head sharply to the right, as if I had the strength to tear it off.

Teresa cried out, stumbling forward then falling to her knees. "Please, please…" she sobbed.

"Put the zombies to bed. Now."

The creatures behind Teresa stilled, including the horde still churning around Kett.

"You won't kill him," she whispered. "You won't risk the wrath of the Convocation."

"Pearl has already sent an extraction team, necromancer," I said, blocking out the way my heart twisted with every sob torn from her. "Your resistance was anticipated. Release the vampire, quell the horde, and I'll testify on your behalf. I'll plead for leniency."

Teresa snorted through her tears. "The vampire is dead. Torn to pieces."

Then behind her, the pile of corpses exploded.

Body parts burst forth in every direction, raining down in pieces all over the graveyard and pelting our heads and shoulders. Bile rose up in my throat, but I swallowed it down. Now was not the time to show weakness.

Kett appeared before the necromancer, his clothing hanging off him in shreds. His skin was marred and oddly dented, and his eyes were blazing blood red.

Teresa shrieked, throwing her hands up before her. "Stop!"

Kett froze.

My God.

The necromancer could control him. Just as she controlled Nigel, and as I assumed she controlled Ben.

Slowly, Kett reached forward, inch by inch, closer and closer to Teresa. The necromancer was shaking, struggling to hold him in place with her magic. Tears streamed down her cheeks.

She was looking death in the face. The worst death a necromancer could possibly imagine—a pale, fanged terror who was apparently immune to her command of the undead.

Vampires had slaughtered Teresa Garrick's family. Perhaps it was fitting that she should die in the same way.

Then Kett bopped the necromancer on the nose, playing with her like a cat plays with an unfortunate mouse.

Teresa's eyes rolled up in her head, and she slumped sideways in a faint.

The vampire threw his head back and laughed. That warm, joyful sound reverberated around the cemetery, echoing off churned earth, decayed corpses, the stone of the low outer walls—and chilling me through to the bone.

He was a pale smudge in the dark graveyard as he leaned over Teresa, whispering in her ear, "Two can play the mind control game, necromancer."

Teresa woke from her faint with a scream stopped in her throat. She scrambled away from Kett, making it to her feet and halfway across the churned earth between us.

I was still holding Ben, though I'd pulled my bracelet away from him. The teen had gone almost catatonic in my arms, unable to tear his gaze from his mother but barely even flinching when she had tried to control Kett and failed. The zombies that surrounded us were still all seemingly on pause.

"Stop," Kett said.

His command flowed through me. Had I been moving, I would have heeded him without question. Just as Teresa did.

The necromancer stared at us, her eyes wide with terror.

Ben began to sob silently in my arms, so that I was cradling him more than holding him captive.

"Give me your hand," Kett said.

Teresa pivoted away from us, lifting her arm.

Kett stepped up to her with his own hand outstretched. His skin had smoothed over, pristinely healed. If his clothes hadn't still been ripped to shreds, I would have had no idea that he'd just been overwhelmed by a zombie horde.

Moving as if in a dream, the necromancer placed her hand in Kett's. He raised her palm to his face, drawing her closer to him, inhaling her scent.

I found my voice. "Kett…" But then not knowing what I could possibly say, I fell hopelessly silent again.

Ben clutched my arm. His grip hurt, but I didn't shake him off.

Teresa began to shake, tears still streaming down her face. "Please…please," she whispered. "Don't kill me in front of Ben. Please don't kill me in front of my boy."

Kett dropped her hand, stepping away to the side. He wasn't playing anymore. The change in his demeanor was startling.

But before I could sigh in relief and start trying to salvage the situation, the vampire's gaze fell on Ben kneeling before me.

"You mistake me," Kett said, flicking his silvered gaze to me. "I collect power. I don't snuff it out."

The necromancer let out a shuddering breath. "But...Ben."

"Yes, Ben," Kett said, echoing her. "Ben is a problem. You've created a monster, Teresa Garrick. And a monster must be powerful in order to justify its existence. Like me."

He glanced sideways at the necromancer. "Like you."

Then he turned his gaze to me.

I tightened my hold on Ben, knowing I couldn't actually stop Kett if it came to it.

"Ben is next to nothing," Kett said. But his tone was smooth despite the harshness of his words. "Not human, and not truly a vampire. When you realized what you had done, you should have taken care of it. You should have killed him."

"I know..." Teresa's admission came as a strangled cry. "But he's mine. He's all I have. I couldn't. I couldn't go on without him."

"And so we are here."

"You..." Teresa clamped her mouth shut on whatever she was going to say, but then she forced herself to speak. "You are powerful. More powerful than I thought a vampire could be. You could...finish the transformation."

Kett laughed.

The dry, sharp sound ran down my spine like someone had walked over my grave. Which was supremely creepy while standing in a cemetery.

"Could that request get any more ironic coming from a vampire hunter?"

Teresa lifted her chin defiantly. "I was nine when my family was slaughtered. I am no vampire hunter."

"We are as we are made, Ms. Garrick," Kett said. "And since that is exactly what makes you valuable to me, I suggest you embrace it."

He lifted his gaze from Ben's bowed head to meet mine. There was something pointedly sardonic, meant solely for me, in his statement, but I had no idea what he was referring to.

"However," Kett continued blithely, "since a single drop of my blood would most likely kill the boy, your suggestion is the same as ending his pathetic existence. I can do that with far less pain to him."

"No!" Teresa cried out, but then she softened her tone. "Please. There must be another way."

"Nigel," I said.

The two of them looked at me in unison, Teresa hopeful, Kett peeved at my interruption.

"Nigel could finish what he started," I said, sounding more sure of myself than I actually was.

"I have need of Nigel," Kett said. "The amount of blood he'd need to give the boy would weaken him. Perhaps even kill him."

"What do you need him for?" I asked quietly. "Do you think he'll want to live another day after all of this?" I waved my hand to indicate the graveyard. "After the deaths of the other boys?"

"That's on Ben's head," Kett said. "That's his burden."

"No," I said, building the idea in my head even as I spoke. "That's Ben's mistake. And it's Teresa's mistake for denying Ben information. But ultimately, Nigel doesn't want to be a monster confined to his basement for decades. He wanted to help Ben if he could. Let him finish."

"He'd never willingly sacrifice himself," Kett said. "He's a coward."

"Ask him."

"I don't need to."

I frowned, not understanding Kett's statement until Nigel appeared between two headstones a dozen steps away. His hands were stuffed into his pockets. I wasn't sure how long he'd been listening in on our conversation, or when he'd chosen to enter the graveyard.

"You could make me do it." Nigel spoke to Kett, who stared back at him impassively.

"What good is the boy to me? He's more of a burden than you will be. Not to mention that it's against Conclave edict to turn one so young, and without the magic needed to survive with his mind intact. If he goes mad, I'll have to kill him. If he cannot control himself, he'll have to be locked away. Possibly for decades. And without any other magic, he will always be weak. Always be lesser than. Prey."

"He's already partially turned," I said. "He's survived this far. And it also isn't your choice, is it? Nigel is only beholden to you as his elder. But you are not his master."

Kett didn't answer, which I understood to mean he had nothing to say. Because I was right.

I was guessing that the Conclave functioned in a similar structure to the Convocation, and to individual covens. The elders of the thirteen strongest covens held seats on the Convocation. My Aunt Rose was the nominal head of the Fairchild coven. Pearl was the head of the Godfrey coven. Each witch in a coven followed the coven elder's advice, but hopefully not blindly.

Kett was an elder of the Conclave, so I assumed he must be someone's master. But not Nigel's.

Nigel glanced at me, then at Ben. He contemplated the churned grass underneath his feet. "I'm not a very good vampire."

"Why did you consent to the change in the first place?" Kett asked.

"I didn't."

Kett stilled. Or grew even more still, in that way he did. But I couldn't tell if he was shocked or simply calculating the best course of action.

"You've already drunk from me," Nigel said. "I assume you saw everything I could show you."

"I did not know you were unwilling."

Nigel stepped closer to Kett, squaring his shoulders to stand taller than the more powerful vampire. His tone hardened. "But you saw my maker? Tasted him in my blood?"

Kett nodded curtly.

"You will avenge my death."

For a long moment, Kett stared at Nigel. Then he glanced over at Teresa Garrick. She was wringing her hands, but she stopped under Kett's gaze.

"Necromancer, whether or not the boy survives, you will do as I say. You will aid me in any way I request. I will never demand your life, but that is all that will be sacred between us."

Teresa nodded. "Yes."

"And if the boy survives and Nigel does not, he will be without a master." Kett swept his hand toward Nigel. "You see how well that works. So Benjamin will be mine to do with as I will. He will follow the edicts of the Conclave. And when he is strong enough, a mentor will be selected for him."

"You..." Teresa began.

"It will not be me. Unless the boy distinguishes himself in some way, he is beneath my attention."

Teresa swallowed, glancing down at Ben. Red streaks of blood had dried on the boy's face. Tears of blood. But the burns on his neck were already healing.

The necromancer squeezed her eyes shut before she spoke. "If I agree, we will move to Vancouver. Deeper into Godfrey territory. I will still need to face a tribunal."

"A fledgling cannot remain with his family—"

"I can control him."

Kett laughed harshly. The corpses of three dead teens were damning evidence against the necromancer's ability to control her son.

Teresa amended her statement. "I can control him now."

"And why would the Godfreys want the trouble a fledgling vampire poses?"

"A necromancer of power is always wanted."

A slow, almost-cruel smile spread across Kett's face. "You think the Godfreys are powerful enough to intervene with the boy? You think they will even take him without my vouching for him?"

"Pearl is the most powerful—"

"Jade," I said, interrupting Teresa's faltering attempt to bargain.

"Don't interfere, witch," Kett said.

I placed my left hand on Ben's head. Getting even more involved in this situation was insane. The teenager had just tried to kill me, and I was shoving myself into the middle of negotiations that had nothing to do with me.

But I remembered what it was like to have my life—my very existence—controlled by the whims of people more powerful than me.

"Jade Godfrey will accept the word of Kettil, elder and executioner of the Conclave." I chose my words and phrasing carefully. "She's a collector, isn't she? Just like you, Kett. Except she factors in friendship, perhaps a little more than you do."

"Jade has never raised a vampire fledgling," Kett said coolly.

"No Adept will ever run unchecked in Vancouver. The Godfrey coven contains more than witches now."

Kett narrowed his eyes at me. Then he looked at Teresa. "Do you understand what you've done, necromancer? What you've allowed to happen?"

"Yes."

"And you know better than anyone what a rogue vampire can do."

The necromancer could only nod.

"Then whether or not you move to Vancouver, the boy is mine to do with what I will."

Teresa grimaced sadly, but she nodded again. "I have one last condition."

"Name it quickly."

"You will hunt down the vampires that slaughtered my family. You will make them pay for what they did."

A genuine smile crossed Kett's face. "Already done."

Teresa looked shocked.

"The Conclave was always aware of your family's activities. Had it not been so, you would not have been allowed to continue them for so many generations."

Kett held out his hand to the necromancer. She clasped it without hesitation, sealing the bargain.

"Now put your horde to bed, necromancer." Kett glanced back at me, smirking. "As the witch already demanded."

There was some deeper meaning behind his smirk, but I was too tired and drained to worry about it.

Teresa nodded, closing her eyes. I was buffeted by a lighter brush of the energy I'd felt before the chaos erupted. Then the inert corpses spread across the graveyard began to shift, piecing themselves together and moving back toward their graves. It was sickeningly mesmerizing.

"They'll go now," Teresa said, spent and swaying on her feet.

Kett nodded, then turned to Nigel, who had been waiting patiently for his fate to be decided. "I will avenge your death."

Nigel took a deep breath. Then he knelt in the grass and held his arms out to Benjamin.

I loosened my hold on the teenager, but he hesitated.

"Come, Ben," Nigel said. "Come to me...my child."

Teresa began to sob in earnest. Her son looked up at her. She stepped toward him, trying to wipe the dried blood from his face.

"I love you," she whispered. "I love you, my boy. Please forgive me. Please, please."

Ben grabbed her hand, holding her tightly. "I don't want to be weak," he said. "I don't want to die. I'm tired of dying."

Teresa nodded. "Go to Nigel, then. Go."

She disengaged herself from her son, then turned to walk away through the zombies reclaiming their graves and disappearing into the darkness.

"Wisteria," Kett said quietly. "Go with her. Please."

I nodded, turning away before I had any chance to see Ben crawl into Nigel's arms. Before I could watch one or both of them die.

Maybe I was the coward. Brave enough to bandy words with a vampire, arrogant enough to bargain with Nigel's, Ben's, and Teresa's lives. But too weak to watch the results of my interference play out.

Out of all the Adepts in this graveyard, maybe I was the weakest in spirit.

By the time we crossed beyond the stone wall that marked the boundary of the cemetery, the zombies had returned to their graves, but the cemetery itself still looked like a war zone. The Convocation was going to need to bring in a cleanup crew—or make a hefty donation to atone for the apparent vandalism that was sure to be discovered by morning.

Jasmine was pacing along the sidewalk by the front gate, her phone pressed to her ear. She looked up as Teresa crossed out of the cemetery ahead of me. The necromancer climbed into the back seat of the white SUV parked at the curb without a word. Nigel's green Accord was behind it. Jasmine and Nigel must have gone back for the vehicles while Kett and I were fleeing zombies.

My cousin stared at me. "What the hell happened? Where's Kett?"

I glanced back at the cemetery, which looked exactly the same as it had when I'd first seen it. Then I narrowed my eyes, looking through the magic with which Jasmine had cloaked the entrance. I could see the destroyed headstones along the edge of the main path. The graveyard looked smaller from outside than it had felt while within it.

"Nice spell," I said.

"Yeah, well, it won't last through the dawn." Jasmine was now texting madly with someone.

"Neither will Ben and Nigel," I said. "One of them, anyway."

Jasmine snorted.

I wasn't joking.

Jasmine looked at me, concern flooding her face. "Oh, Betty-Sue..." she whispered. "You're really hurt."

"Yes." I lifted my right hand. "I'm pretty sure at least one bone is broken in my hand. I punched Ben."

Jasmine stared at me as if I were insane. "You...punched a vampire?"

"Well, he wasn't fully a vampire at the time, according to Kett. So I guess I was lucky. Oh! Pencils do not kill vampires. Three pints isn't enough. It all makes sense. That's why the pink pencil was enough to unbind the magic animating Colby."

"Wisteria, you're rambling. Or possibly drunk."

"Yeah. I might have a concussion."

Jasmine swore a fanciful blue streak, reaching for me while somehow still texting with one hand at the same time. "I've got a healer coming."

"My apartment would be better, maybe?" I was rapidly losing my grip on reality. The dark houses and half-lit street were sliding sideways. "I'd like to sleep."

"No sleeping with a maybe-concussion." Jasmine's voice was far away, though she was steering me toward Nigel's car. She forced me into the front passenger seat, leaving the door open though the night was cool.

I sat there, toying with the tiny platinum houses on my bracelet and feeling the magic of it tickling my fingers. I shouldn't have been playing with it, though. I should have been shutting down my senses, gathering and reinforcing my mental shields to avoid further exposure to magic.

Except I remembered the way the bracelet had glowed on my wrist. I remembered the pulse of power—the force of my amplified magic—as I'd smashed my fist into Ben's nose, then wrestled him to the ground.

I touched a little platinum fence, then a tiny tree. The bracelet was meant to be ironic. A 'screw you' to my family, and to all the dark secrets contained behind the perfect facades of their perfect homes.

But really, it was an acknowledgment that even though I might spend years living purposefully, following the rules, keeping my magic contained and trying to be useful—I would always be a Fairchild. I would always choose my own life and the lives of those I loved—as short a list as that might be—over everything and everyone else.

A person like me, capable of what I was capable of, didn't deserve a white picket fence or the family that came with it.

Kett appeared at the cemetery gate. He was cradling Ben in his arms. The unconscious teenager was deathly pale. But if the transformation worked, it made sense that he was supposed to be.

Jasmine hustled over to the SUV, opening the back door. Teresa half-stepped out of the back seat, reaching for her son.

"You may text Pearl now," Kett said to Jasmine.

"Already done." Jasmine's tone was stiff and accusatory. "The second I saw the state Wisteria is in."

I squeezed my eyes shut, wrapping my hand around the bracelet until it cut into the flesh of my wrist. Pain shot through my hand, clearing my hazy head. I eased my grip.

Jade Godfrey had unwittingly saved my life tonight. I certainly wasn't going to sit around being morose about it.

I glanced around the sidewalk and vehicles.

Kett was gone.

As Jasmine climbed into the car, I closed the passenger-side door. "Ben's alive," she said, starting the engine. "Kett says the tinted windows in the SUV will only protect him from the predawn. So they have to get him underground, or at least better protected right away."

"And Nigel?"

Jasmine looked grim. Then she nodded toward the cemetery. I followed her gaze.

Beyond the screen of Jasmine's magic, fire flickered among the gravestones.

"More vandalism," I muttered sarcastically. My heart felt oddly heavy given that I hadn't really known Nigel at all, and how he had tried to rip my throat out when he'd first laid eyes on me. Though he'd been driven to that act by all the things beyond his control. I knew the feeling.

"It was what he wanted, though."

I looked over at my cousin. "He told you?"

She shrugged. "He told all of us. Look at how he was living."

"He was forced." As I whispered the words, unbidden tears finally began to roll down my face.

Jasmine nodded, intuitively understanding that my sorrow was a reflection of the elements of our shared past—and how those elements had paralleled Nigel's life.

Brushing moisture away from her own eyes with one hand, she gripped the steering wheel with the other. I wrapped my hand around hers. Shared pain was always easier to handle.

A car pulled up behind us. The Convocation cleanup crew had arrived.

I dropped my hand, automatically reaching for a Kleenex in my bag before realizing I didn't have it. I used my sleeve to wipe my face instead. The crew would collect my purse and get it back to me.

The white SUV slipped away from the curb with Kett at the wheel. I hadn't seen him return.

Jasmine waved to the two witches climbing out of the car behind us, then put the car into gear and pulled away. "The healer is meeting us at your place," she said.

"Okay." I allowed myself to settle back against the seat and the headrest. "I found your birthday gift."

"Yeah? Cool."

Silence fell as we drove out of the suburbs and back into the city. But then, Jasmine and I had never really needed to talk.

Chapter Thirteen

The en-suite bathroom was the reason I'd bought my apartment two years ago. I still wasn't sure that Seattle was where I wanted to settle permanently, but the city suited me for right now—good food, international airport, and no snow. Not considering Hawaii or Alaska, it was pretty much as far away as I could get from my family without leaving the country. I wasn't a cook, and I didn't have any hobbies other than crafting my oyster-shell cubes, nor did I entertain. So the gourmet kitchen went unused, my living room furniture was sparse, and the view went mostly unnoticed.

But the bathroom off my bedroom was my luxury and my solace. Heated floors of white slate tile, towel warmer, walk-in glassed shower, and the most glorious freestanding soaker tub.

Even the waterfall tub filler was divine.

In the aftermath of everything that had happened, Jasmine stayed with me for two weeks, sorting out the incident with the Garricks and making sure every last scrape or bruise I'd collected in the cemetery was healed. We'd celebrated her birthday at Canlis, an expensive but incredibly decadent restaurant, and I'd given her the reconstruction from Jade's bakery. The peaceful smile that had lightened her face upon viewing it almost made up for the events that had summoned me to Vancouver in the first place.

Jasmine had taken a cab to the airport earlier in the day, heading back to San Francisco on Convocation business.

I didn't mind having some alone time. I was more accustomed to being alone than not. But I was still glad my cousin was planning to come back for Thanksgiving at the end of November.

Every time something traumatic happened in her life or mine, I thought about asking Jasmine to move in with me, or at least to think about relocating to Seattle. But I never did. I wasn't sure she'd be happy here full-time with only me for company. Plus, I would ruin all her electronics.

Happily, the hot water heater was located beside the main bathroom on the opposite side of the apartment, so as long as I didn't touch it, I could luxuriate in as many baths as I wanted.

I added a dollop of a brand-new bubble bath that Jasmine had purchased for my birthday the previous month from the witch who made her skin cream and hair conditioner. It was brewed with raspberry and tarragon, which I would have thought an odd combination. However, it was supposed to be supremely relaxing.

Delightfully, it was also exceedingly sudsy.

I climbed into the tub, taking a moment to let my feet and legs grow accustomed to the heat before lowering my body all the way in. Then I leaned back. The tilt of the tub was perfectly angled. Not so shallow that I felt as though I had to keep myself from slipping down into the water, and not so deep that I couldn't rest my neck on the tub's rounded edge.

The bubbles covered every part of me from the neck down, except for my right arm, which I kept out of the water along the edge of the tub. I hadn't taken my bracelet off since the incident in the graveyard. Actually, I hadn't taken it off since Jade infused it with her alchemy. But it was an unaccustomed feeling of comfort, rather than fear, that kept it on me.

I flicked my wrist quickly twice, shifting the bracelet until the two tiny oyster-shell cubes sat on top of my hand. I triggered one of the reconstructions with less effort than it took me to breathe. It was already a part of me, embedded within my soul, but I wanted to see it...to see him...with my own eyes tonight.

A dark-haired teenaged boy with golden hazel eyes appeared above my wrist as the magic of the reconstruction unfolded. He looked back over his shoulder and winked. The sight of his tanned face, his easy grin and sparkling eyes was momentarily heart wrenching.

I squeezed my eyes shut, but then I forced myself to look. I had wanted to see him. I'd wanted to have him near me tonight.

Declan.

In the magic I'd collected, Jasmine's half-brother was a year or so younger than Ben and his friends, though he looked older. Matured by his rocky life, which—though he had a permanent roof over his head and all the food he could eat—wasn't much better under the care of the Fairchild witches than it had been after he'd been abandoned by his mother to the streets of New Orleans.

It was twilight in Seattle, as it was within the twelve-year-old reconstruction.

Declan held his hand up, magic shimmering around his fingers. Pinpoints of blue and green launched upward, exploding into a brilliant display of miniature fireworks a few feet above his head.

It was a trick he had practiced all that summer. For me.

His darkly tanned skin had been hot underneath my touch that night. His hair was damp from swimming all day. A rare day during which the two of us had been alone and not at lessons.

He had lain down next to me in the grass with the sparks of his magic still floating over our heads. I opened my arms and asked him to kiss me, to touch me, the two of us giving ourselves to each other rather than having our affections taken and twisted into some terrible and powerful perversion. We had deliberately broken one of our uncle's cardinal rules. Our purity would no longer fuel his spells after that night.

Declan's caresses had been firm and needy at the same time. Magic danced beneath our skins. And we had loved each other as no one had ever truly loved us.

Three days later, I had left Declan and Jasmine in a hospital, both of them broken and bruised, forced by my family to walk away from them. My silence was their only guarantee of safety. My absence was the only way I could deal with abandoning them.

I had collected the reconstruction I played back now only moments before walking away with nothing but my clothing and my name. As far as Declan knew, I hadn't even visited him in the hospital.

We had almost died. We'd made a bid for freedom, and we'd won. But not together.

We'd never be Betty-Sue, Betty-Lou, and Bubba. We'd never have our white picket fence. Not together.

But we had thwarted my uncle's bid for power and survived. That was going to have to be enough.

I passed my wet hand across my face, washing away the tears that had gathered on my cheeks. Reaching above my head for a charcoal cotton towel, I dried my face.

Then I triggered the reconstruction again, watching Declan's fireworks with joy once more and trying to let the pain of the remembrance that accompanied it fade away. Twelve years was too long to carry so much pain. I just wanted to remember the good parts, the laughter and the love.

A vampire was sitting on the edge of the tub. White blond hair, blue-gray cashmere V-neck, distressed black jeans, and all.

I stifled a shriek, forcing my body to stay down beneath the blanket of bubbles rather than flinging myself naked out of the bathroom.

The reconstruction winked out.

"Your new wards are...interesting," the vampire said.

"Kett." I forced myself to speak calmly, hoping he hadn't ruined the protective magic I had just paid several thousand dollars to have installed around the apartment. "Try knocking."

A smile slowly transformed his chiseled features. He reached over to the vanity, then rapped one of the dark cupboard doors lightly with his knuckles.

I jutted out my chin and kept my shoulders underneath the bubbles, though I seriously wanted to cross my arms over my breasts. "How may I help you?"

He touched my right hand lightly, his fingers feeling like ice against the steamy air that surrounded the bathtub. "You've recovered? Wholly?"

"Why does that sound like a loaded question?"

Kett smiled but didn't elaborate.

"Yes," I said begrudgingly. "I have recovered. How is Ben?"

"Alive." The vampire cast his gaze around the bathroom, taking in the candles and the low light. He frowned. "Are you expecting someone?"

"No."

He nodded, slowly tapping his fingers on the edge of the tub. He was nervous.

I didn't like that he was nervous.

"Jasmine isn't here." I blurted the words, but then quickly moderated my tone. "If you were looking for her?"

"I do not seek Jasmine Fairchild," he said. "Not tonight. Not for this."

I had no idea what that meant, but I was starting to get peeved that my lovely evening had been interrupted. "You can't just come in to someone's bathroom," I said. "It's not done. It's rude."

He raised an eyebrow. "Ah, I see. People will think we're having sex?"

My jaw dropped. "No one will think we're having sex! Who would even know you're here but me?"

Kett shook his head. "The rules of the twenty-first century have no sense of logic. What applies in one situation doesn't apply in another."

"Bursting into anyone's bathroom is always rude, in any century."

"Point taken."

He didn't leave, though. His gaze was pinned to the black-and-white photo of an eagle hanging over the wall-mounted toilet. The raptor's eye was the only thing in focus in the shot, its wings a blur all around its head. But I was fairly certain the executioner of the Conclave wasn't hanging out in my bathroom to discuss photography.

"Shall we move to the living room?" I asked.

Kett turned his silver-blue gaze to me, taking in my face, then looking down at the bracelet on my arm. "No," he said. "I'm not staying."

He pulled a thick ream of parchment out of thin air by his left hip, which made me realize that he must have been wearing an invisible satchel of some sort.

I was immediately jealous, but such complicated magic wouldn't stay intact if worn by me.

The vampire touched the thick bundle of pages to the back of my hand. "Delivered and accepted?" He looked at me questioningly.

I started to turn my hand, to take the letter or whatever it was from him.

"Don't get it wet," he said chidingly.

I almost laughed, but Kett's entire demeanor was…off. Solemn and excited. Almost edgy and unsure.

"Is acceptance binding?" I asked.

"What is held within was binding for you the moment it was written and signed," he said. "But I'm delivering it to you formally now."

My heart was suddenly lodged in my throat. "All right," I said, expecting to feel some kind of magic pass between us. But it didn't.

Kett nodded, placing the parchment on the vanity counter. He looked back at me, casting his gaze over my face again in that oddly deliberate way. As if he was memorizing my features. Then he nodded as if satisfied.

I had no idea what the hell was going on. And my bubble bath was getting a trifle thin around the edges.

"I was exceedingly impressed by your conduct in the cemetery," he said. "That you persevered and focused on the target, despite your fear, despite the great odds. That you got the boy under control and leveraged the necromancer into releasing me."

"Is that a thank you?" I said dryly.

He smirked. "An acknowledgement that you are more than I took you for, magically and psychologically. That you are…deserving of my attention."

My heart was back in my chest now, but thumping wildly. I tried to swallow the fear away. I was unsuccessful.

"I don't know what you mean," I whispered. "Are you...are you interested in me?"

Kett laughed quietly, then straightened from the edge of the tub and crossed toward the door.

I reached up while his back was turned, retrieving a large bath towel and holding it to my chest as I sat up in the tub.

When Kett turned back in the doorway, his marble-chiseled features were almost sorrowful. "Might I suggest that the next time you depose a coven leader, you make it official."

My stomach churned with dread. The vampire was talking about my uncle, Jasper Fairchild. He was still the head of the Fairchild coven—for reasons of power and politics—even though my Aunt Rose sat on the Convocation and oversaw the coven's day-to-day operations.

"I'm not a member of the Fairchild coven," I said. "I want nothing to do with them."

"You are blood. You will always be blood, even if you chose to wipe every single one of them off the face of the earth. Even if you are the last Fairchild, everlasting." He smiled wryly. "Your vengeance would be a glorious thing to behold, Wisteria."

My gaze shifted to the thick ream of parchment sitting like an untriggered malignant spell just across from me.

"Might I also suggest you take the document to a lawyer," Kett said. "I understand you went to the Academy with Ember Pine. She practices here in Seattle, and is well versed in Adept contract law."

Then he was gone.

I climbed out of the bath, dragging the soaking wet towel with me and flooding the warm tiled floor. I reached for the stack of parchment before noting with some detachment that my hand was soaking wet. So I grabbed a second towel and dried both my arms.

With the remainder of my body still dripping wet, I opened the thick document and scanned the first page.

It was handwritten, a heavy script in black ink. I could see the magic within the words without even trying. The title on the first page declared it to be an application for membership to the Conclave. The remainder of the pages were filled with legal jargon, some of which appeared to be written in Latin.

That didn't make any sense. I didn't want to be a vampire. I hadn't made any sort of application. Why would Kett give this to me?

I flipped to the final page, noting a shakily scrawled name and a signature: *Jasper James Charles Fairchild.* Dated: *August 24, 2014.*

"Oh God, no," I whispered. Then I clamped down on the moan of fear evoked by even the idea of my uncle reincarnated as a vampire.

The middle section of the final page—under the heading *For Consideration*—contained a list of handwritten names. A long, exhaustive list. Each and every one was a Fairchild, including my and Jasmine's parents. Some of the names were such distant relations that I'd never even met them.

Each name was written in Jasper's cramped, shaky hand. Each name had been carefully struck through and initialed with the letter K in dark-red ink.

K for Kett?

And I was fairly certain that wasn't actually ink.

The fourth-to-last name crossed off the list was Jasmine Belinda Joan Fairchild.

The last three names were Declan Grey Fairchild Benoit, Wisteria Elizabeth Marie Fairchild, and Jasper James Charles Fairchild.

I stumbled back, barely managing to sit down on the toilet before my legs gave out. I stared at the final three names.

Declan's full name. My full name. Jasper's full name. Knowing someone's entire name held weight in the magical universe. Our second middle names weren't even written down in the family chronicle. They were known only to our parents and ourselves. For our own protection.

My coven leader had somehow coerced my true name from my parents. Or, knowing my mother, he had simply bargained for it. Then he had added that name to the appendix of a contract for application to the Conclave. Without my permission. As if I was just fodder in yet another of his absolutely insane power plays.

Every other name had been crossed off except the last three.

Jasper wanted to be turned—to be remade—into a vampire. With my mind racing, I could barely do more than scan the text, but I pieced together enough to understand that for some reason, some condition enforced by the Conclave, he had to offer up the entire Fairchild coven for consideration.

Kett was going to turn one of us into a vampire.

The case we had just completed—the reconstructions, tracking the boys down, finding and thwarting the necromancer—had been a test.

Jasmine had somehow failed it.

And I had passed.

It was utterly ridiculous.

It couldn't possibly be legally binding.

I didn't want to be a vampire. The idea was abhorrent to me. I'd been running from that kind of darkness since I was sixteen.

But if that was the case, then why wasn't I afraid?

Acknowledgements

With thanks to:

My story & line editor
Scott Fitzgerald Gray

My proofreader
Pauline Nolet

My beta readers
Terry Daigle, Angela Flannery, Gael Fleming,
Desi Hartzel, and Heather Lewis.

**For their continual encouragement,
feedback, & general advice**
Kira Mundhenk—for her suggestion of Elie Tahari
Heather Doidge-Sidhu—for once again
refereeing the final proof
The Office

Meghan Ciana Doidge is an award-winning writer based out of Salt Spring Island, British Columbia, Canada. She has a penchant for bloody love stories, superheroes, and the supernatural. She also has a thing for chocolate, potatoes, and cashmere yarn.

NOVELS

After the Virus
Spirit Binder
Time Walker
Cupcakes, Trinkets, and Other Deadly Magic (Dowser 1)
Trinkets, Treasures, and Other Bloody Magic (Dowser 2)
Treasures, Demons, and Other Black Magic (Dowser 3)
I See Me (Oracle 1)
Shadows, Maps, and Other Ancient Magic (Dowser 4)
Maps, Artifacts, and Other Arcane Magic (Dowser 5)
I See You (Oracle 2)
Artifacts, Dragons, and Other Lethal Magic (Dowser 6)
I See Us (Oracle 3)
Catching Echoes (Reconstructionist 1)

NOVELLAS/SHORTS

Love Lies Bleeding
The Graveyard Kiss

For recipes, giveaways, news, and glimpses of upcoming stories, please connect with Meghan on her:
Personal blog, www.madebymeghan.ca
Twitter, @mcdoidge
Facebook, Meghan Ciana Doidge
Email, info@madebymeghan.ca

Please also consider leaving an honest review at your point of sale outlet.

OTHER BOOKS BY MEGHAN CIANA DOIDGE

WWW.MADEBYMEGHAN.CA